INDENTURED DAUGHTER

Ruth Ann Cornelson

Happy Reading!
Christmas 2023
Ruth Ann Cornelson

Contents

PROLOGUE

England 1840

In the summer of her twelfth year, Sarah Blake's world changed forever. She stood looking out of the upstairs bedroom window, one hand fidgeting with the ragged edge of a faded blue curtain, the other twirling the end of her long, golden braid. The bright sunshine streaming in the window mocked the gloom in her heart. Tears fell like raindrops, splashing on the chipped paint of the windowsill. She watched the lane with unblinking eyes, waiting. Today, they would come for her. Today, she would leave all she knew and loved.

"Sarah," her father spoke quietly from the open door of her room. "Are your things packed? They will soon be here."

Sarah wiped the tears quickly and turned to greet her father. "Yes, Father." She looked at the two small bags on the floor beside the bed.

He followed her gaze. "I know it is not much, but I am sure the Tompkins will provide whatever else you need. They come well recommended. They will treat you well."

Sarah sensed that he was trying to reassure himself as well as her. *Was this actually going to happen?!* "Father, must I really go?" She questioned him, her emerald eyes begging him to answer no.

Arthur Blake walked slowly towards his daughter, feet leaden, shoulders stooped. Gray streaks stood out in his dark brown hair, making him look far older than his 34 years. Placing large, gentle hands on her shoulders, he answered slowly, "Sarah, darling, if there were any other way, we would have found it. With your mother so ill and the new master unwilling to let the church stand on his land, this is all that is left to us. Without a parish, we are set for the poor house, and we will not have that for you, Sarah girl. We cannot bear to have you there. God has provided this opportunity for you to find a new life, a better life. And you will be back in a few years. Come now," he took her hand, tugging her gently out of the room, "Your mother wishes to talk with you."

Sarah walked beside her father, loving the feeling of her small hand engulfed in his large, capable one. Her father could do anything. She looked up at him, love and confidence shining in her eyes. *He would still find a way to change this.*

Catching her gaze, Arthur stopped, kneeling to meet her eye-to-eye. He spoke as if reading her mind, "I cannot make this go away, Sarah. I know I am supposed to be able to fix anything," he paused and swallowed, "but I cannot fix this." A sheen covered his eyes, and Sarah stared, stunned to see a tear run down her father's cheek. He put his arms around her, holding her close for a moment. "I am so sorry, Sweetheart." He stood, taking her hand again, "Let's go see your mother with a smile, shall we?"

Sarah's smile quivered a little, but she held it forcefully. She could do this. She could help. The money her parents had received for her eight years of service to the Tompkins would be used to take her mother to a hospital in Bath, where she would have the expert medical care she needed. Bath was known for the healing power of its mineral springs. Perhaps they would help. *Please, Lord, let the money from the Tompkins be enough to help Mother get well,* she prayed.

Stopping at the door, she saw her mother lying on the bed, propped up on pillows and covered with a beautiful quilt. Sarah remembered watching her make it, fingers moving quickly as she sewed each square. Now, her hands lay idly beside her. Sarah smiled in greeting, but her heart sank as she watched the tiny, frail woman attempt to push herself up into a sitting position. Her father hurried to his wife's side and easily lifted her to the chair beside the bed.

Sarah watched them from the doorway. *How could she leave now? What would Mother do without her?* She ran over, kneeling down by the chair, hugging her mother's knees, looking up into uncharacteristically pale, blue eyes. Her heart skipped a beat, questioning, *would this be the last time she saw her mother?* "Mother, I do not think I should leave you now. I want to be here to help you get well," she pled.

Slowly lifting a weak hand to rest on Sarah's head, Margaret Blake responded, "Darling, I won't be getting well right away. You can help me when you get back." She smiled at her daughter. The words sounded reassuring but didn't ring true.

With a tremulous smile, Sarah answered, "Yes, Mother, I will help you when I get back. I will miss you so much, but I am excited to go on the ship and see America." Her words rang no truer than her mother's had, but they pretended they did, each for the other's sake.

It was then that they heard the carriage arriving. Their eyes met instantly, sorrow and determination reflected in them all. They embraced each other tightly, surrounding the small woman in the chair. "Lord, give us all strength," Sarah's father prayed quickly and then rose to answer the door.

Part 1

Rescued

CHAPTER 1

Virginia 1846

Sarah dropped the wet cloth into the washtub and straightened slowly, brushing the back of a small, chapped hand across her forehead. Tiny rivulets ran down once round, dimpled cheeks, now hollow, matching the gaunt frame covered by a too large, faded dress.

It had been a lovely green with lace around the scooped neckline when she brought it with her from England six years ago, hoping to keep it for church meetings and holiday parties.

A hollow laugh choked from her parched throat, and was quickly blown away by the scorching wind. Oh, the naiveté of her young 12-year-old self, so pleased with the new dress she had received to bring on her journey. Clearly, she had not understood what life as an indentured servant to Master and Mistress Tompkin would be like.

Sarah smoothed back wisps of dark blonde hair, hair the color of the wash water. It had been over a week since she had been allowed enough water for a proper bath and hair wash. Her naturally soft, honey-blonde hair was now coated with dust and sweat. Perhaps tonight, she would be granted more than one bucket of water with which to wash herself and the heavy, offending curls that reached almost to her waist.

Bending back over the washtub with a small groan, tears fell into the murky water. She wiped them angrily. She would not give in to despair. But two more years! Could she survive two more years? The first year after they arrived, the Tompkins had received a message that her mother had never recovered, and just a year later, another saying that her father had passed away from an illness, or a broken heart, Sarah thought. Now, she was truly alone. She took a deep breath and prayed silently, *Lord. Please help me endure. Sometimes, I just don't think I can do it. I need you. Where are you?* She hated to admit it but sometimes she felt like God had stayed in England when she left; He seemed so far away.

"Sarah! Get in here!" Mistress Tompkin's loud shriek made her jump.

"Yes, Mistress," Sarah called back, wondering what could be wrong. *What had she done? Or not done?* Leaving the wash, she hurried to the house, a long, single-story structure shining white in the hot sun. A covered verandah stretched the length of the house with a pillar at each end. Sarah was not permitted to use the front entrance and turned to go to the back of the house.

"I said get in here!" Mistress Tompkin yelled, waving frantically at her. Stopping abruptly, the girl turned back towards the angry woman, walking hesitantly to the verandah. Mistress Tompkin glared at her when she reached the front steps, then turned and walked briskly into the house.

Sarah followed, head down, feet shuffling.

"Sit down," the harsh woman snapped.

Sit down? On one of the family chairs? Sarah glanced around the room in front of her. The Tompkins had brought many beautiful things from England with which to furnish the house; plush carpets covered the smooth wood floors, brocade upholstered chairs and couches had dark cherry wood tables beside them. Oil lamps that Sarah lit each evening were attached to the walls, highlighting beautiful paintings of the English countryside. Against the main wall was a large but surprisingly tasteful fireplace, framed by a carved white mantle with a large painting of the somewhat younger and slimmer Tompkins hanging prominently above it.

"Sarah! I said sit down!" The angry command startled her. She searched for a stool or bench on which to sit but, seeing none, sat down hesitantly on one of the beautiful chairs, eyes fixed on the heavy-set, scowling woman in front of her.

Mistress Tompkin paced in front of the frightened servant, waving a piece of paper she held. "We have received an interesting message; apparently, you have a cousin from London who has arrived in Norfolk looking for you." She held the note up to her face, squinting to read it. "A Gra... Oh, such terrible penmanship! I can't make it out, possibly Grace Attwood? What do you know of this?"

Sarah was puzzled, her mind blank. Attwood? The name meant nothing. A cousin? Closing her eyes, she wracked her brain for any memory of a cousin but could think of nothing. It made no sense. Why would someone from London come looking for her? In all honesty, she replied, "I do not know. I know nothing of a cousin, Mistress."

Her answer was not well received. "It seems unlikely that you would never have met your own relative," was the sharp retort. Mistress Tompkin studied her suspiciously.

Sarah's brow furrowed. She could not recall any relatives at home. Her grandparents had died when she was young. Aunts and Uncles? She scoured her memory again. *Wait! There was something. She did vaguely recall meeting an aunt once, her mother's older sister,* she thought. She had been so young at the time. She could not recall any mention of a child. If there was a cousin, they had never met.

"Well, never mind, then. It makes no difference," the impatient mistress declared. "This message was just delivered. It says that you *do* have a cousin who wishes to redeem your indenture early." Sarah stared at the woman in confusion. "Oh goodness! Do you know nothing?" Mistress Tompkin snapped, still pacing. "That means your cousin wishes to pay us the price of your next two years of service, buying you back, freeing you from your bond to us," she explained.

Sarah's mouth hung agape. *Was that possible? Could someone else pay the price of her debt and free her?*

"Oh, close your mouth, you snippet. Yes, they can do that," Mistress Tompkin answered the unasked question. "Your parents insisted that your indenture agreement contain a clause requiring us to release you to a relative should one wish to redeem you. And now, apparently a cousin has appeared wishing to do just that. I cannot imagine why. Who would pay the price for someone else's freedom? Ridiculous!"

Mistress Tompkin talked primarily to herself as she paced, folding, and unfolding the message in pudgy, ring-laden hands. "And what about me?! What am I supposed to do if I have to let you go? I have worked so hard all these years getting you trained and now, when you are finally of some use to me, this cousin expects to just take you away! There must be some way to prevent this."

The woman stopped pacing suddenly, a devious smile on her lips. She stood in front of Sarah, hands resting heavily on ample hips. Leaning towards the girl, she spoke softly, "Your cousin probably doesn't really want you. She probably feels guilty now that your mother and father are both dead, and you have no one to return to when your time here is done. Perhaps we could offer to keep you here as a free servant. Yes, we could offer that. That might be even better." She beamed now, pleased with her plan, outlining it to herself. "By paying for your last two years, your cousin can free you, but by leaving you with us as a free servant, she can be rid of the bother of taking you back and dealing with you there. And I won't have to bother about finding and training a new girl. Yes, we can turn this around somehow.

The woman's smile disappeared in heavy jowls as she focused on her servant, "Of course, you will have to tell them that you do not want to go to England now that your parents are gone." She leaned down and spoke almost kindly, "After all, why would you want to go to a strange place when you have a home here?"

Sarah gasped. The stinging slap caught her off guard.

"Don't even think it, you snippet. You will reject the offer. You still belong to us!" Mistress Tompkin opened the paper she held and re-read the message, informing Sarah, "We are requested to bring you to Norfolk tomorrow at four o'clock to work out an agreement. It is too late to send a message saying that you do not wish to go, and we do want to get the money for you."

Whirling back to Sarah, the woman snapped, "Go! Get ready to leave in the morning. You do not need to pack much since you will not be leaving, but bring some night things. Mr. Tompkin and I will want to stay in the city a few days, and it will be good to have you there to help me." The Mistress dismissed Sarah with a flick of her plump wrist.

Sarah left, eager to get away, her mind whirring with all she had just heard. She went quickly to her room, a small space tacked on to the back of the kitchen after the Tompkins arrived with an unexpected servant. A tiny bureau, a little rope bed, and a rickety straight-back chair in one corner barely fit into the room.

Sinking down on the hard straw mattress, the weary girl pulled her legs up under her, planted bony elbows on her knees and cupped her chin in her hands, contemplating. *What was the mistress thinking to even suggest that she should decline her cousin's offer? Who would reject an offer to have someone else pay their debt and purchase their freedom?* She frowned. It was true, though; she had no idea what would become of her if she went back to England. She no longer knew anything about life there and nothing of this cousin. Why would they want to take her back, indeed? Life with the Tompkins was almost unbearable at times, but at least she knew what to expect and what was expected of her.

She sighed deeply. Mrs. Tompkin would never really give her a choice anyway. If the mistress wanted her to stay, she would find a way to make her stay. However, Sarah thought with determination, the woman might be surprised to find that her demure servant still had something of a mind of her own left. But she must wait until they are in Norfolk to say anything about her intention to leave, or they might refuse to take her at all. Sarah gasped out loud at the thought, then reasoned that the greedy couple wanted the money badly enough; they would take her.

Pulling an old carpet bag from under the rope bed, she went to the little bureau across the room and emptied it of its meager contents. She had two extra skirts. If she wore one underneath her baggy dress, she felt sure it would not be noticed and she could bring all her things for her journey. Once done packing, Sarah crawled into the hard, narrow cot and covered herself with a thin, scratchy blanket, clasping the only possession she truly valued tightly against her: the Bible her parents had given her before she left England.

"Read it every day, Sarah," her father had said.

When she first arrived, she had read it often because it reminded her of home, and gave her hope that she would be back there someday. Now, with her hope waning, she read the precious book only occasionally because her father had asked her to. But, in fact, she did find comfort in the words of love she read there. She had heard few enough of those these last years.

Lying in the dark, eyes wide open, she stared at the familiar rough wood ceiling. Soon she would be leaving here and going home! Home - the word was so foreign to her now. What would home be like? Did she even have a home? With both of her parents gone, where would she live? She had nothing, no one. How could she leave here? Maybe the mistress was right. Maybe it would be better if she stayed, even as a free servant with no end to her term and no hope of ever leaving.

A tear slipped out of the corner of her eye. In a few hours everything had changed. Once again, her life was turned upside down. *God, help me trust you more. I know you are with me, but I am afraid,* she prayed, turning into her flat pillow, and crying herself into an exhausted sleep.

CHAPTER 2

He lay on the bunk, his 6'3" frame stretching from end to end. His legs were crossed, boots still on. Strong hands, fingers interlaced, cradled his head in a tight grip. Although his eyes were closed, there was a tautness about him that belied sleep or even relaxation. Grayson Attwood was a man with a great deal on his mind.

Dash it all! Six months ago, he had never heard of this girl and now his future rests in her hands. Grayson scowled bitterly at the thought. Even in death, Bethany reaches out to cause him trouble. Since she married his father 8 years ago, Bethany has brought nothing but grief and strife to him: conniving her way into his father's heart, getting him to marry her, and then convincing the enamored man to send his own son away to manage the shipyard in London, and finally persuading him to leave the entire estate to her! Anger and pain gripped his heart. But it was not his father's fault. It was that woman, always Bethany! And now, after she is finally gone, she rests her conscience on him. She had no thought of her niece in life, but in death, to appease her own guilt, she leaves the burden of the girl's plight on him.

Grayson swung his legs over the side of the bed and stood up. He needed to move, to think, to plan. Striding across the polished wood floor, he stomped up the stairs, his broad shoulders grazing the sides of the narrow stairwell. Out on deck, the air was still, hot, and close, pressing against him. Grayson shook his dark, collar-length hair, creating his own breeze. He suddenly

19

longed for England, for the cool nights and gentle breezes. He longed for this whole ordeal to be done with!

Tomorrow, he would meet the girl and begin the trip home. Grayson wondered about her then. He had never really given her much thought. Did she know anything of the situation? He had said as little as possible in the message he had sent. There had been no response and his messenger had not seen the girl, only the people to whom she was indentured. Grayson could only assume that they intended to turn Sarah over to him the next afternoon.

Sarah. He seldom thought of her by name. Until now, she had only been an irritation he had to deal with. Now she was about to become a reality in his life. A reality, but no less an irritation! Leaning against the deck rail, looking down at the inky black water lapping at the side of his ship, he wondered how Sarah had dealt with the news. From his message, she would know only that a cousin had come to free her and return her to England. She would not have any more memory of him than he had of her. They were cousins only by the unfortunate marriage of her aunt to his father. His full lips tightened into a thin line. Likely the girl did not even remember her aunt, her one fortunate condition. He would certainly consider himself fortunate had he never known Sarah's Aunt Bethany.

"Pardon me, Sir."

"What is it, Harper?" Grayson pushed away from the rail, turning to the old, weather-worn first mate who had been at his side on many a voyage. He was a valued sailor and trusted friend.

"The room is ready. I think it will be quite suitable for yer new charge." There was a smile in Harper's voice, picturing his large, strapping Captain as guardian to a young girl. "C'mon, Cap'n, come see the room. Make sure it meets your approval."

As this was a cargo ship, there had been no space for the girl. There was, however, a storage room that Grayson had ordered to be converted into quarters for her. He followed Harper's uneven gait down the stairs, past his own cabin, to the end of the hallway. Harper raised the lantern he carried to illumine the entry to the room. "Here ye be, Sir," he said with pride as he opened the door for Grayson. The tall man ducked to avoid the low doorframe as he entered the small room.

There was a bed against one wall with a small chest beside it, which would serve as a nightstand and bureau. On the opposite wall the old sailor had hung a curtain across the corner, forming a private area and had also put hooks on the wall so the girl could hang up some of her frocks. Grayson grimaced at the thought of frocks hanging in his ship. There was a space for her trunks and Harper had hung a small mirror above it. Grayson's eyes paused there.

"Where'd you get the mirror, Harper?" Grayson knew all of the furnishings on his ship and suspected what the answer would be.

Harper gulped but smiled when he said, "From the looks of ye, I didn't think ye was makin' much use of it." His smile was greeted with an answering frown. "Ah, Cap'n, she's a woman. Every woman wants a mirror around. And you have that hand mirror if you ever take to wantin' to comb that wild hair of your'n."

Grayson ran a hand through his thick hair. He kept it clean, but he would admit that the curls made it a bit unruly, and he didn't bother much about that. *Maybe he should tie it back more often and keep it out of the way.* He shook his head, scowling at that thought. *Having a female on board was not going to change anything! Especially not him!*

"She is not a woman, Old Man. She is just a girl. But all right, keep the mirror," he growled at his first mate. "Let her look in it as much as she likes. It will keep her out of my way." He surveyed the room again, then shook Harper's shoulder vigorously. "You have done a fine job of this. There are no better quarters on the ship save mine."

"Thank 'e, Sir." Harper led the way out of the room and back down the hall, stopping at Grayson's door, looking back at the man behind him, "Let me come in and talk for a minute, my boy."

Grayson nodded, opening the door to his cabin. He stopped in the entry, surveying the room before him. He loved this room, his refuge, his solace. It was by far the most spacious on the ship where everything was compact. The rich oak wood lining the walls gave a golden glow to the room in the lamplight.

His bed was secured against one wall, built large enough to fit his frame.

Against the far wall was his desk, a large table with thick curved legs staked to the floor. Grayson walked slowly over to it, rubbing his hand against the smooth, dark mahogany wood. The deep, rich grain carried his burdens, his responsibilities. No man knew him like this desk did. A rack of the same wood hung on the wall beside the desk, built especially for his rolls of maps. He absentmindedly ran a hand over them, drawing comfort from them. They were his guides. Some he had sketched himself on his voyages.

"Good memories in those maps, eh?" Harper's voice brought Grayson back to the present.

"Indeed, there are. We've been on many an adventure following them." He regarded his friend seriously. "What kind of adventure am I starting on now, Harper? I feel more uncertain in these waters than I have in the most dangerous seas of the Atlantic." Dropping down into the large chair behind his desk, the troubled man motioned to another chair, inviting Harper to join him, "Sit, please. Talk to me."

Harper sat down, offering what little advice he could, "There's nothing more to be done about it until tomorrow when you meet her. Even then, there's nothing to be done about it. You have no other option. Thinkin' on it more will not accomplish anything. Sleep now, meet her tomorrow."

"More easily said than done." Grayson shoved his chair back, ignoring the loud screech of wood on wood. "What do I tell her?" He paced across the room and back. "Do I tell her that I have come to rescue her because I cannot claim my inheritance otherwise?" he asked bitterly. "Because that's the truth of it. I wouldn't have even known about her if she hadn't come up in the will. And even if I had known, it is unlikely that I would have taken it upon myself to free her. She is a servant! And not even a blood relative! I am only claiming to be her cousin because the contract says that only a relative can free her." He threw his head back, running both hands through his hair. Stopping in front of Harper, Grayson pounded his fist on the desk, leaning close, "She probably has me pictured as a generous benefactor. I do not want to deal with it, I tell you! I do not want her gratitude. I can't be bothered with some female fawning at my feet. I have too many concerns while we are at sea. I have to tend the ship."

Harper hesitated before answering. "It is a dashed, awkward situation, my boy, but you know she can't help but be thankful. She has no doubt been in very hard times these past years. Ye've seen the condition of many an indentured servant. Of course, she must be relieved at the thought of being free. So ye'll have to deal with that. Ye've never been one to be so modest, has ye? Ye're doing a good thing, Grayson. Forget about why. Just let her be grateful."

Harper strode over to stand beside his captain. He was overshadowed by the younger man who stood a good foot taller than he. Looking up at his friend, he advised, "There's no need to be discussin' the will with her. Just tell her the simple truth - that it was her aunt's dyin' request that ye free her from her bondage and that you're pleased to do so."

Grayson nodded, "I will tell her what you say then, and no more. And," he snapped, striding to the door, his words punctuated by the click of boots on the hardwood floor, "I will tell her to leave me be when we are on the ship. My responsibilities here take precedence over anything regarding her. Any questions she has will be answered when we arrive in England." Grayson opened the cabin door for Harper to leave and then called after him, "I will be wanting you by my side at the meeting tomorrow."

Harper stopped, turning back to see his tall, strong friend leaning against the small doorframe. He had never seen Grayson without an air of complete confidence, but now there was a hesitancy, even timidity, about him standing there alone. "Grayson, I will stand at your side whenever you need me," he assured the troubled man. "Sleep now. We will see what the morrow brings."

Grayson nodded, "Sure, sure, old man. Let me be then so I can get some of this sleep you keep talking about. Tomorrow it is. Good night." He paused and then added, "Thank you, Harper."

CHAPTER 3

Sarah woke with a start. It was dark outside, the house still silent, but the occasional twitter of a bird awakening signaled that morning was approaching. She must be ready when the time came to leave. Mistress Tompkin would not abide tardiness, and Sarah did not want to bear any bruises today when she met her cousin. She touched her cheek, hoping the slap from last night had not left a mark.

Jumping out of bed, she splashed her face with cold water before pulling an old comb through her tangled hair. She had been allowed enough water for a bath and hair wash last night, and the long golden strands glistened as she braided them together into a thick braid, winding it into a bun at the base of her neck and securing it with a few pins. She dressed quickly, putting an extra skirt and shirtwaist on first, then slipped her dress over the top so that the mistress would not notice that she was bringing extra clothes.

With no mirror to check the results, Sarah could only hope that her cousin would not be too dismayed when they met. She knew her skin was not fashionably fair but had tanned from long hours spent in the hot sun. What she did not realize was that the golden tan made her green eyes startling, and the contrast with her blonde hair was striking. She had grown into a lovely woman.

"Sarah!" She jumped at the call. "Aren't you ready yet?"

"Yes, Mistress, I am ready," she called back, looking once more inside the bag she had packed the night before to make sure that there was nothing visible that would cause suspicion. She grabbed her Bible off the bed and put it inside, closed the bag and went to meet Mistress Tompkin.

Upon seeing her, the woman snapped, "There you are, finally! Now turn around, let me see you." Sarah turned slowly, breathing a sigh of relief when nothing was said about her clothes.

"There is a smudge on your face. Go wash and make a lunch to take along," the woman ordered, shoving the girl towards the door. "We must leave within the hour if we are to be in Norfolk by afternoon."

After packing some bread and cheese and a few apples, Sarah grabbed her bag and went out to the wagon where the Tompkins waited impatiently. She crawled up without a hand from Master Tompkin, who flicked the reins as soon as she stepped in. The horses sprang forward at his yell, "Ha!" knocking her down against the hard bench.

After they stopped for lunch, they began to see an occasional farmhouse in the distance, and soon houses began to appear more frequently until finally they could see the city ahead. As tired as she was, Sarah watched with excitement as they drove into the city. Buggies and horses lined the sides of the streets. People were bustling about the boardwalks carrying baskets of goods. The women wore lovely dresses of all colors, their hair done up with ringlets   hanging   around   their   faces.   Sarah absentmindedly reached up to touch her own now dust-coated hair and smoothed the skirt of her no longer clean dress.

The meeting with her cousin was to be at a small dining house at four o'clock that afternoon. Near the dining house was a hotel where the Tompkins had secured a room for the night. The room was on the second floor with six other rooms and a shared privy at the end of the hall. There was also a bathing room where one could have a bath prepared for an extra quarter.

Once in the room, Sarah went eagerly to the window to watch the activity below. "Sarah quit gawking and bring up the rest of our things and unpack them," Mrs. Tompkin instructed. "But be quiet about it. We are going to lie down for a rest."

A rest sounded lovely, but Sarah knew she would not have time for that and turned to leave and retrieve the Tompkin's bags. She only hoped that there might be a way for her to wash up and change out of her dress. She would feel more confident in the skirt and shirtwaist she wore underneath. They would at least be less dusty. The bun at the back of her head had long since fallen down. Pieces of hair had escaped the tight braid and hung around her in tangled strands. If she just had a few minutes, she could surely make herself more presentable than she was now.

"Sarah, inform the man at the desk that we want a bath brought up at three o'clock. It must be at three if we are to be ready in time. Do you understand?" Mrs. Tompkin's sharp command stopped her at the door.

"Yes, Mistress. I will get the things now." Sarah closed the door quietly behind her. Hauling the Tompkin's large bags out of the wagon was difficult for the small girl, and she struggled with the weight of them on the stairs, dragging them up one at a time and then her small bag as well. By the time she finished, the Tompkins were alternately filling the room with loud snores. Sarah unpacked their things carefully, watching that she did not wake them. She looked forward to an hour by herself and would surely not get it if they woke.

Creeping out the door, she carefully pulled it closed behind her, then froze! "Oh!" Her eyes widened. She clamped a hand over her mouth to stifle the gasp. She had completely forgotten to ask for Mistress Tompkin bath water. She didn't know what time it was but prayed there would still be time for the water to be ready at 3:00. Hurtling down the stairs at break-neck speed, thinking only of the bath water, the desperate girl failed to notice the tall man at the bottom just beginning his ascent, and crashed directly into him.

She might as well have run into a brick wall. With an outcry, she fell back against the rail when her arms were grasped by two large, strong hands that lifted her off the steps and set her firmly on the floor. Sarah looked up into dark, stormy blue eyes and felt like she was drowning in them.

CHAPTER 4

Grayson had just taken a few steps up the stairs when he heard a tremendous clatter and glanced up just in time to see a blur before the girl slammed into him. Catching her before she fell, he set her down on the floor in front of him. She weighed next to nothing and was really hardly worth noticing, he thought, quickly taking in her shapeless dress and messy hair. "Are you alright?" His voice came out low and gruff.

The girl did not reply but stood staring at the floor, "Are you alright?" he repeated, impatient with her silence. And then she looked up. He was startled for a moment, his breath catching. Her face was as dirt and sweat streaked as her clothing, but her eyes were so remarkable he hardly noticed. Too big for the small face, they stood out like two emerald jewels.

Grayson forced his eyes away and stepped back. He did not have time for this. Leaning against the banister, arms crossed, he waited for a reply to his inquiry.

"I.. I.. I think I'm alright," Sarah stuttered, looking at the floor again. "I am sorry. I wasn't watching where I was going."

"Obviously," was his stunted reply.

Harper stepped up from behind him, placing a calming hand on Grayson's shoulder. "Don't scare the poor girl. She didn't mean any harm." He then turned to the little thing, speaking kindly, "Where are you off to in such a hurry, Miss?"

"I need to order a bath," Sarah answered quietly.

Well, at least she knows it, Grayson thought, looking her over and assessing her slowly. "Obviously," he responded dryly. He heard her small gasp and suddenly realized how he must sound. *Why was he being so harsh with the girl? But what did it matter anyway? She had nothing to do with him. He had much more important things on his mind.*

Sarah refused to look at him. She knew she was a mess, but there was no need for him to be so rude. She felt her face flush red, and uncharacteristically small sparks of anger pricked at her insides. *It was just too much! Who was this man to be critical of her? It was enough that the Tompkins were always angry and criticizing her. He should have moved before she crashed into him. He wasn't watching what he was doing either. Obviously!*

She glared at him, green darts shooting from her eyes, then quickly turned away, but not before Grayson caught a glimpse of those sharp daggers. He chuckled and said, "Please excuse my rudeness. I have a great deal on my mind."

Sarah nodded and turned her attention to the older man, took a deep, calming breath and explained, "I need to order the bath for my mistress. I must have it prepared by three o'clock."

Grayson heard the desperation in her voice and saw a flicker of fear cross her remarkable eyes.

He had been upset when she came hurtling down the stairs, crashing into him, but now he found himself somewhat moved by her obvious distress over her mistress.

Calling the proprietor over, Grayson told him, "We need bath water on the second floor at three, please."

"Yes, of course, Mr. Attwood. We have some water warming now."

Grayson glanced at Sarah again. He couldn't imagine the girl had any money from the look of her and slapped a quarter on the counter.

The ever-considerate Harper stepped up, putting another quarter down, requesting, "If you have some water heating now, could we please have a bucket in the bathing room on this floor for the Miss while she waits?"

The proprietor assured them that he could spare a bucket of water and still have a bath upstairs in twenty minutes.

CHAPTER 5

Sarah turned to the men, including both the older man and the large tyrant in her quiet, "Thank you, Sirs. I am very grateful." She then swallowed her pride and addressed the dark-haired man directly, "Please accept my apologies for running into you."

"Yes, well, no harm done," he quipped. "We must be going now. We have a meeting shortly. Farewell." With that, he turned and walked away, the older man following.

Sarah watched them leave, then heard the proprietor calling to her, "The water is in the bathing room down the hall for you now, Miss."

Sarah gave him a brilliant smile, "Thank you." She paused, suddenly concerned, "Will you please be sure that the bath water is upstairs in time?" She couldn't help feeling nervous that the Tompkins would be looking for her, wondering where she was. The bath would keep them busy and give her a little more time for herself.

"Yes, Miss. Do not worry," the man assured her. "Come with me now. I will show you the room."

Sarah followed him down the hall and entered the door he opened for her. There were two buckets full of warm water on the floor beside an empty claw-foot tub. On a bench in the corner lay a fresh towel and a bar of soap. Sarah was overwhelmed, tears pricking in her eyes. She thanked the proprietor and locked the door behind him.

Once she removed her dress, she discovered that the skirt underneath had fared quite well, with just some dust around the hem. The shirtwaist had telltale damp spots from the heat of the day, but Sarah hoped much of that would dry, and she would be acceptable. After shaking out the clothes, she hung them on some hooks on the wall.

Picking up one of the buckets of water, she eagerly stepped into the tub. She poured the water over herself carefully at first and then, seeing the other bucket waiting, more liberally. Such bounty! The soap had a hint of lavender in it, and she used it liberally as well, then rinsed off with the second bucket.

Suddenly, she realized that as lovely as this all was, she could not luxuriate over it. She had spent too much time already. She really must hurry now. Grabbing the towel, she took a moment to rub her hand over its softness, then dried off quickly.

How fortunate it had been that she ran into the two men on the stairs. If only the tall man had not been so upset about it. It was an accident, after all. It's not as though she planned to crash into him. Oh well, she needn't trouble herself about it. She would never see him again. It had all ended up very well for her. She smiled and quietly thanked God in her heart.

A frown quickly replaced her happy smile when she reached up to touch her hair and felt the dirt and grime from the dusty road they had traveled. It was such a pity when it had been shiny and clean just this morning. What could she do with it? There was no time to wash it. She had very little time to finish before the Tompkins realized how long she had been gone. The thought touched a chord of fear. How would she explain her bath as it was, let alone if she arrived late? She couldn't do much with her hair, but she had to get some of the dirt out. She quickly undid the braid, shaking the golden mass out. A small cloud of dust surrounded her, falling to the floor. She leaned forward, flipping the hair over her head to shake even more of the dust off and then used the damp towel to rub it down.

She was dismayed at the brown film that covered the formerly white towel, but surely that meant her hair looked considerably better than it had. Running her fingers through the tangles, she pulled the hair back loosely, leaving a few shorter tendrils to curl down the sides of her face, then braided the rest quickly with practiced fingers. She shaped the braid into a honey-gold twist and pinned it high on her head. Sarah wished she could see herself. She had never bothered about that much before, but she had never had such an important day in her life before, either.

Grabbing the shirt off the hook, she checked it over. It was dry, and she slipped it on, following up with the dull brown skirt which hung loosely on her slight frame. She quickly wiped the dust off her shoes with the already dirty towel. With everything done and in place, Sarah felt quite presentable and much more prepared to meet her cousin than she had ever hoped.

Rolling up her dress and tucking it under her arm, she left the room happily. She prayed that the Tompkin's rest and baths had put them in a good frame of mind. Perhaps they had been busy enough not to have noticed her absence. She knew that was very unlikely and took a deep breath, raising her chin slightly. Soon, they would not have any power over her ever again.

Rushing down the hall, she paused to thank the proprietor. He looked up from the desk, his eyes widening when he noticed her. He greeted her with a smile, "You look very nice, Miss, if I may say so." A blush touched her cheeks, and she thanked the man quickly before hurrying up the stairs.

Amazing, the proprietor thought. What a change in the girl! She was really quite attractive, all cleaned up like that. What a shame that Mr. Attwood couldn't see her now.

CHAPTER 6

The Tompkins were almost ready to go when Sarah came rushing in. The mistress must have had a difficult time deciding what to wear. Clothes were strewn all around the room while toiletries littered the top of the bureau.

Mrs. Tompkin was looking in the mirror and did not bother to turn around to greet Sarah but immediately snapped, "Where have you been? I had to get dressed by myself. Come here and help me with my hair and button my dress. We don't have any time to spare."

While the woman continued to examine herself, Sarah quickly stuffed the dirty dress into her bag and then rushed over to help her mistress, tugging the sides of the too-tight dress together in order to button it around the well-padded waist. That done, she quickly started trying to fashion the thin, graying hair into something Mistress Tompkin would find acceptable.

After a glance in the mirror, the woman nodded, "It will have to do. Quickly now, it is almost 4:00. We must leave.

As Sarah turned towards the door, Mistress Tompkin reached out and grabbed her arm in a tight grip. "Remember, Sarah," she said smoothly but forcefully, "You are not going anywhere. You are going to meet your cousin and politely explain that you do not wish to go away to England," she emphasized her point by squeezing Sarah's arm ever tighter as she spoke. "Mr. Tompkin and I will manage all the negotiations and discussions. You will be silent. Do you understand that?" Her face was close, her eyes glaring into Sarah's.

Sarah's arm was hurting now, but she left it in the grip without flinching. She was sure she was going to have bruises. "Yes, Ma'am," the frightened girl answered quietly.

"Good! You still belong to us! Don't forget that. Come now!" The command included Mr. Tompkin, who stood quietly in the background, watching the scene unfold before him. He quickly came to his wife's side, politely holding her elbow as they went down the stairs. Sarah followed demurely behind.

The dining house where the meeting was to be held was directly next door to the hotel, and the little entourage was soon entering the establishment. Sarah scanned the room. There were a few tables occupied by other customers: a family of four, a young couple holding hands across the table, and an older couple ignoring each other. None of them appeared to be her cousin. They were shown to a table to wait.

Sarah was suddenly nervous. The time had finally arrived. She was about to meet her cousin. This meeting was all that had occupied her mind since she heard the news a day ago. She had been so excited to meet this person, but now that the time had come, she was afraid.

She glanced surreptitiously at the Tompkins, who were watching the door unwaveringly. All these years, she has had no affection for them. How could she have? And yet, they are really all she knows. She is about to leave everything behind again. She wouldn't be sorry to go, but it would still be a parting, the second drastic parting in her young life. She squeezed her eyes tightly shut. Surely, God had a part in all this, but Sarah felt as though she had been completely left out of the plans. A small voice inside her said, *Trust me.* Her heart answered *I'm trying,*

Just then, she felt the Tompkins sit up straighter in their chairs. Sarah tried to peer around them, but they blocked her view. She was certain that her cousin had arrived. The Tompkins stood up, and now she could see nothing but their backs. Footsteps approached their table, stopping in front of it. Her heart beat faster.

A deep voice questioned, "Mr. and Mrs. Tompkin?"

Sarah jumped up, stretching to see over the couple's heads, but could only see shiny dark hair falling forward like a curtain, hiding the face of the man who had bent down to greet the couple. Then the head lifted, and the hair parted. Her eyes locked with a pair of deep blue eyes, green looking into blue, both widening in shock. Time stopped. Neither Grayson nor Sarah moved.

Sarah's breath caught in her throat when she met the deep blue eyes. Her eyes roved over his face, taking in the brown hair curling over his forehead and down to touch his collar. He was undoubtedly the same man she had crashed into a few hours ago. *Why was he here talking to the Tompkins?*

Grayson stared into the green eyes, easily identifiable, although the face that held them seemed different somehow. Had the dirt really disguised this soft, glowing skin? Had her hair been that honey-gold color a few hours ago? Even her clothing was different. Certainly not fashionable, but not covered in dust and dirt either. But she was clearly the same girl who had run into him on the stairs. *What was she doing here?*

CHAPTER 7

An angry shout startled them both. "What are you doing, Girl? Stop bothering the gentleman!" Sarah moved back, shrinking away from the angry woman beside her.

"Sit down," Mrs. Tompkin exclaimed, reaching out to grab Sarah and pull her down when a strong hand clamped onto her arm.

"Leave her be. She is not bothering me," Grayson said sternly to the short, plump woman.

Mrs. Tompkin sputtered in protest but, looking at the imposing gentleman beside her, thought better of arguing.

Mr. Tompkin then stepped forward, making a meager attempt at defending his wife, "Now see here, Sir, my wife has every right to speak to the girl however she wishes. The girl belongs to us. She is our servant. We are waiting for a guest, so it would be best if you leave now."

The Tompkins turned away from Grayson and watched the door intently. Grayson followed their look. He was exasperated with the whole situation. He heard the condescension in his own voice when he spoke, "I believe I may be the person for whom you are watching. Let me introduce myself. I am Grayson Attwood. I am here to meet Mr. and Mrs. Tompkin and my cousin, Miss Sarah Blake."

Sarah's gasp filled the quiet room. Mrs. Tompkin reached out, yanking her arm. "Sit down and be quiet!

We will handle this," she hissed. Sarah sat, looking away from the man in front of her, fidgeting quietly with the tablecloth.

Mr. Tompkin replied to Grayson, "Yes, I am Mr. Tompkin, and this is my wife. Sarah is our servant."

Grayson gave a quick nod to Mr. Tompkin, acknowledging his introduction, and then sat down at the table across from Sarah. "Miss Blake," he began, "I sent a message yesterday informing you of my arrival. I am here to return you to England."

Sarah stared at him, confused. She looked over to the door of the dining house again.

"Miss Blake, you needn't continue to watch the door." His voice was brusque. "I am the person you are waiting for."

She was bewildered at his words, delicate brows drawing together. "But... I thought... Are you sure?"

Grayson hadn't known what to expect, but he found this reticence to accept him annoying. "Please enlighten me, what did you think?"

Sarah shifted uncomfortably under his gaze. "I was expecting my cousin to be a woman," she stammered.

Grayson ran his hand through his hair, "Indeed. And why would you expect that? Do you know of a woman who is your cousin? I know of no other relatives."

"Mrs. Tompkin said your name was Grace," Sarah hesitantly explained.

Mrs. Tompkin quickly defended herself, "I said I could not make out the name on your message and thought it was possibly Grace. The girl simply jumped to conclusions."

Leaning forward, Grayson looked Sarah directly in the eye, "It appears we have both been misinformed. You were expecting a woman, and I was expecting a young girl. How old are you anyway?"

The girl's thin shoulders slumped as she lowered her eyes, unshed tears shining in them.

Perhaps he had spoken a bit harshly, Grayson considered momentarily. His hand tightened into a fist on the table. *Was he going to have to continually be worrying about this female sensitivity? He has come all this way to rescue her, and yet she is crying!*

Sarah took a deep breath before answering, "I am eighteen and will be nineteen later this year. I am hardly a child."

Grayson was both happy that she was not a child he would have to play nanny to and unhappy that she was a woman he would have to be guardian over. However, he was seven years her senior, which would establish his authority.

CHAPTER 8

"Sarah!" Mrs. Tompkin's shout startled everyone, and all eyes snapped to her. "That is no way for you to speak to Mr. Attwood. I know you do not want to go to England, but that is no reason for this kind of behavior."

Sarah's head snapped up with a small gasp.

"Mrs. Tompkin," Grayson interjected, ignoring the woman's comment, "I believe we can quickly accomplish the business we have, after which Sarah can come with us to the ship." With that, Grayson reached into the pocket of his jacket and pulled out a large wad of bills.

"No, no, Mr. Attwood," the woman said. "Let us not be hasty. We should sit down and have a cup of coffee as we discuss the matter. Sarah, you go back to the hotel. We do not need you here."

Sarah hesitated, looking first at Harper and then at Grayson. Clearly, she wanted to stay, to hear what was said. Grayson went over to stand beside her. "Sarah, please sit down. You should be here while we discuss this," he stated, in direct contradiction to Mrs. Tompkin's order.

The woman sat down with a loud "Hmpf!" the chair creaking in protest.

Grayson gave her a curt nod as he and Harper were seated. "I believe things will be settled easily enough. I offer a fair price for the final two years of Miss

Blake's service. I have here a copy of the indenture agreement stating my right to buy her back." He pulled a neatly folded piece of paper out of his pocket and opened the aged document carefully, setting it in the middle of the table. Everyone leaned forward to view the document. Grayson pointed to a small paragraph at the bottom. "You can see here a clause stating that if a relative of Sarah Blake wishes to redeem her before her full tenure, they must be permitted to do so." The document was signed by both the Blakes and the Tompkins and witnessed by a legal barrister. "I believe that is clear enough," he stated firmly, daring anyone to disagree.

"We do not wish to contest your right to redeem Sarah, Mr. Attwood. We have a copy of the agreement also," the timid Mr. Tompkin stated.

"Well then, I will give you your payment and Harper can go with Miss Blake to retrieve her things and take her to the ship." Grayson took the money from his pocket again and began counting it out on the table.

Mr. Tompkin put a hand on his arm, "Mr. Attwood, there are some things we would like to discuss with you first. Sarah has expressed that she does not want to return to England. Haven't you Sarah?"

Immediately, everyone's attention was riveted on the small figure across the table. All color had drained from her already pale face. Even her eyes had faded to a dull green

She turned from one pair of eyes to the next, obviously distressed, not knowing what to say.

"You see how afraid she is at the idea of leaving?" Mrs. Tompkin declared. "And can you blame her? She has no home in England, does not know anyone, and for that matter, she does not even know you, Mr. Attwood, and you are about to take her away on a very long voyage. Of course she does not want to go!"

Grayson was surprised at the almost protective feeling that came over him as he watched Sarah, who did indeed appear to be afraid, but of what he was not sure. Of leaving? Or possibly staying? Whatever the reason, it was essential that she come with him. He spoke to her gently, "Sarah, you do not need to fear coming to England. I believe you will be happy there. I will take care of you."

"But surely you do not wish to take her back to England with you, Sir," Mrs. Tompkin interjected. "Look at her! She is barely strong enough to do housework and would make a poor servant for you."

Grayson looked at the woman with disdain, "I do not lack for servants, Madam. I have no need of another."

Mrs. Tompkin squirmed, uncomfortable at having suggested such a thing to the fine gentleman before her. "Yes, yes, of course not," she stammered. "I only meant that it is a lot of work for you to take her back and train her in English ways. We would be willing to keep her here and spare you that bother. You can pay for her last years of service, freeing her of her bond, and then we will take her off your hands and keep her here as a free servant. You may rest assured that we will pay her a fair wage, and she would be free to leave whenever she wishes.

It will work out well for everyone: she won't have to leave, you won't have to take care of her, and we will have our servant." Mrs. Tompkin laid out her proposal, never blanching at the scowl directed her way.

Grayson admitted to himself that the Tompkin's plan to leave Sarah here had a certain appeal. The girl would be a bother, but without returning her to England, he could not claim his fortune. The stipulation in Bethany's will was not that he simply free her but that he return her to England and provide for her there. Always that document! Plaguing him! Regardless of how inconvenient it was, Sarah was coming with him.

He spoke firmly to Mrs. Tompkin but focused on Sarah, "Miss Blake is my cousin, Madam. I need no further reason for wanting to take her home." There, that should make the girl willing to come with him, he thought, watching Sarah digest the comment.

Sarah had been sitting silently, listening to them bartering for her, but snapped to attention when Grayson spoke. *He was willing to do all this simply because she was family?!* Her throat tightened. She had forgotten what it meant to be family. She looked at him, her expression full of surprise and gratitude.

Grayson was disturbed by her look. He did not want her to think of him as a generous benefactor. In an effort to correct that impression, he explained, "I became aware of Sarah's plight through her aunt, who wanted to correct the wrong done six years ago and have the girl returned to her rightful home. It was her aunt's dying wish and my responsibility to complete." *There, that should clear it up. She can see that it is not he but her aunt who wants her release. She could be grateful to Bethany all she wanted. It was time to get this done.* "There is no more discussion necessary. Here is your money," he said firmly to the Tompkins. He began counting the bills one by one on the table.

Halfway through the wad, Mrs. Tompkin put her hand on his arm, "That is fine. I can see that it is all there. If you are sure you want to take the girl, then get on with it," the woman huffed, "You will find you've gotten the worse part of the bargain."

Grayson turned to Harper, "Take Sarah back to the hotel. I will finish here, then bring the cart to transport her things to the ship."

"Yes, Sir, Cap'n." Harper smiled broadly as he took Sarah's arm to help her up from the table. "Come along, missy."

Sarah stopped at the door, staring at the Tompkins, uncertain what to do. *Were they really going to let her go?* They were huddled over the table with her cousin, happily counting their money.

Mrs. Tompkin looked up from the table to see her standing there. "Are you still here? For goodness sakes, go! Get your things, and don't leave a mess. I do not want to have to clean up after you."

There was not a moment of kindness in her voice or face. *The mistress is eager to be rid of me now,* Sarah thought. She had never been able to do anything right for them. At first, she had tried so hard because she wanted them to like her. Later, she tried hard so they wouldn't punish her. Even then, she hoped they might at least come to value her work. Maybe even now, in this last moment, she still wanted them to show some feeling for her, to say something kind, to look at her with some care.

The Mistress turned and saw her still there. "I told you to leave! I don't want you in the room when we get back to the hotel. Do you understand? At least we won't have to worry about what to do with you tonight."

Harper took Sarah's arm and tugged her gently toward the door. "Come along now. Let's go to the hotel and get ye ready."

Sarah walked silently beside the kindly old man, head lowered, feet dragging. Slowly, she stood straighter, her steps firm, her head finally up, and she walked almost confidently. "I'm done with them," she said quietly but with determination. "They can't hurt me anymore. God has given me a chance to start over again."

"That He has, Miss," Harper agreed.

Sarah glanced over at him, eyes slightly puffy and red-rimmed, but she gave him a small smile. "I am just going to be thankful and do my best. I do not want Mr. Attwood to regret doing this."

"Ah..hmm," Harper cleared his throat, "No, Miss, I'm quite sure he will have no regrets about bringing you back to England. Don't you worry none about that?"

The hotel was just up ahead, and Grayson was already there, leaning against a wagon out front. "Come along, Sarah," the old man said, hurrying her along. "The captain'll be wantin' to get on board now that this is all done with. Are all yer things packed?"

Sarah gave a little dry laugh as she answered Harper. "Yes, ALL my things are packed. We should not have any trouble getting down to the ship quite quickly."

Grayson pushed away from the wagon and strode over to meet them, clearly anxious to leave. "Let's get her things and get down to the ship. Morning can't come soon enough, and we can leave this place behind. Sarah, can the three of us get your things downstairs and into the wagon, or should I get one of the men to help?" He glanced over her shabby condition, "I don't expect you have much more than one trunk," he observed.

"Your assessment of me is correct, Mr. Attwood. I do not have much. In fact, you and Harper can wait down here, and I will get my things and be right down," Sarah answered quickly. She was tired of it all, too. Little pricks of anger poked inside her, and she looked away before they shot out of her eyes again. What was it about this man that irritated her so easily? She was surprised to hear a deep, rumbling laugh coming from the rogue in front of her.

Grayson had not heard Sarah speak much. She had just sort of been there, in the background, quietly letting her world take shape around her. The snappish response surprised him, just like the little green darts he had seen earlier. In fact, he was pleased to see that little Sarah had some spunk in her and told her so, "My, my, Miss Blake, not all meek and mild now with your new-found freedom. That is good. You will need all the strength you have got to get you through the voyage ahead. However, whether or not you feel strong enough to get your own things, we will assist you in bringing them down."

Sarah was too tired and emotionally drained to try and explain further. She simply turned and trudged ahead of them up the stairs to the Tompkin's room. She stepped one foot inside and froze. With everything going on, she had forgotten how the room looked when they had left for the meeting. Mrs. Tompkin's things were still scattered everywhere.

Grayson and Harper stared at the room, their faces showing surprise at what they saw. They turned to her simultaneously.

Sarah suddenly looked at the room through their eyes. They had no way of knowing that she did not have a room of her own. Naturally, they would assume the things scattered around were hers. She went to her bag, picked it up and turned to face them, "I am ready. We can go."

"What of all this should we bring?" Grayson waved a hand over the room. "You said you were ready, but never mind that now. We are all tired. We will help you pack these things and be off."

"I have my things here. I am ready to go," Sarah re-iterated, lifting the bag to show them.

"Come now, surely that is not all," Harper spoke up.

"You forget, both of you," Sarah said, irritated once again. After taking a calming breath, she explained slowly, "I am a servant. This is not my room. I do not have a room. That rug on the floor would have been my bed tonight."

As she spoke, Grayson realized it all made sense. He should not have been surprised that she had so little. Women usually had so many trappings that he had just assumed she would also, forgetting that she was not in the position to have the things most women had, especially the women he knew. A picture of Lydia flashed into his mind. He doubted if she wore the same dress more than once a week.

Observing Sarah standing there, so small and gaunt, he suddenly recalled the way he had talked to her earlier, scorning her appearance. He had never really thought about her, how she felt about the things happening around her, happening to her. Did she have feelings? She hugged her little bag to herself, her face fluctuating with looks of embarrassment, defiance, and fear. His groan came from deep inside. Without question, he had his faults, but he was generally not completely insensitive!

Sarah cowered back at his groan, "I am sorry, Mr. Attwood. I should not have talked like that. It really might be best if we leave now. My Mistress said she did not want me here when she got back. If I were not leaving with you, I expect I would be getting the strap for all this mess."

"You certainly would be getting the strap, you snippet." The familiar, unpleasant voice came from the door. Sarah, Harper and Grayson turned as one to see the Tompkins standing there. All the color drained from Sarah's face, and Grayson stepped quickly to her side when she began to sway.

CHAPTER 9

"I told you to be gone when we got here, Sarah! And, I believe I said, don't leave a mess," Mrs. Tompkin said, looking around the room and back at the girl.

Grayson stepped forward, "We were just leaving. Sarah has her things. The rest," he surveyed the room with disgust, "I believe is yours." He took Sarah's arm and nodded at Harper to follow.

When they reached the door, Mr. Tompkin reached out and touched Sarah's arm, stopping her, "Oh, Sarah, I think you left something at home that you will be wanting."

Sarah paused, wondering what Mr. Tompkin could be referring to. She had brought everything. "No, Sir, I can think of nothing I left behind."

"Strange," he said, cocking his small, bald head to one side, looking every bit like a crow eyeing his prey. "I am sure I saw that Bible of yours on the table just before I went to get the wagon. I know you put a lot of stock in it, so I remember it surprised me to see it lying there so casually like you didn't want it."

Sarah grabbed onto Grayson's arm to steady herself. Why is the master saying that? Of course, she wouldn't leave her Bible behind; the one thing that mattered to her, the only stable thing in her life. She distinctly recalled putting it in her valise. She looked up at Grayson, "My valise. It is in my valise."

Grayson picked up the small bag from the floor where she had dropped it. "We will look through your bag now. I am certain it is there if you say you put it there." The look he gave Mr. Tompkin was menacing. They have put her through enough, he thought. If they are up to something, they will have to deal with him.

Sarah began looking through her things calmly, then more anxiously, then desperately, emptying the contents. "It was here! It was. Where is it?" She begged Mrs. Tompkin with pleading eyes, "Where is it?"

Mrs. Tompkin huffed, "Calm down, Sarah. If it isn't in your valise, then obviously you have left it behind, as Mr. Tompkin said. Crying about it is not going to help anything.

Sarah went over to lean against the wall beside Harper. Grayson followed her. "Sarah, I can get you another Bible. In fact," he put a hand on his first mate's shoulder, "old Harper here probably has an extra one on the ship. He certainly quotes enough of it at me that it would not surprise me if he has them all over the ship." He hoped the casual comment might lighten the moment and console her enough that they could leave.

But Sarah just kept shaking her bowed head. He could barely hear her stuttering words, "My parents gave it to me to bring to America. It is all I have of them." She looked up at Grayson, the life gone out of her eyes, "I will go back with the Tompkins. You needn't wait. I will stay as their servant."

Grayson put his hand on her shoulder, speaking firmly, "Sarah, I came to bring you home, and that I intend to do. I will settle this."

He strode over to the Tompkins, towering over the now pale couple. He most certainly was not going to let Sarah go anywhere with them. They could easily disappear into the countryside, and he would never find her again.

"I will delay our departure," he informed them. "At daylight tomorrow, I will escort you myself to your home, retrieve the Bible, and will be back on board my ship by early afternoon and then set sail."

The Tompkins were visibly dismayed at his suggestion. That would not do at all. They turned to each other, whispering quietly.

Mrs. Tompkin walked across the room, speaking as she went, "Amidst all this turmoil, I had completely forgotten that I also saw the Bible lying on the table, and realizing how important it is to Sarah, I picked it up on my way to the wagon. If I am not mistaken, I put it in my reticule as I left. Let me just check." She picked up a cloth handbag, rustled around inside, and pulled out the small black book with worn gold edging.

Sarah ran across the room, taking Mrs. Tompkin's hands in her own, the Bible between them. "Thank you, Mistress. Thank you so much." She rested her head on their clasped hands.

"Oh, for goodness sake, Girl, leave me be!" Mrs. Tompkins pushed her away, relinquishing the Bible, which Sarah instantly clutched to herself.

Grayson came to her side, "We will be leaving now. You owe no thanks to these people, and even God does not seem to have been of much help to you," he remarked cynically.

"You have no idea," Sarah said, wanting to tell him how wrong he was about that, but not now. Now, she would do all she could to help him get to his ship as quickly as possible. She glanced up, meeting those deep blue eyes. She smiled at him then, trust and gratitude shining in her eyes.

Trust and gratitude - two things Grayson Attwood knew he did not deserve. As much as he was disturbed by Sarah's look of trust, Grayson was taken by her sweet smile: full, naturally pink lips turned up to reveal small, straight white teeth. He had not seen her smile much. Of course, she didn't have much to smile about then, did she? He looked into her eyes; he had seen them well with tears, widen in fear, lower in shame, but never shine with happiness. At that moment, he found himself hoping that she would have many more reasons to smile once he got her away from these people and onto the ship with him.

He turned his head away, shoving that thought out of his mind. *This was not about making her happy! She was in his care because he needed her there to acquire his inheritance.* He took the bag out of her hands rather abruptly, but she never moved, letting him remove it without any resistance.

"Come, let's get out of here and on our way to the ship. Harper, take Sarah's bag to the wagon. I will come with her in a minute," he instructed, handing the bag to Harper.

Sarah still had not moved. She stood staring at the Tompkin's hard, cruel faces. "Sarah, come," Grayson spoke firmly but softly, turning her towards the door, guiding her with his arm around her waist. He could feel her tenseness. What was the matter with her? She was leaving a terrible situation. He was anxious to get going and becoming impatient. He felt her turning back to look at the Tompkins. "Careful," he whispered, "You'll turn into a pillar of salt."

Sarah stopped abruptly at his words. Her mind was suddenly full of images from the Bible story when Lot's wife looked back and turned into a pillar of salt. Maybe she had felt this way, realizing that everything she knew was back in Sodom. As awful as that city was, Lot's wife did not know what lay ahead and would not trust God enough to not look back to that security.

Now, I don't know what lies ahead. Do I trust God enough to not look back? Will I put all my security in Him even without knowing? Sarah wondered. That quiet voice inside her said, *"Trust me."*

"There is nothing for you here," Grayson said as kindly as he could. "That woman never cared about you. She was only using you so that she could look rich and important." Sarah's face blanched, and her eyes sparkled with unshed tears.

Dash it all! He hadn't meant to upset her. He wanted to make her look ahead to better days when she would be…, be…., what? He swallowed hard. *Be used again? A means to an end again?* He clenched his hand into a fist by his side. *She must never discover that he was, in essence, doing the same thing the Tompkins had done! Using her for his own gain.*

Sarah's tears spilled over, running down hollow cheeks. Grayson shook his head hoping to clear his mind. He didn't want to think about it anymore, didn't want to face the truth of what he was doing. She was going to be better off regardless of his motives. He took her arm gently and directed her to the door, down the steps and into the cool evening air.

Harper was waiting in the wagon, reins in hand when they came out. Grayson helped Sarah into the wagon, and then climbed up beside her. "Let's go, Harper," he said, and with a slap of the reins, the wagon moved slowly forward. Sarah stifled a yawn as she settled down on the hard bench.

Grayson glanced up at the evening sky, "We'll need to travel quickly now. We can still make it before dark. It is but a half hour from here." He observed the tired girl beside him and warned her, "I'm sorry, but the road is rough."

Sarah assured him, "You do not need to worry about me. I have been on rough roads before. I will be fine."

One dark eyebrow rose, "Indeed? That is good to know." He had no intention of worrying about her, so was glad to hear that she had no such expectation.

The wagon rolled on. The steady gait of the horses and the sway of the wagon were somehow soothing, and Sarah relaxed, suddenly so very tired. Before long, she had leaned against Grayson, resting her head on his shoulder, her soft curves pressing against him. Grayson quickly realized that he had been wrong when he said she was a girl and not a woman. He nudged her with his elbow to wake her. She snapped up straight, "Oh! The sway of the wagon made me sleepy."

"Good," Grayson replied, "Let's hope that the sway of the ship has the same effect." He loved the feel of the ship, had never been sea-sick a day in his life. He certainly hoped that this girl was not the sickly type. There were no nurse maids on his ship. She would be on her own if she did get sick.

Silence settled over the wagon, and everyone was lost in their own thoughts, all focused on getting to the ship and beginning the voyage ahead of them. It was not long before Harper pulled on the reins, bringing the horses to a stop at the top of a knoll looking out over the harbor.

"There she is, the Sea Wolf." The pride in Grayson's voice was unmistakable. The ship was silhouetted against the sunset sky, tall masts standing straight and strong.

Sarah gasped when she saw it, looking away from the boat and staring down at the floor of the wagon.

With everything that had happened today, she had not really had time to think about going back to England. It had been such a shock to discover that this man was her cousin. She had pictured her cousin as someone who would be a friend, someone to talk to and confide in. *This man was not that person*, she thought, glancing at him from beneath lowered lashes. Now, with the sight of the ship, the journey to England was thrust before her. *She was, indeed, going to England, on that ship, with this man.* A shiver ran through her. She heard Mrs. Tompkin voice in her head, taunting her, "They probably don't even really want you there. And why would you want to go to live with relatives you don't even know?" Maybe the mistress had been right after all. Was she doing the right thing? It didn't really matter now; she was here, looking at the ship that would carry her away. Leaning forward, she put her elbows on her knees and rested her forehead on the palms of her hands, praying earnestly for strength and peace.

"You don't like my ship, Sarah?" Grayson's sardonic question broke the silence. The girl baffled him. Not once had she reacted with joy during this day. He recalled his concern of the night before that this girl he was going to free would be overzealous in her thankfulness to him, bothering him with her gratitude. Now, he wondered if she was really thankful at all. At every turn, she seemed somehow displeased. He was tired, and he'd had enough of this day. He longed to be at the helm, steering his ship into the cool night breeze, smelling of the sea he loved.

Part 2

The Voyage

CHAPTER 10

Two men came to greet them when they arrived at the dock. Jumping down from the wagon, Harper handed the reins to one, issuing instructions for returning the wagon and horses. Grayson greeted the other man, handing him Sarah's bag while confirming that the ship had been loaded with the cargo and fresh supplies and was prepared for the voyage.

When Grayson walked back to the wagon, Sarah stood quickly, preparing to get down. She had just set one small foot on the first step when strong hands circled her waist, lifting her easily out of the wagon. She looked up at Grayson, a thank you on her lips, but he stopped her with a quick nod. Placing her hand in the crook of his arm, he pulled her forward to walk with him to the waiting vessel.

Grayson's stride was long, and he walked quickly, eager to be aboard. Even with two quick steps to match his one, Sarah was having difficulty keeping up. He did not notice her situation until she stumbled and grabbed onto him to keep from falling. He stopped immediately and steadied her, realizing that he must have been half dragging her, walking as he did. Whether he liked it or not, she was a woman, and he would need to be a bit careful of her at times. With a deep sigh, he reached for her hand, tucked it back in his arm, and walked forward at a much slower pace.

At the gangplank, Grayson guided her up the narrow board. He jumped down onto the deck. Ahhh, it was good to be back. He turned and lifted the tired girl down to stand beside him. With a slight bow and a sweep of his hand around the deck, he said, "Welcome to the Sea Wolf, Sarah."

"Thank you, Mr. Attwood," she replied softly.

Something grated him about the 'Mr. Attwood.' He called her by her first name, yet she always addressed him so formally.

Just then, Harper came over with a large smile, hand outstretched to Sarah. She moved to meet him, taking his hand. "Good to have you aboard, Sarah girl," the older man said in welcome.

Sarah's smile was genuine, and she answered with enthusiasm, "Thank you, Harper. It is good to be here." She was surprised to realize that she meant it. Turning slowly, she looked over the ship, stopping when her eyes ran into a pair of dark blue eyes watching her.

"Good then," Grayson said. "Everyone is happy to be aboard, but it is getting late, and I think we should show Sarah her cabin so she can get to bed, and we also. Bring her along, Harper."

He turned, walking briskly past Harper and Sarah and the small audience of sailors that had gathered to watch their captain's return to the ship. They had gotten more than they expected, having not known that they were taking on a passenger, a woman at that. They stared openly at Sarah as she and Harper walked by until Harper stopped and commanded them, "Back to work with ye all now," and they quickly scattered. Harper stopped one sailor, ordering him to bring a keg of fresh water down to the cabin on the lower deck and then directed Sarah to the stairwell where Grayson waited.

After descending the steep stairway, the three walked single file down the hallway to the room at the end. Harper opened the door, stepped inside, and held the lantern high to illumine the doorway. "Careful of the step," he warned, reaching a hand to help Sarah.

Grayson followed, bending to avoid the low beam, his tall frame blocking the doorway. Sarah stood staring at him. His eyes locked with hers, both recognizing that this moment marked the end of one existence and the beginning of another.

CHAPTER 11

A knock at the door broke the spell between Grayson and Sarah. They quickly looked away from one another as a young sailor entered, carrying a keg of water. Harper instructed him to put it behind the curtain in the far corner.

The boy couldn't resist looking at Sarah as he crossed the room. He would be the center of attention in the crew quarters tonight, having had the opportunity to see the passenger up close. Everyone would want to hear about her. He didn't see much to talk about, though; a quiet little thing, looking down at the floor. He couldn't tell much about her looks with her hair back in a bun and some ugly brown clothing hanging on her; looked like a tired brown mouse, she did. He'd have to do some exaggerating to make the story interesting, he figured.

On his way out, he gathered his courage and stopped as he passed her, managing to croak out a nervous, "Good night, Miss," despite the stern, watchful eye his captain had fixed on him. Sarah looked up and smiled. The boy's eyes widened. He wouldn't have to do quite so much exaggerating as he had thought. She was right pretty up close, with beautiful green eyes and soft tan skin. She returned his good night quietly, her eyes dropping back to the floor. The growl of Grayson clearing his throat made the sailor jump. One glimpse of the Captain's face had the boy saluting and quickly disappearing out the door.

Grayson turned his stern look on Sarah. What he did not need was for the men to be preoccupied by her presence. Before long, they would be vying for her attention. She would distract them from their duties, and he would have to deal with the consequences. Would this day never end? He longed for the solitude of his quarters. He needed time alone to think, plan, and hopefully, sleep.

Sarah sensed his eyes on her bowed head and slowly lifted her face to look at him. He saw his own tiredness reflected in her eyes, mixed with confusion at his stern glare. His look softened as he walked over to stand in front of her. None of this was her fault any more than it was his. He pictured Bethany, the real cause of all this. Sarah was really just a pawn in it all. She had actually held up quite well, considering all that this interminable day had thrown at her. In fact, he was quite impressed with her ability to handle the unexpected, and often unpleasant, events she had faced. Hopefully, that bode well for the voyage ahead.

The thought of the voyage brought him back to attention and he spoke quickly, "There are some things I must attend to before we set sail in the morning so I will bid you good night, Sarah."

"I should be going also," Harper agreed. "I hope you will find your room suitable, although it is a mite small."

"I'm sure I shall," Sarah responded. "At the Tompkins, I had a very small space. I do not require much."

She looked around the room. It really was nice. Although the ceiling was low, almost touching Grayson's head, the light color of the unfinished wood brightened the small space, making it seem larger. "This is more than enough."

"The Captain ordered it especially fixed up for you," Harper interjected. "It was a storage room, filled right up, but we moved everything out, so you'd have a proper cabin." The proud smile Harper turned on Grayson was unreciprocated.

Sarah peered up at the tall man beside her, a small smile on her lips, "Thank you Captain Attwood. It really is very nice. I'm sorry if I seemed ungrateful. You have done so much for me already. I don't really know how to thank you," she said gently.

With a quick nod, Grayson acknowledged her thanks, repeated his good night, and stepped out the doorway. A moment later he reappeared. "We will be setting sail early. I prefer that you stay below deck until we are under way, Sarah. Someone will inform you when you may come topside. I trust you will sleep well. Good night."

Her quiet "good night" drifted unheard through the doorway in his wake. The room seemed so empty without his commanding presence. Sarah found herself watching the door, hopeful, maybe, that he might suddenly reappear. She shook her head. What was she thinking?! She certainly did not want him returning to issue more orders to her. Stay below deck, indeed!

She turned abruptly away from the door to find Harper watching her curiously, his eyes thoughtful. "Looks to be an interesting voyage we have before us," he chuckled, glancing from Sarah to the empty door and back. Sarah followed his look, uncertain of what he found so amusing. Harper just smiled at her and said, "I'll be off now, Girlie. Have a look around the cabin. If there's anything ye're needing, tell me tomorrow and I'll see what I can do." He handed her the lantern he carried as he left, cautioning her to be sure to extinguish it before going to sleep and to put it in the drawer of the nightstand.

"Thank you so much, Harper, for everything. Tell Captain Attwood that I will stay here until someone lets me know that I am free to move about tomorrow."

From the look on her face and the slightly sarcastic edge to her voice, Harper doubted her words. Grayson had better not make her stay below deck too long. She was obviously used to work and activity. Sitting in a room waiting didn't seem likely to suit her well. Harper promised to give Grayson her message and assured her that the Captain would be happy to hear it. An interesting voyage indeed, he thought with a grin as he walked to the stairwell.

Sarah closed the door behind Harper and leaned against it with a sigh, glad of the quiet, glad to be alone. She had often been alone at the Tompkins and had grown used to silence, listening to her own thoughts. The constant company and commotion of this day had left her emotionally and physically drained.

After a moment, she perused the room. Against the far wall was a large shape she recognized from her voyage to America to be the bed. It was like a large cradle, shaped like a V with a deep bottom and high sides. The peculiar design helped keep passengers secure when the weather got rough.

Sarah then went to investigate behind the curtain in the corner. Pulling it back, she saw hooks on the wall where she could hang her things. The keg of water the sailor had brought was on the floor, tied in place by a thick rope. Beside it was a small chest. Opening the chest, Sarah found a metal basin and cup, a bar of soap, a towel, an old but clean hairbrush, and even some tooth powder. She was stunned! All this, for her? She closed the chest and sat down on it for a moment. Her mind worked furiously to comprehend this day: such kindness mixed with severity, so much loss competing with unexpected gain, everything changed.

Getting up, she walked slowly to the bed. Her bag lay on the floor, but she was too tired to unpack it tonight. After pulling out her nightgown and changing, she went back to get a drink of water from the barrel. After taking a small drink, she dampened a cloth, wiping her face with the cool fabric, a sigh of pleasure escaping her lips.

She took the hairbrush to the bed with her. Settling down into the contraption, she pulled the brush through her hair, delighting in the scratch of the bristles against her scalp. She brushed the long curls for several minutes before braiding them into one thick braid down her back and then reached for her Bible, clasping it tightly to herself, quietly murmuring a prayer of thankfulness. God had not stayed in England when she left after all. He had been with her all this time, even when she did not feel Him there. "Please stay with me now," she whispered. Opening the little book, she saw her father's inscription inside:

To our darling Sarah, God will be with you and keep you in His care while we are parted from one another. Until we meet again.

Lovingly, Mother and Father.

Proverbs 3:23, 24 Then you will walk in your way securely, and your foot will not stumble. When you lie down you will not be afraid; when you lie down your sleep will be sweet.

She had read the dedication many times before, but her eyes welled with tears now. She was finally coming home but they weren't there. She knew she would meet them again one day, but right now she didn't want to wait until Heaven. Right now she wished they would be in England, waiting with outstretched arms to welcome her. A tear splashed on her father's writing.

In the quiet darkness she slid down into the bed. It wasn't comfortable, but Sarah liked the secure feeling of the sides pressing against her, holding her in, keeping her safe. Behind closed eyelids a picture of Grayson appeared. She heard him promising her that she didn't need to be afraid, that he would take care of her in England. She felt his strong hand taking hers to prevent her from falling as they walked to the ship. Her hand curled under her cheek. She barely heard the quiet whisper on her lips before she fell asleep, "Thank you Lord, for bringing Grayson to rescue me."

CHAPTER 12

Sarah groaned, rolling over onto her stomach, throwing an arm up over her head, covering her ears. Why are they shouting, and what is all the banging? Her eyes snapped open, and she sat up quickly, heart pounding. Oh no, they are angry. She'd overslept. Any minute the Mistress will throw the door open and yank her out of bed, yelling about the bread not being set and breakfast not ready.

Quickly Sarah swung her legs around and encountered the side of the bed with a loud thump. "Ouch," she yelled, holding her throbbing foot. She looked around, slightly disoriented, brain still fuzzy from sleep. Slowly the events of the past evening returned to her. Her breathing slowed as she recognized the cabin.

She studied the plank board ceiling, hearing the pounding of heavy footsteps running back and forth, louder thuds of objects being dropped, the creak of wood rubbing on wood, a cacophony of sounds she did not recognize, all accompanied by loud voices and shouted commands.

Sarah carefully lifted her feet up over the side of the bed before she jumped out. A moment ago she had been afraid, dreading the day ahead. Suddenly she was excited. The energy from above radiated down through the ceiling, catching hold of her, and she was eager to get dressed and go up. Tossing the dusty brown skirt from the day before aside, she reached into her bag pulled out the faded dress she had worn on the trip to Norfolk and tossed it aside, also. Reaching back inside, she found the black skirt. It would look fine with the clean shirtwaist she pulled out.

After dressing quickly, Sarah brushed her hair, twisting it into a bun at the back of her head. As she crossed the room, she saw the mirror hanging on the wall. Curiosity drew her to it. Large green eyes fringed with dark lashes and topped with delicate arched brows stared back at her. Her skin was smooth and clear with a healthy glow from the golden tan. High cheek bones stood out prominently in her too-thin face. A spattering of freckles crossed the bridge of a small, straight nose. All-in-all she thought she appeared much younger than her 18 years, like a schoolgirl who had played out in the sun too long. No wonder Grayson thought he could order her about. She lifted her chin and with a glare turned away from the mirror, chastising herself for bothering with it in the first place.

She was at the door, hand poised to open it before she remembered Grayson's final instructions of the night before, "stay below deck until someone comes for you." She hesitated, hand on the latch. Slowly she let go and turned away. The click of the heels on her worn shoes became more punctuated with each step as she paced across the room. How long would it be before someone came for her? She couldn't just sit here waiting.

Stopping by the bed, she noticed her bag on the floor. Unpacking it would occupy a few minutes. With a sigh, she picked the bag up and carried it to the curtained corner, dropping it on the floor with a loud thud. She hung her dress and shirtwaist on the hooks. The rest of her things she put inside the chest on the floor.

She sat down on the bench next to her bed, feeling at a loss for anything else to do. After a few minutes, she began to fidget, eyes glued on the door, waiting for the knock that would signal her release. Surely, enough time had passed so that she could go out on deck now. Grayson could not possibly have really meant she had to wait until someone came for her. With all the activity on deck, it would be very easy for him to forget to send someone, she reasoned. She sat very still, listening carefully. Much of the activity above had ceased. She could feel the ship moving beneath her. They were definitely underway. Surely, Grayson must realize that she would want to watch the departure. Would he remember that she was down here now that the ship was underway, remember that she waited below for his permission to leave? A grimace passed over her face at the word *permission*. She was so tired of someone else controlling everything she did, telling her if, and when, she could or could not do something.

With a deep sigh she leaned forward resting her forehead in the palms of her hands. A low rumble interrupted her thoughts. Sarah looked down and put a hand over her stomach as if to silence it, suddenly realizing that she was hungry. Did he intend to keep her unfed as well as shuttered away?! Her freshly cleaned, white teeth nibbled nervously on her lower lip. No, he had simply forgotten that he was going to send someone for her. She must go above to remind him. Standing up, she squared her shoulders and walked determinedly to the door, opening it without further hesitation.

74

Peeking out quietly, she examined the hallway before stepping out and closing the door behind her. She leaned against it, hesitant again, heart thumping. She really had no desire to make Grayson angry, but it seemed unreasonable of him to make her stay below for so long. The stairwell at the end of the hall beckoned to her. Sunshine streamed down, bathing the stairs in a golden glow. An almost overwhelming need to feel that sunshine on her face came over her. Perhaps she could simply go up the stairs and take a look. That couldn't hurt. She wouldn't go all the way up, just poke her head out and have a quick look around.

Sarah had completely convinced herself that there could be no problem with that as she walked down the hall, barely conscious that she held her breath and tiptoed as she passed the door to Grayson's cabin. At the stairwell, she glanced back at that door before setting her foot on the first step and beginning the short climb up. She slowly poked her head out into the open air. She could smell the sea and the sun warmed the top of her hair. Closing her eyes, she lifted her face to meet it, letting the warmth drift over her. She had spent much of her time out in the sun these last six years, and it had become a friend to her. She smiled happily, greeting it.

Sarah heard heavy steps, and Grayson came striding into view. She glanced back down the steps she had just climbed, considering her possibility of escape, but it was too late.

Grayson crouched down by the nervous girl. "Sarah," his voice was so low it rumbled in her ear. She took a deep breath but kept her head lowered. "Sarah," he said more firmly, "Look at me."

Unable to avoid the command, she turned to him. He greeted her, his tone firm, but not angry. "Good morning, Sarah."

She was uneasy but decided that she must not back down. She was away from the Tompkins now. It would be best if he understood straight away that she had not left one prison only to find herself in another. With all the strength she could muster, Sarah straightened her shoulders, took one step up, and with a hint of a smile lifted her chin, greeting him lightly, "Good morning, Captain Attwood."

Their eyes were on a level now, Sarah halfway out of the stairwell and he, crouching down on the deck. "Sarah, I believe I asked you to stay below until I sent someone for you." His voice was steely. "Did you forget that?"

"No Sir." Sarah was pleased to hear the strong, firm voice that came out of her mouth, although she felt the flush of embarrassment move over her face. Grayson did not flinch, simply waited. She turned away, taking a deep, calming breath before looking back up at him, explaining, "When the ship started moving and still no one had come, I was sure it would be all right to come above. I thought you had forgotten I was down there."

"I seldom forget an order I have given, Sarah. It will be best if you remember that in the future." He stood in one fluid movement and held out his hand to her. "Since you are here now, please do come up."

She reached up and his powerful hand grasped hers, helping her up the last few steps until she stood on the deck beside him. A breeze blew over her face. The wind tugged at her skirt. The sun warmed her back; a perfect day to mark her first taste of freedom. She turned slowly, looking over the ship. Tilting her head back, she followed the tall center mast to the top. Large sails billowed in the wind, starkly white against a bright blue sky dotted with small white clouds.

Sarah's forehead puckered, a hint of a memory pricking behind her eyes and she suddenly smiled. She'd had a dress just like that once, as a child, blue with white polka dots and a big white square collar that hung over her shoulders. How she had loved that dress! She remembered her mother sewing it, bent over the pretty fabric, sewing dainty stitches. The sails flapped in the wind. Sarah reached as if to smooth that big white collar and laughed when she realized there was no collar on her blouse.

Lowering her eyes, she gazed out across the bow. Green-blue water stretched out as far as she could see, gentle waves rippling the top like the washboard she had spent so many hours bent over. Bright sunshine glistened on the water, ricocheting back into her eyes. She squinted against the brilliance for a moment, then closed her eyes, letting the warmth drift over her.

Sarah opened her eyes to find Grayson watching her. He smiled, strong white teeth showing between full lips. Her breath caught in her throat. For a moment, she simply stared at this man who had so suddenly entered her life. He stood in the sun, his long, wavy brown hair blowing back from his face, tangling in the breeze. Dark eyebrows and deeply tanned skin surrounded striking blue eyes, brightened by the reflection of the sky. A straight nose topped firm, full lips. He was clean-shaven, his jaw strong. A loose white shirt fluttered across his broad chest. The sleeves were rolled up to his elbows, revealing muscled forearms and large, capable hands. Grayson Attwood was an extremely attractive man. His smile brought life to his chiseled good looks, making him seem approachable, likeable even, two words which just yesterday Sarah would never have thought to associate with this man.

CHAPTER 13

Grayson watched Sarah as she looked around the ship, up at the sails, out to the sea. His lips turned up when he heard her tinkling laugh. What had she found to laugh at, he wondered. It felt good to see her like this, happy, carefree, away from those awful people.

"Sarah." His voice startled her. "I actually was just on my way down to get you. I thought you might like something to eat." Her eyes brightened at the suggestion, and he chuckled. "Come along then. I have already eaten but have a few minutes to spare. I will take you to the galley." He began walking as he explained, "We don't always eat well when we are at sea, but since we have only just left port, you will have something better than hard tack this morning."

Sarah followed at his heels, once again unable to match his long stride. He looked back and, with a grunt to himself, slowed to half speed. Further down the deck, Grayson announced, "Here we are," and disappeared down a stairwell, reaching back to help her.

The room was long, with the kitchen at the far end. Rough benches and tables formed two rows on either side of the room. It was hot despite the breeze Sarah knew was blowing above. Grayson led the way to a table near the kitchen, seemingly unbothered by the heat. Of course, he wasn't wearing a petticoat and a long black skirt. Sarah sighed, lifting the offending skirts to avoid the spills and spatters left behind after the crew had eaten earlier.

They were just barely seated when a heavy-set man appeared from the kitchen, wiping greasy hands on a smeared apron. His hair, what there was of it, lay in dark streaks plastered against the round dome of his head. His eyes were small brown buttons and after a quick glance at Sarah, he lowered them to the floor. A bulbous nose and round cheeks shone red from the heat and sweat ran down his jowls into the rolls of his neck. He shuffled surprisingly small feet back and forth.

Grayson instructed the cook to bring whatever was left from breakfast for her. The man nodded, eagerly leaving for his kitchen. A short while later he returned with a plate of half warm scrambled eggs and a big slab of bread.

"Do you drink coffee, Sarah?" Grayson asked before the man left.

"No, but if you have some tea, I would love some." Sarah replied, feeling a twinge of guilt for asking when she looked up at the tired cook who stood waiting beside her. The poor man returned to his hot kitchen and brought her a cup of tea. Sarah thought of the kitchen at the Tompkins, remembered the heat, and visualized herself wiping her own sweat-streaked face with a smudged apron before bringing tea to them in their nice dining room. They had seldom even acknowledged her presence. At that memory, Sarah deliberately smiled up at the cook and thanked him.

Grayson cleared his throat, realizing that he had not made introductions. "Sarah, this is Clarence. He's not much to look at, but he's the best ship cook you'll find." Grayson affectionately grasped the large man's shoulder as he spoke, and Clarence grinned broadly, not offended by the comment about his looks and pleased at the compliment from his Captain. "Clarence," Grayson nodded towards Sarah, "Miss Sarah Blake."

Clarence smiled, revealing small, slightly crooked teeth with a wide gap between the front two but his smile was big and friendly. "Good morning, Miss Blake. I have been hearing a lot of talk about our passenger while the men were eating. It's a pleasure to meet you. Welcome aboard." He bowed slightly and Sarah couldn't help but smile back as she greeted him. After checking with Grayson if there was anything else they needed, Clarence returned to the kitchen.

Sarah then folded her hands, bowed her head and silently thanked God for the food. She looked up to find Grayson's eyes on her. "I am the one who provided those eggs for you, Sarah."

Sarah looked down at her plate, then back up at him, feeling like a chastised child. After a breath, she answered, "And I thank you also, Captain Attwood. God uses many tools to accomplish His will."

His eyes broadened at her comment and a deep laugh rumbled from his chest. He observed her puzzled expression and barely resisted laughing again. She did amuse him when she suddenly turned from the demure, introverted little thing she generally appeared to be into the somewhat snappy, confident woman he saw just now.

"A tool then, am I, Sarah?" He lifted one eyebrow, "We shall see. Right now, I am the master of

81

this vessel and must go see to her. When you are finished eating, you may walk around the deck if you wish." All amusement was gone from his voice when he continued sternly, "Just stay out of the way of the men. They have duties to attend to. I do not want them distracted while we are at sail." He spoke abruptly and left likewise.

Sarah watched Grayson leave. She ate slowly, suddenly not nearly as hungry as she had thought she was. Her thoughts were as scrambled as the cold eggs she ate. He was often so harsh with her and yet the room felt empty when he left. Turning her mind away from him, Sarah wondered what time it was. How long had it been since she woke up this morning? She was lost without her routine. Life had always been so structured, always something to do, some place to be. She had felt useful, even if not appreciated. She pushed her plate away, folded her arms on the rough table and rested her head on them.

That is how Clarence found her a half hour later when he came back with a mop and pail, a towel tossed over his shoulder.

Sarah hopped up quickly when she heard him come in. "Oh, I'm sorry, Clarence. I was just dallying."

"That is no problem, Miss. I am just going to clean up before I get lunch started." He scanned the littered floor and messy tables. "The men do leave a bit of a mess behind."

"Please let me help you," Sarah offered, following his look around the room.

"Oh no," he objected quickly, "It is my job. I'm used to it."

"I'm used to it too, Clarence. Cleaning and cooking are all I have been doing for the past six years. It feels strange to watch someone else doing it," Sarah explained to him. "I'd really like to help you," she smiled but couldn't help but notice the dubious look that crossed his face.

Fingering the cloth he held, Clarence sputtered, "Uh, well, I'm not rightly sure how the captain would feel about that, Miss."

"I'm sure he won't mind. I am supposed to keep out of his way as well as that of the men. This will be the perfect place for me to pass the time. I will come down after meals and clean up while you start preparing the next meal." Sarah explained, pleased with her plan. "Now, just tell me what needs to be done." Clarence was relieved when Harper came in right then, and he could escape to his kitchen.

"Good morning, Harper," Sarah greeted him happily. "I was just telling Clarence that I'd like to help him in the kitchen." She was surprised and unhappy to see the disapproving look on Harper's face. She tried to explain, "I need something to do, Harper. I will go crazy on such a long voyage if I have nothing to keep me busy. This is what I know how to do. I am used to it. I want to do it."

Harper's look did not change. "I don't think Grayson would approve of you cooking and cleaning the floors, Sarah. Perhaps we can find something more appropriate for you to do. I will look into it, but I must ask you to stop this. Just be patient. Relax and rest for a time. You might find that you enjoy having nothing to do more than you imagine."

Unable to persuade him, Sarah followed him up to the deck. She walked over to the rail and stared out across the water. Harper came and stood beside her. She could still faintly make out the land in the distance. She stood completely still, watching as her life faded away with the coast. "There it goes, Harper, my life for the past six years." She was quiet again, thinking. Her new life was a mystery before her. A wave of insecurity washed over her.

Harper sensed her uncertainty, "It will be alright, Sarah girl," he comforted. "Things won't be perfect on the road ahead, but I truly believe they will be better for ye."

Sarah listened to the kind man beside her. "Thank you, Harper. I'm so glad you are here," she told him.

Harper put an arm across her shoulders, assuring her, "I will help you any way I can. You can call on me any time." They talked for a few more minutes, and Sarah felt much better when Harper left to attend to his duties.

Grayson stood on the upper deck at the wheel, looking down on the two friends talking so easily. Something in him envied Harper's friendship with Sarah. He reminded himself again that she was nothing but a means to an end for him, but his eyes lingered on the small figure standing at the rail gazing out at the sea, knowing that her eyes exactly matched the green water rolling by.

CHAPTER 14

Sarah left the rail, staring at the sight in front of her. The deck was nothing but a jumble of lines and ropes. Young sailors ran around the deck barefoot or scampered aloft on the riggings and masts like monkeys. She wandered carefully around the deck, avoiding the ropes at her feet, and staying out of the way of any of the sailors, recalling Grayson's strict order to not distract the men.

Finding a quiet ledge out of the way, she sat down, surrounded by the sound and smell of the sea, the shouts of sailors and the cry of gulls playing on the wind. She took it all in; this was her world now.

And that is where Grayson happened upon her a week later. He stopped abruptly, surprised to see her there. He kept expecting to find her bent over the rail somewhere, moaning in sickness. It was a relief to find her here instead. He watched her for a moment, lost in her solitude, absorbing her surroundings.

Sarah jumped when he turned to go, sensing the movement behind her. "Oh! Hello Captain Attwood. I hope it is all right if I sit here. It is out of the way. I didn't think I would be interfering with anything." She spoke quickly, nervously, as if expecting a reprimand.

"It is perfectly all right for you to sit there, Sarah. I'm glad to see you are enjoying the sun. I had thought you might be in your cabin feeling ill, but you seem to be fine.

"I am feeling fine. It is different not to have any duties, but I am enjoying getting used to life on the ship."

"I am happy to hear that. I must attend to some duties now. Good bye, Sarah."

As he turned to go, Sarah answered, "Good bye, Captain Attwood."

He stopped abruptly. "Enough of this, Sarah. As you are aware, my name is Grayson. I call you Sarah. You call Harper by his given name. We are relatives. I wish you to call me by my name."

Sarah's mouth hung agape. He wanted her to be so familiar? She tried to explain, "I did not want to seem presumptuous. I recognize the difference in our positions. I do not think it is my place to call you by your given name, Captain Attwood."

"Sarah," he was concentrating on being calm, "I did not ask you what you think. I asked you to call me by my name. I appreciate that you recognize my position. I also realize that you have had little reason to trust anyone in authority, but I am not your master. I do not want you to fear me. I would like you to call me by my name. Do you understand that?" He asked again.

"Yes, thank you, I understand," Sarah replied quietly.

"Then do so, please," he instructed.

Sarah's eyes widened, and she stared up at him. With a swallow, she answered, "Yes, I understand... Grayson." It sounded so strange when she said it out loud. She used it in her mind all the time, but saying it was different, personal.

For Grayson, it was also strange to hear it coming from her lips, in her soft, sweet voice. He found he liked the sound of it, the familiarity, as though a wall between them was broken. His jaw clenched. What was he doing? He did not want more familiarity with this woman he was deceiving. Perhaps this was not such a good idea after all. But it was too late to retract it.

"Come with me now. I will take you back to your cabin." He held out his arm for her, and she took it without dissent.

They walked in silence to the stairwell. He preceded her down, ready to assist her, but she refused any assistance and followed him down the hall to her room.

She began to shut the door, preparing to say good night when he spoke. "Do you have everything you need? Are you comfortable?"

Sarah was a little surprised at his interest. "Everything is going well, Grayson, thank you. Everyone has been kind and helpful. I am getting used to the ship."

"I'm glad to hear that."

"However, there is something I want to talk to you about. My days are very lazy, I'm afraid," Sarah said.

"It is a bit difficult to become used to having nothing to do. I was thinking that I would like to help Clarence in the kitchen to pass the time. In an odd way, sometimes I miss the hard work, the constant chores and duties I had. The mistress would be so angry if she found me resting, doing nothing." Sarah shrank back at the memory, shriveling before his eyes, her pain flowing out to him.

Without thinking, Grayson stepped closer, gently laying a hand on her shoulder, assuring her, "You do not need to be afraid now, Sarah, but I cannot permit you to help in the kitchen. You are an Attwood now and must act as such. Just try and enjoy your time of having nothing to do, no schedule to keep."

Sarah could tell it would do no good to argue with him now and so just responded, "How could I not enjoy being out here with nothing but the sea and sky, so open, so free." She paused, adding, "I have found the nicest place to sit. I love sitting in the sun and listening to the sounds of the ocean."

"Yes, I believe I found you in your spot earlier. You should be careful about sitting in the sun. It reflects off the water and can cause a bad burn," he advised.

Sarah's smile faded. She reached up and touched her cheek, her hand trailing down her neck. "My skin has become very accustomed to the sun and has built up a resistance to sunburn. I am afraid that I won't fit in well with the ladies in England." Her eyes dropped to the floor as she spoke.

Grayson had no comforting answer for her. She was right, of course. Her tanned skin and unstyled hair would set her apart instantly, not to mention her pauper clothing. It seemed she had been wearing the same faded dress and brown skirt since he met her.

As he watched her standing there, head bent, looking at the tips of her worn shoes, he thought for the first time about what it would be like to arrive in England with her. He had not really thought ahead to that point. Obviously, she had. Her fear of meeting the people in England was justified. And how would he feel presenting her? He was a man of position and status. His crowd was made up of the wealthy and elite.

He suddenly had a vision of introducing Sarah to Lydia. Proud and vain Lydia, always dressed in the best and latest fashions from head to toe. He pictured the soft, white skin that she valued so highly, always holding one of those silly, ruffled parasols when they walked in the sun. And, she had a right to her vanity. She was a beauty, full of fun and life, with brown topaz eyes and deep auburn hair that glinted red when the sun touched it. Beautiful Lydia, waiting for him, waiting for the proposal he was not yet ready to give. He frowned, his brows drawing together. She was his match in every way, in appearance and position, wealth and heritage. They shared the same backgrounds and the same lifestyle of the privileged. Their combined wealth would give them the power and position they both craved. Why did he hesitate? He had asked himself that question many times and still had no answer.

Grayson scrutinized Sarah, seeing her through Lydia's eyes. The contrast was stark. The simple delicacy of Sarah would be swallowed up in the vibrancy of Lydia. He wished he could believe that Lydia would take Sarah under her wing, help her adjust and be accepted. If Lydia gave Sarah her stamp of approval, everyone else would follow. But she would not. She would never associate with someone so beneath her. And he could not fault her because, in his heart, he recognized that he was embarrassed to present this shabby waif to his friends. Would he even stand by her?

At that moment, Sarah lifted her eyes to meet his. She saw the question there, the hint of embarrassment, maybe regret, that he had brought her into his life. Her brows puckered in perplexity. He had just said that it had been his pleasure to free her and she had believed him, but his eyes didn't say that now. She stepped towards him, reaching a small, work-worn hand to rest on his arm, speaking as if she read his mind. "Grayson, I do not want to be a burden to you. You have your life and friends. I do not want to intrude. You have already done so much for me."

Grayson raised a hand to stop her, but she continued, "Perhaps I can find a position as a maid or governess in London, and you can return to your home, free of me. I am sure you know people in London who would be happy to have a good servant, and I would be glad to have the work. I would be far more comfortable in such a position than trying to be something I am not among your friends. Truly I would. I do not expect you to include me in your life. God will take care of me as He always has."

Grayson was amazed at the peace he saw come over her. She really did not care! She would be content to be in a lowly position and had no desire for the wealth and comfort he could give her. Suddenly, he found that he genuinely wanted to help her, to give her the pleasure that his money and position could offer. "Sarah, I will take care of you," he assured her. "It seems to me that God has not done such a good job of that, as He did not do for me when I needed Him. Why you are so confident in Him, I cannot understand. But never mind about that. I will not abandon you in London. You will come home with me as I have said." Grayson straightened up, realizing that they had been standing at Sarah's door for some time. He turned to leave and then back to her. "I would like you to dine with Harper and me on Tuesday." Sarah was surprised as a picture of the galley came to her mind. Grayson read her look and laughed, explaining, "We do have a dining room on board. I sometimes entertain important guests when we dock in different ports."

Sarah had no time to do more than nod in acknowledgement before he had left the room, pulling the door closed behind him. Tuesday was only a few days away. She wondered what dinner would be like, in the dining room where he entertained important guests. After locking the door, she prepared for bed and fell asleep immediately, a smile of contentment and peace on her lips. Her last thought was, *Grayson is so wrong. God has been so good to me! Here I am, a servant a few weeks ago and now free, on a ship sailing to my homeland, soon to have dinner with my cousin, the captain, and his first mate!*

CHAPTER 15

Harper had shown her where and how to wash and dry her clothes, and Sarah busied herself with that the next day. She had to wash in salt water, of course, but if she shook the clothes out well after they were dry, the salt crystals fell off and the clothes were just fine.

On Tuesday, Sarah woke slowly, a feeling of anticipation surrounding her. Her eyes flew open, and she sat up straight. This was the day Grayson had asked her to have dinner with Harper and him. What should I wear, she wondered and laughed at herself. Of her three choices, her dress seemed the best. It was clean, the ruffles still faintly green. If only there was a way to fix it up some, to do something different with it, but there was not. It didn't matter anyway. Grayson wouldn't notice even if she did do something special.

She decided to wash her hair. That, at least, would help. After she was done, she took her brush and went on deck to her alcove and brushed the long curls until they were smooth and glistening.

Soon, the sun was dropping on the horizon and Sarah saw faint pink blushing the clouds, signaling that evening had come. She had spent most of the day outside enjoying the warmth. Reaching up she touched her hot cheeks, realizing that likely they were red from the sun, and just after Grayson had warned her about getting burned. She went down to her room to assess the damage and get ready.

After washing her face in lovely cool water, Sarah put on the dress. Although it had only been a few weeks, with regular meals to eat the dress now fit more snuggly. She tied the ribbon around her waist tightly, accenting the smallness.

She pinned half her hair into a bun on top of her head, leaving the rest to fall in a shiny curtain down her back.

Finally ready, she checked the mirror. Her cheeks were somewhat pinker from the sun but it made her eyes greener and matched her naturally pink lips. She felt a new surge of confidence. She could go to dinner holding her head just a little higher.

With nothing left to do but wait for Grayson to come for her, she sat down on the chair by her bed. It had been a long day, and the wind and sun had left her tired. Her eyes were stinging, and her head seemed almost too heavy to hold up. She leaned it back against the wall and shut her eyes for just a minute to ease the sting, assuring herself that she had no reason to be nervous.

Her eyes flew open at the sound of pounding and a deep voice calling her name. "Sarah! For goodness sake, open this door."

Sarah jumped up. Oh no, it couldn't be! She had fallen asleep waiting. Shaking out her skirt and patting her hair in the back where she'd leaned against the wall, she went quickly to the door. When she opened it, Grayson's fist was raised to pound again.

She jumped back, and he dropped it quickly, "Oh, Sarah, for goodness sake. I'm not going to hit you.

I've never given you a reason to think I would. I've been standing out here knocking on your door for quite some time. I expected you to be ready when I came." Sarah opened her mouth to reply, but he stopped her. "It doesn't matter. Follow me." He turned and went out the door.

By the time she was out, he was halfway down the hall, and she hurried after him. He stopped, and she bumped into his hard back. He turned around immediately, commanding sternly, "Lock it."

She stammered, "I was just trying to follow you."

He held up his hand. "Did I not tell you to always lock your door?" At her nod, he instructed, "Please do so and then we will go. I would have waited for you at the stairs, Sarah."

Sarah went back to lock her door. Grayson stalked on ahead. He had questions on his mind. He had thought she would be ready, waiting eagerly for him to arrive. He had planned this dinner as a diversion for her, something entertaining for her. There were other things he could be doing. They would be arriving in Boston in a day or two, depending on the wind. It had been unusually still the past several days, and he needed to be watching to give directions for the sails to be shifted to catch the best wind. But he had taken time to have this meal with her. It irritated him that she had not been ready and waiting, looking forward to it. He glanced back to see that she was following him and waited at the stairs to help her up. On deck, he offered her his arm to make sure she would not trip over something in the dark. Sarah took it hesitantly. They were silent as they walked, tension between them. The air was still and warm, the sky star-studded, and the moon brilliant, but they walked purposefully, not noticing.

Halfway across the deck, Grayson stopped to open a door for her, leading her up a few stairs into a room unlike any other Sarah had seen on the ship. She stopped in the doorway to take it in. The ceiling was high, giving an open feeling, unlike the close compactness of the rest of the vessel. Golden maple wood lined the walls, with a matching floor polished to a high gloss. Lamps stood guard on either side of three portholes across both side walls. The lamps were burning just brightly enough to light the room with a soft glow. The portholes open just enough to let some fresh air in. In the center of the room, a large oval carpet with swirls of deep red and golden yellow lay underneath an oval table of rich mahogany with thick pedestal legs. Eight tall back chairs sat around the table, the seats padded and upholstered in deep red, matching the carpet below. A crisp white cloth covered the far end of the table and a silver-tiered candlestick holding 6 white candles sat in the middle. There were three places set with white china plates and shining silverware.

A large, curved bar of the same mahogany, etched with a pattern of deep lines and intricate carvings down the front, stood across the corner at the back of the long room. Large oval mirrors in silver frames graced the walls on each side of the bar. Grayson left Sarah transfixed at the door and went over to the bar, opening a cupboard underneath to remove two stemmed glasses and a bottle of deep red wine.

"Would you care for some wine, Sarah?" His voice startled her.

She hesitated for a moment. She hadn't had many opportunities to have wine but somehow it seemed fitting and so she answered, "Yes, thank you," as she walked slowly across the room, around the big table, trailing delicate fingers over the smooth tops of the chairs.

He met her halfway and held the glass out to her, "Here you are." She peered up at him and he was stunned again by her eyes, deeper green even than he recalled. Her hair shone, slightly lighter than the walls around them, glowing in the lamplight, the bun revealing her delicate neck. He knew he had seen the simple, worn-out dress many times, but he could not help but notice the womanly curves it revealed tonight. It might be harder to ignore this woman than he had ever imagined.

"You look very nice tonight." He said it without thinking and was almost as surprised as she at the words.

Her eyes widened and her lips turned up in a soft smile. "Thank you, Grayson." He was looking particularly attractive tonight, himself, she thought. Beneath a waist-length fitted vest he wore an ivory shirt that complimented his deep tan. The vest was navy blue with tiny gold threads in the fabric, giving it a rich sheen. A thin gold braid outlined a wide collar running down the front to his trim waist. His eyes picked up the color of the vest making them hypnotizing pools of dark blue. His hair was tied back but several strands fell forward around his ruggedly handsome face. He somehow managed to have the look of both a gentleman and a rogue, a captain and a pirate.

Sarah's heart beat a little faster and she turned away quickly, looking around the room again. "This room is beautiful, Grayson. The wood makes it feel so warm and comfortable, but at the same time the deep colors make it so elegant."

"Thank you." He was pleased that she liked the room. "It is a favorite of mine. I brought some of the wood home from my travels and had the table and bar built to fit the room. I entertain dignitaries from the various ports we visit in this room. I like it to look worthy of nobility."

"Ah, you are here already." The loud, cheerful voice intruded on the two. Harper came rushing into the room towards them. "Sorry if I'm late."

"That's fine, Harper," Grayson replied. "I will ring for Clarence now. Help yourself to some wine." He walked over to the wall and pulled on a tasseled cord in the corner.

They couldn't hear it, but Sarah knew that down in the kitchen, a bell had rung, and Clarence would be hurrying about to bring things up. The Tompkins used to ring for her in that same manner when they had guests for dinner. She could never have imagined back then that she would soon be a guest rather than a servant.

98

CHAPTER 16

Sarah smiled at Harper as he came over and put an arm casually around her shoulders. "Hello, Sarah. It is good to see you. It has been a while. How are you faring?" With his arm still around her shoulders he took her with him over to the bar and got himself a glass of wine. They talked comfortably about what they had been doing for the last while.

Grayson saw Sarah's smile and Harper putting his arm around her shoulder as they greeted each other. He watched them walking to the bar, talking like old friends. When he saw them together, he always sensed that they had a connection that he did not have with Sarah. He regretted that somehow. But that was not to be for Sarah and him. When they got to England, after she was settled and had some friends and activities, he would set her up in the guest cottage, separate from the house, where she could have her own life and he, his. He walked over to the bar to join the two.

"I was just telling Sarah how lovely she looks tonight," Harper said, like a proud parent. "Don't you think so, Grayson?"

"Yes, Harper, I have already told Sarah that she looks nice tonight.

Just then, a door next to the bar opened, and the server came in. He carried a large tray with covered platters and bowls. A delicious smell preceded him into the room and the three followed him to the table, carrying their glasses with them. Grayson pulled out a chair and motioned for Sarah to sit down. Harper moved to the other side and took his place while Grayson was seated at the head. As the server picked up a platter of golden-brown roast chicken and prepared to serve Sarah, Grayson ordered, "Just leave the food on the table, and we will serve ourselves." The man set the chicken down and then uncovered a bowl of fluffy mashed potatoes and a gravy boat filled with steaming gravy. Another bowl held bright orange carrots. He set down a basket of warm, thick slices of bread and butter beside Grayson and stood at attention. Grayson thanked him and dismissed him.

Grayson watched Sarah as she ate, surprised at her good manners. She used the right utensils and ate delicately. Where had she learned that? She was quite acceptable at the table. She actually fit fairly well in this environment. As he observed her, it suddenly occurred to Grayson that with some proper clothing and fixing up, Sarah could possibly be reasonably presentable in England. They were soon to dock in Boston. If he could get her outfitted there, she may be passable among the people he knew. Yes, he would take Sarah to Rose and have Rose buy dresses and shoes and fripperies, whatever it was that women needed to compete with other women for the most compliments. Grayson relaxed visibly at his plan. He would be able to proceed on to England without the fear of embarrassment when he introduced this urchin to society.

Sarah sensed Grayson's gaze and looked up to meet his eyes. What was that look she saw? Approval maybe? Hope? Relief? Whatever it was, it seemed to be positive, and she smiled softly into his eyes.

Grayson's breath caught. She always disarmed him when she smiled. He recalled how little she had smiled when he first met her with the Tompkins, the fear in her eyes when that woman spoke to her, the meek look of defeat the rest of the time. He felt it then, and he felt it again now. He wanted to see her smile more often, to give her a reason to smile. He shook his head, trying to shake away those thoughts and feelings. There was only one reason she was here, on his ship, in his dining room – to get his fortune for him.

Sarah watched the look of approval fade and quickly looked down at the table, away from the man at her side.

Grayson glanced at his silent companion. She sat with her head bent, both hands folded in her lap. He pulled a pocket watch from his jacket and clicked it open. "It is not really so late. Let us have some of the pudding Clarence made before we leave. He will be quite disappointed if it is not eaten." Reaching for the bowl of soft yellow custard, he spooned some into small bowls for each of them.

Sarah took the bowl of custard and thanked him quietly. What was he thinking, she wondered? Why was he lingering here with her? What would they talk about? Harper had discreetly slipped out a while ago. They were alone. She surveyed the room around them. Several of the oil lamps on the walls were out; the remaining ones burned low and cast an almost ethereal glow over the room. The candles on the table illuminated only the immediate area around the couple, giving the feeling that they existed in a world apart from everything else.

CHAPTER 17

After a brief time, Sarah broke the silence, asking Grayson something she had been wondering about since she met him, "Grayson, tell me about my aunt. I don't know anything about her. I had no idea that I still had any family alive, and now here I am, sitting beside my cousin. It meant so much to me to hear that I still had family. When I learned that both my parents had died, I felt so alone. I almost lost hope. I barely remembered that my mother had an older sister. I only met her once when I was very young. I did not remember her having a child, but now I discover that my aunt had a son. You." She paused. He could almost hear her thinking. "You said that my aunt had passed on." Her eyes suddenly widened, and she spoke her thoughts out loud, "If you are my aunt's son, then that would mean your mother…." She stopped, a touch of sadness crossing her face. "I am sorry, Grayson. I know how it feels to lose your mother."

Grayson scowled. Confound it all! Why was she bringing this up now? He did not want to get into the family relationship, didn't want her sharp little mind pondering on the gaps. And she was smart. He wasn't sure why that had surprised him. Probably because he, like most others of his set, simply assumed that servants did not have any brains to speak of. Ridiculous superiority! As though wealth made them more intelligent somehow.

Sarah cleared her throat delicately. Grayson realized that he had been lost in thought and she was still waiting for his answer. "Sarah, it really is all a bit tangled. We do not need to get into all the intricacies of family relationships tonight. Let me take you back to your room now so you can get some sleep and prepare for Boston tomorrow." He hoped mention of Boston would distract her.

Sarah watched him intently. "Untangle it for me, Grayson?" Her voice was sweet and quiet.

"Sarah!" It came out harsher than he intended. He began again, deliberately keeping his voice calm. "Sarah, your aunt was not my mother."

Sarah tried to grasp what he had said, "My aunt was not your mother?" She paused, her face reflecting her confusion. "But you are my cousin. You said that we are cousins. My father didn't have any siblings and my mother just had one sister. In order for you to be my cousin your mother had to be my mother's sister," she reasoned.

Grayson knew he was going to have to explain. "Sarah, we are not blood-related. We are cousins only by law. My mother died when I was 16 and your aunt, your mother's sister, somehow convinced my father to marry her a year later." Try as he might, he could not disguise the bitterness that he felt.

Sarah's eyes widened at the irritation in his voice. "You appear to have had no affection for my aunt." She paused, watching him. "And yet you carried out her wish to free me. Why?"

"For goodness sake, Sarah! The woman was dying. Regardless of my feelings towards her, I have some decency. She had been my stepmother for nine very long years. How could I refuse her final request?" He paused. This could go on no longer. "Leave it be, Sarah. I'm sorry if it distresses you to discover that we share no blood, that you have no blood family left. We are still family. I see no reason to dismiss our family ties because of this. We are legally cousins. There is really nothing more to say." He rose from his chair, holding out his hand to assist her. Clearly, the discussion had ended.

They walked in hurried silence back to her cabin. Sarah quickly unlocked the door and then turned to him, confusion still clouding her eyes, but she smiled up at him. "Grayson, I don't understand why you came to rescue me when we have no true family ties. You had no real obligation to do it. It seems I have more reason than ever to thank you. You did not even like my aunt, and yet you came to free me."

Grayson placed his large hands on her shoulders and pushed her somewhat abruptly into the room, his voice brusque. "It is no different, Sarah. I did what I did because it was asked of me. Nothing more or less than that. Go to sleep now. We hope to arrive in Boston tomorrow should the wind cooperate. Good night."

"Good night, Grayson." He was already walking down the hall, but she called after him, "Thank you for dinner."

He turned, gave her a small smile and brief nod and went into his cabin.

Sarah did the same, leaning against the door as it closed behind her. Her head dropped back with a quiet thunk. A sigh escaped softly smiling lips, but behind her eyes there was still a question mark. She had learned so many new things tonight, things she couldn't quite put together. Somehow, Grayson did not really seem the type to let the wishes of a dying woman he had no liking for take precedence over his own plans and desires.

She shoved herself away from the door, shaking her head hard enough to loosen some of the pins holding her heavy hair up. The blonde mass fell down around her. She pushed it back, away from her face. Walking in long strides across the room she chastised herself. *Stop it, Sarah! You're not being fair. Just because Grayson is harsh sometimes does not mean he could not do something good without ulterior motives. Don't be so judgmental. He is your cousin, after...* The sentence trailed off.

She stopped abruptly in the middle of the room, pulling her tousled hair together at the back of her neck, thinking. He is not my cousin. What a strange thought. She hadn't wanted him to be her cousin when she first met him, but now that she had become used to the idea it was a shock to hear that he was not. She had grown to like knowing that there would be someone in England with her who had ties to her parents and even that Grayson would be that person. It made it all less frightening somehow. But he had no real ties to her family. Why should he bother to take care of her? And yet, he had said that things were no different. "We are still cousins, even if only by law," that is what he had said. But still, somehow it did change things.

She moved about the room preparing for bed, pondering all she had learned. *Grayson had said she looked nice, very nice, if she recalled correctly.* She smiled at the memory – a compliment from him; now that was something to be remembered. Of course, he was just being a polite gentleman, saying the polite thing. But she would remember it anyway.

She crawled into bed. Would she ever fall asleep with all the thoughts of the evening rambling around in her head? She had seen surprise, even acceptance in Grayson's eyes. She had lost a cousin but possibly gained this man's approval. They had just begun to bond as family. Could they bond as simply a man and a woman thrown together by unexpected circumstances? Just for a moment, when she closed her eyes, she pictured dark blue eyes looking at her with a light of approval. Perhaps they could, she thought and with a soft sigh fell asleep.

CHAPTER 18

The wind blew in their favor that night and when Sarah went up on deck in the morning the sails were fully billowed, and the place was bustling. Sarah caught the excited mood around her and stood staring out across the water, wondering when Boston would come into view.

"Sarah," Grayson called from behind her. She turned and he continued, "I am glad to find you. I had something I wanted to speak to you about. I know that you will want to spend some time ashore while we are in Boston, and I would like you to stay with a friend of mine. She has been a friend of my family for many years. In fact, she went to school with my mother. I am sure you will enjoy sleeping in a real bed and having firm ground under your feet for a few days."

Sarah was unprepared for this. She wasn't ready to meet new people, especially a fine lady. "I really prefer to stay on the ship, Grayson. I can go ashore during the day," she told him.

"I do not have time to talk about this right now. We will be taking on Cargo and supplies while we are there, and no one will be available to go ashore with you, and you cannot go alone. You will stay with Rose. Be ready to disembark shortly after we dock." He disappeared before she could object further.

Shortly after the ship's bell rang three o'clock Sarah noticed that many of the men were stopping at the rail on the other side of the ship. She ran over to see if land was in sight. Off in the distance, she could make out the shape of a shoreline. She found a place out of the way to sit and watch the approaching shore.

As they got closer to the harbor, sea gulls appeared, crying overhead as they followed the ship. The sails of another large ship already in the harbor were visible and the excitement in the air was palpable. Some of the men scampered overhead, working among the lines and sails, and others on the deck rushed about at their various duties.

Sarah stared out across the water, watching the land get closer and closer. The men were shouting to each other as they directed the ship into port, and some of her excitement returned when the ship stopped moving and they had officially docked.

The pier was a busy, noisy place, with men from the other ships rushing around and people from town standing by watching the arrival of the large vessels. When the gang plank was in place, the sailors started to disembark, running down eagerly. Many of them had been to Boston before and had friends waiting for them.

When things had settled down and it seemed that most of the men had gone ashore, she went to her room to make sure she was ready when Grayson returned. It took only a short while to get her things together and with a bag in hand, she returned to wait near the gangplank. She sat down on a ledge and, before long rested her head back, feeling the warm sun on her face. She closed her eyes, listening to the sounds of people, birds, dogs barking, smelling smoke, food, and fish. She smiled, taking it all in.

"Am I finding you sleeping again, Sarah?" She opened her eyes to see Grayson looking down on her.

Without moving she smiled up at him. "No Grayson, not sleeping, just enjoying the sounds and smells of land, of people and life." She stood up, "Are we ready to go ashore now?" She paused for a moment, adding, "I would still prefer to come back to the ship at night. I wish you would reconsider."

"Sarah," his voice was firm and clipped, "I will not reconsider. The ship is not a place for you to be while we are in port. Although there are guards posted around the ship, I cannot be sure that only our men will get on board. There are often less than savory men hanging around the docks, full of liquor and too much revelry. Frankly, I do not want you traveling back and forth from the ship or being on board at night. I have a good, safe place for you to stay, where you will have the company of a woman to talk to and see the city with, and that is what you will do. We are leaving now." He picked up her bag and began walking to the gang plank without looking back, knowing she would follow.

"Here we are," he said, opening the door to a waiting black buggy and helping her in. Grayson spoke to the driver and then got in on the other side, his bulk filling up the small space. As the buggy bumped over the cobblestone street, Sarah stared out the small window in the door, taking in the sights of this large city. The sidewalks were busy with people going about their business. Many of the buildings were several stories high and contained a large variety of stores and offices. Before long they were away from the main bustle of town and into a residential area. Rows of beautiful, matching brick homes lined the street.

Shortly past the streets of row houses, they turned into a long drive lined with trees, stopping in front of a two-story red brick house with windows across the front, framed by dark green shutters. Grayson paid the driver and then helped Sarah down. Taking her bag, he led her down a flower-lined brick path, up matching stairs to a lovely, covered porch with white pillars periodically placed to support the roof. At the door, Grayson rapped the brass knocker several times.

A man in a crisp white shirt opened the door and immediately recognized Grayson, "Mr. Attwood. Come right in, Sir. Miss Rose is expecting you."

"Thank you, Charles," Grayson said as he ushered Sarah into the house, stopping to make introductions. "Charles, I would like to introduce Miss Sarah Blake." Turning to Sarah he reciprocated, "Sarah, this is Charles, the best butler in all of Boston."

Charles acknowledged the compliment with a large smile and a slight bow. "Pleased to meet you, Miss." Before Sarah could reply he ushered them into the front parlor. "Please sit down. I will tell Miss Rose that you have arrived."

Sarah studied the bright, cheery room. A bay window with a fitted seat set into it faced the street. In the middle of the far wall, there was a rather delicate fireplace with a white carved mantle surrounding it. The white contrasted nicely with the soft blue walls. A settee with scrolled arms and arched back was upholstered in a darker blue brocade. Two mahogany high-back chairs with curved arms and legs were upholstered in matching fabric.

Sarah and Grayson each chose to sit on one of the chairs rather than sharing the couch. They were barely settled before a young girl wearing an apron and carrying a tray came in. She set down the heavy tray, which held a china teapot, teacups, a cream and sugar set, and dainty silver spoons. The girl didn't say anything, but with a slight curtsey left the room, only to return a few minutes later with another tray, this one holding a plate of lovely little cakes and biscuits. Sarah let out a little gasp of delight at the sight.

The girl turned to her with a smile and curtsied quickly toward Sarah, asking, "Is there anything you need, Miss?"

"Oh, no," Sarah answered, explaining, "The cakes look so delicious."

"Thank you, Miss. Cook will be pleased. I hope you enjoy them."

"I'm sure we will." Sarah stood and went over to the girl, "Hello, my name is Sarah. I will be staying here for a few days so we might as well be acquainted."

"Yes, I heard we were to have a guest. Thank you, Miss. I am pleased to meet you," the maid said with another curtsey.

"Mary, I see you have brought the tea." Everyone turned to the door. A tall, slim woman stood in the doorway, a smile of welcome on her face.

CHAPTER 19

Grayson rose when he heard the voice and strode across the room to meet the woman. She seemed to glide towards him, so graceful and smooth were her movements. The two met with obvious pleasure, clasping hands tightly. "Rose, it is so good to see you!" Grayson pulled her into a quick hug and then set her back, looking at her carefully. "You look well and lovelier than ever."

With a tinkling laugh, Rose greeted the man, "Grayson, my dear, ever the charmer, thank you. I can easily say the same back to you. You get more handsome each time I see you. More like your father every year." Her voice trailed off slightly and a soft, far-away look came to her eyes.

Grayson kept his arm around her shoulders and guided her over to Sarah. "Rose, may I present my cousin, Sarah Blake."

Before he could complete the introduction, Rose stepped up and took Sarah's hand, a smile of welcome covering her face, "Yes, Sarah. I am so happy to meet you. I was delighted when Grayson sent a message saying he would be stopping in Boston and would grant me the pleasure of hosting his newly discovered cousin."

Sarah watched the woman as she spoke. She was on the young side of middle-aged, in her early fifties, Sarah judged. Perhaps she had been named for the red hair, only slightly laced with gray, which was caught up on her head in a variety of intricate twists. Her eyes were a bright shade of blue, verging on turquoise, and were quite striking set in the pale skin of most red heads. Although her skin was pale her cheeks were a natural shade of pink that matched her smiling lips. She was obviously prone to smiling as evidenced by the fine lines at the corners of her lips and eyes. Her dress was simple, with puffed sleeves to her elbows, a fitted bodice that was obviously hand-tailored to her slender frame, and a full skirt gathered just slightly at the waist to flare out over slim hips. The dress was a soft lavender shade with dainty lace trim across the top of the square neckline and around the cuffed sleeves. Rose was the picture of delicate elegance and Sarah stood entranced by her.

The gentle voice beside her startled Sarah out of her trance. "Sarah, dear, I was just suggesting that we have our tea and cakes now. Would you like to have a seat? I will pour."

Without thinking, Sarah blurted out, "Oh, I will pour. Please, you and Grayson sit and visit." It was one thing to have the maid wait on her, but it would be far too strange to be served by this lovely woman.

Rose seemed to understand and agreed. "Yes, Dear, that would be fine. I will have sugar and milk with mine and, although tea would not be Grayson's choice of beverage," she glanced over at Grayson who smiled back, "he will have just a small spoon of sugar with his."

Grayson and Rose were sitting together on the settee quietly talking when Sarah delivered their tea, followed by the plate of cookies and cakes. Once they were served, she got her own tea and a delicious-looking small cake covered in pink icing and sat down in one of the chairs across from the two. They continued their conversation and barely noticed when Sarah sat down.

"Oh, Grayson," Rose said, reaching to pull a pink envelope off a table beside the settee. "Before I forget, I want to be sure to give you this letter." She waved the envelope near her nose and sniffed appreciatively. Smiling, she passed the letter to Grayson, "I believe it is from the beautiful Lydia. Captain Williams delivered it on his way through a week ago. She must be quite anxious for your return."

Grayson almost snatched the letter from Rose, glancing over at Sarah who was staring at the pink envelope with her cup paused halfway to her lips. Quickly tucking the envelope inside his jacket, Grayson turned to Rose. "Perhaps Sarah would like to see her room now. It is starting to get dark and I should be getting back to the ship soon."

"Oh, certainly," Rose rang a small bell on the table beside her and almost immediately, Mary appeared at the door.

"Yes, Mum?"

"Mary, please take Sarah to her room now," Rose instructed.

With a quick curtsy, Mary turned to Sarah, "Come with me, Miss.

Grayson came over to stand beside Sarah. "I will be leaving now. It is unlikely that I will see you tomorrow, possibly even the day after. You are in good hands with Rose and if not before, I will come for you in three days' time to go back to the ship." He took her hand in his and their eyes met when she glanced up at him. "Good night now, Sarah. Have some fun before we are back on the ship and out to sea."

Sarah peered into his dark blue eyes seeing comfort and concern there. "Thank you for bringing me here, Grayson. Goodnight."

At the quick break in conversation the little maid jumped in, "Follow me now, Miss." Without waiting to see if Sarah was following, the girl turned and walked out of the room.

Once they were gone and Grayson could see the two walking up the stairs, he turned to Rose, taking her hand and pulling her back into the room. "Rose, I have a request of you. I think now that you have met Sarah you will understand." They sat back down on the settee, facing each other.

"What is it, Grayson? I am happy to have her here. She seems quiet, but quite delightful. I will help in any way I can. What do you need?"

With a deep breath, Grayson began, "I cannot take her back to England looking like that, Rose. Perhaps it is snobbish of me and petty, but I don't want to present her to my set in her current state." He touched the pocket where he had put the letter. "Can you imagine Lydia meeting her?"

Rose reached over and put her hand over the ones that lay twisting in his lap. "Grayson, dear, it is alright if you are uncomfortable, embarrassed even, to take her back. I understand. She is a bit shabby, but quite lovely behind it all. What can I do to help?"

Grayson took the small hand in his and squeezed it lovingly. "Ah Rose, I knew I could count on you. I would like you to take Sarah in hand and outfit her with everything she will need to be presentable in England. Buy whatever you think she will need and all the fripperies to go along as well. Have the merchants keep a tab. They all know me and will have no trouble trusting me for payment. Don't hesitate to buy whatever is needed."

The expression on Rose's face changed several times as he spoke, from surprise to concern to excitement. "It is a splendid idea, Grayson, although there is not really enough time to do a good job of it. I know a couple of excellent seamstresses and a few shops that even carry some ready-made items, so I suppose it is possible."

Grayson could almost see the wheels turning in her attractive head and smiled. Her bright blue eyes were sparkling but turned serious for a moment. "I will have her for three days you said." She waited for his confirmation and, at his nod continued. "That will be tomorrow, the day after and the day after that. Then you will leave on the following morning."

"Actually, I was planning to take her back to the ship on the afternoon of the third day so that we could set sail early the next morning. So, you will have her for two full days and a half," Grayson explained.

"No, no, that won't do. She must stay here the third night also and I can send her to the ship early the following morning." Her tone brooked no argument and Grayson agreed in resignation. Suddenly, she brightened again and jumped up, clasping her hands together. "I have a wonderful idea. On the last night I will have a special dinner for some of the important people here in Boston. You know most of them and they would love to see you. It will be a coming-out party, of sorts, for Sarah. We can see how she does in society."

Now, Grayson's expression went through a series of emotions, ending with a concerned look. "Rose, I don't know if she will be ready for something like that so quickly. Even if you can get her the right clothes, to have her ready for a formal dinner seems unlikely. I think it will be enough to get her outfitted and leave it be until England."

Rose patted his hand, assuring him, "It is alright, Grayson, dear. Do not be concerned. If you can trust me with her clothing, you can trust me not to let her attend a dinner for which she is not ready. If I feel she will not be able to handle herself appropriately, I will simply let her have dinner in her room. You, however, will still want to see the people you know. You must plan on dinner here the night before you sail. And bring that old first mate of yours. Harper, isn't it? Yes, bring him, but you must dress him up as well." Her musical laughter rang out.

Grayson sighed, "I never can refuse you, my dear. You are just like my mother. I never could get around her either." He pulled her into a hug. "We will be here for dinner. Thank you, Rose." He stepped back and smiled fondly at her. "Good night then. I will see you in three days. If you need me before then just send a message to the ship."

"Good night, dear boy. I must get busy." A hand brushed over her perfect hair, mussing it slightly. "I must make a list of what we need, where we should go. She does not seem to have much."

Grayson interrupted her, "She most certainly does not and everything she has should be burned. Do not let her keep any of it. If I ever see that mouse brown skirt again, I will throw it overboard and her in it." He pounded his fist against the doorframe.

Rose laughed, "Don't worry about the brown skirt, Grayson. Get some rest. You appear to need it." She pushed him gently out of the door.

He turned back, speaking softly, "Thank you, Rose. I really do not know how Dad let you get away."

Rose reached up to touch his cheek with a dainty hand, "Old history, my dear. It wasn't meant to be. Go on, now. Don't worry. I'll take care of your little Sarah."

Grayson shook his head, protesting, "She is not my little Sarah. This is just something I had to do. I made a promise on Bethany's death bed."

"Yes, of course. I understand." She smiled as he leaned over and gave her a quick kiss on her cheek.

"Good night, Rose. I will see you in three days."

CHAPTER 20

As soon as the door closed Rose rang for Charles who appeared instantly. "Charles, bring me some paper and ink, please. Just leave them in here. I must speak with our guest but will return shortly. Oh, and I will need the carriage first thing in the morning."

"Yes, Ma'am," Charles replied and left to do her bidding.

Rose followed him out of the drawing room and went up the long staircase to Sarah's room.

Sarah opened the door to the light knock. "Oh Rose, come in."

"I just wanted to make sure you were settled and invite you to join me for dinner in an hour."

"Thank you, Rose. I would love to," Sarah replied as Rose left the room, pulling the door shut behind her.

After putting her things away, Sarah climbed up onto the bed, piled high with feather comforters and covered with a quilt in patterns of yellow and green squares. She jumped when she heard a knock, crawling off the bed as she called, "Come in."

Mary opened the door, smiling when she noticed Sarah's sleepy eyes and mussed hair. "Had a little nap did we, Miss? That's good. Come along now then. Supper is ready."

Sarah ran a hand over her hair, shook out her wrinkled skirt and followed the maid down the hall to the dining room. Rose was already seated at a long, glossy table when they came in. She smiled, waving Sarah over to have a seat beside her.

As they ate, Sarah and Rose talked like old friends, maybe like mother and daughter. Sarah wondered about that for a moment. What would it be like to talk with her mother, woman to woman rather than as a child? She would never know.

"You look sad, Dear," the perceptive woman commented. "Would you like to tell me about it?"

Sarah felt instantly comfortable with the older woman and found herself telling Rose things about her life that she thought she would never tell anyone.

She then asked Rose about herself, hoping to hear how she had come to know Grayson and be so close to him, but although Rose talked about her life, she never spoke about her relationship with Grayson.

After they had finished dinner, Rose stood gracefully, folding her napkin neatly and setting it beside her plate. "I am tired now, Dear. I think I will go to bed. You must be tired also and I do hope you will enjoy sleeping in a real bed without the floor moving beneath you." She laughed softly.

Sarah wanted to hear more but graciously agreed, getting up from the table to join the older woman.

"Yes, I am ready for bed, and it will be wonderful to sleep on the bed upstairs rather than the tight little cradle onboard ship."

They left the room together. At the stairs, Rose stopped, turning to Sarah with a bright smile, "I almost forgot to tell you. We are going into town tomorrow to do some shopping. I've asked Charles to have the carriage ready at nine. I will have Mary bring you a tray at eight. I hope you sleep well. Good night, Sarah, darling." She turned and Sarah watched the slender figure glide down the hall.

CHAPTER 21

The sun was shining through yellow curtains when Sarah opened her eyes. She stretched and smiled at the warm sunshine and thought about how life had changed for her in these last weeks. She could wake up happy, unafraid of what the day might hold. She seldom thought of her days with the Tompkins anymore. She had begun to believe that they really were gone. It seemed so long since she had been yelled at or hit, and now, she was waking up in a beautiful room, knowing that a kind, caring woman was waiting to spend the day with her.

She lifted her face into the sun and spoke out loud, "Thank you, Lord God. Your mercies are indeed new every morning." Just as she was climbing down from the fluffy bed, she heard a knock at her door.

Mary was there with a tray. "I was to wake you at 8:00, Miss. Here is your breakfast. Miss Rose has ordered the carriage to be ready at 9:00."

Sarah nodded, "Yes, thank you, Mary. I will be ready." She dressed while she drank her tea and nibbled on crisp toast with jam. She wrapped her hair in a bun, smoothed the front of the brown skirt as she left the room and ran down the stairs to wait by the door.

Rose was soon there, followed immediately by Charles announcing the arrival of the carriage. Rose thanked him and moved to take Sarah's arm, following the butler out the door. "It's a lovely day to see a bit of the city and do some shopping."

Sarah agreed about the day but said nothing in regard to shopping. She would not be doing any shopping, but she was happy to go along and watch while Rose shopped.

The driver had his orders, and it was not long before they were in the city, stopping by a board sidewalk. The driver immediately jumped down and helped the women out. "Please return for us at 4:00," Rose instructed him and then turned to Sarah eagerly. "Come along Sarah, dear. My seamstress is just a few shops down. We will stop there first." She took Sarah's arm and began walking briskly down the street.

Sarah gazed in the shop windows as they walked, slowing Rose to a more leisurely pace. There were shops with shoes displayed in the window, one with beautiful jewelry locked in a case with a glass top, and some with tools and dishes. Although she had walked down the streets of Norfolk with the Tompkins, Sarah had always been carrying things for the Mistress, rushing along behind her and never had the chance to browse the windows.

Rose stopped in front of a store with the most beautiful dress Sarah had ever seen hanging in the window. She stood still, gazing at the dress. A shimmering, almost sheer blue overskirt was gathered in flounces at the bottom revealing a deep green petticoat underneath. The deep green shone through the diaphanous blue, giving it the color and sheen of the sea, while the flounces were reminiscent of waves over the water. Sarah was transfixed and did not notice when Rose came to stand beside her, taking her arm and pulling her gently to the door. "Priscilla is my favorite seamstress. Come inside. She will be able to help us."

Sarah followed her into the shop where bolts of fabric of every color lay out on tables. Rose went to the counter to greet a pleasant, round-faced woman, who smiled cheerfully.

The women talked quietly as Sarah gazed around the store, seeing several dresses displayed. She jumped when Rose called her. "Sarah, Priscilla will show us some ready-made dresses that she thinks will be close to your size. She always has a few made up to show customers what they look like when they are complete. Come with me. There is a dressing room in the back where you can try them on."

Disturbed at Rose's suggestion, Sarah rushed to stop her, "Rose, I have no money for clothes. I thought we were looking for something for you. I am happy to stay out in the store while you try the dresses on."

Rose shook her head and spoke firmly but cheerfully to Sarah, "No, no. I have plenty of things. Today we will look for some clothes for you to take with you to England." She observed Sarah's shirt and worn skirt without any scorn but said with concern, "You really must have some things before you arrive there. You will be uncomfortable going to Grayson's home without something more suitable to wear. I do not mean that unkindly, Dear, but you must trust me on this. You needn't worry about the money. It has all been taken care of."

Sarah was puzzled and shook her head in protest. Priscilla arrived just then with several dresses draped over her arm. "Come with me," she said to Sarah and immediately walked ahead. Rose simply gave the hesitant girl a little push, clearly not intending to discuss it anymore. Sarah had no choice but to follow the woman disappearing down the hall in front of her.

Priscilla had brought a couple of simple day dresses, one a lovely shade of lavender and another in a burnt orange that even Sarah knew would accent her golden tan and blonde hair to its best.

"Shall I help you, Miss?" Priscilla's question interrupted Sarah's thoughts and she quickly turned to the jolly woman.

"No thank you. I will be fine."

"Alright then. Rose would like you to come out when you have the dresses on, and I will need to check them for adjustments."

Sarah felt excitement rising in her as she examined the clothes again. How could she possibly accept anything so extravagant? However, it seemed she had no choice but to at least try them on. She slipped on the orange. It fit surprisingly well. It was a bit large at the waist, but Sarah tied the straps tightly behind her to cinch it in. The square neckline had a small ruffle of creamy lace around it and slightly puffed sleeves ending just above her elbows were finished with a matching ruffle. There was no mirror in the small room, but Sarah knew that the dress was right for her and couldn't hold back the bright smile.

With a deep breath, she smoothed the skirt and went out to show Rose and Priscilla. Rose stared at the woman emerging from the doorway. What a remarkable change clothes can make. Sarah no longer resembled a lost girl beaten by the cares of life. She stood straight and held her head up but there was a slightly shy look in her eyes when she met Rose's, and her hands clenched and unclenched the fabric of the full skirt. "It is perfect," Rose declared. Priscilla was busily inspecting the fit, ultimately declaring that it would not require any adjustment as Sarah was sure to gain at least a little weight and they could simply tie the straps tighter around the waist until then.

"We will take it," Rose said, adding, "You must wear it for the rest of the day, Sarah. Now go and try on the lavender one."

Sarah left to go back to the changing room and barely heard Priscilla call her. She turned to see the seamstress holding the dress from the window out to her, "You must try this on next. We cannot have you arriving in England without at least one gown for parties and balls."

Sarah shook her head and looked at Rose. Surely Rose could not intend for her to try on something so expensive and elegant, but Rose smiled reassuringly, "Take it Sarah. Try it on."

Sarah took the dress somewhat reluctantly, but her heart raced at the thought of putting it on. She had never dreamed of having something so elegant. She put it on carefully. She could not reach all the hooks in the back so would ask for help when she went out. The neckline of the dress was heart-shaped, tastefully covering the rise of her breasts and ending in a V which was modest for the times but still stylish. The neckline was wide but stopped just shy of revealing her shoulders. Short, puffed sleeves left her long, delicate arms bare. The waistline was also heart-shaped emphasizing her tiny waist. The full skirt fell in yards of fabric that swished around her legs as she walked out to show the waiting women.

Rose and Priscilla were both stunned when she came out. The swaying fabric made her walk graceful and showed off her slim figure to perfection. The color was ideal for her creamy complexion and even from a distance her eyes shone like emeralds.

Priscilla again went to check the fit and tucked and pinned. This had to be perfect. It must fit her like it was made for her, not like something hung in the shop window. The alterations would be fairly extensive. While Sarah drifted back to the dressing room feeling like she was in a dream, Priscilla explained to Rose that she could not possibly have the dress altered by that afternoon. She would need a few days.

"I must have it for dinner tomorrow night," Rose insisted. She was envisioning the look on Grayson's face when Sarah walked down the stairs to the dinner she was planning. "I must have it then, Priscilla. Is there no way?"

Priscilla considered carefully and finally agreed that she could get it done. "I will have my niece come and help me tomorrow. But not until tomorrow afternoon, Rose. I simply cannot get it done properly before then."

"Tomorrow afternoon will be fine," Rose agreed. "I will have someone come for it at 3:00. Dinner is at 7:00. That should give us plenty of time to have her ready." Sarah came out wearing the burnt orange dress and carrying her brown skirt and old shirtwaist. Rose took them from her hands, "You won't be needing these now."

Sarah protested, "I can wear them for cleaning. I need to keep them. I might need them on the journey."

However, Rose remained firm, hearing Grayson's orders to get rid of the brown skirt in her head, "burn it," he had said. She gave the clothes to Priscilla without further discussion, agreeing that they would return for the other things later in the afternoon.

By the time they returned Sarah was in a complete daze at all that had transpired. In addition to the things at Priscilla's she had a warm cape, a few pairs of shoes, a couple of hats and even some jewelry, as well as some skirts, blouses, dresses, and undergarments being made. Rose had insisted that she have her hair cut a few inches with some bangs curling on her forehead. She had asked over and over through the day how this was all happening and who was paying for it, but Rose only told her that it was taken care of and not to bother about it.

Sarah leaned her head back as she sat in the swaying carriage. What a day this had been. She thought of her brown skirt back at Priscilla's shop and suddenly tears pricked her eyes. It felt like some of her identity had been left behind with that skirt. Who was she now? She really wasn't a servant girl anymore, but neither was she one of the gentry. She rubbed the soft fabric of the pretty dress she wore and wondered how she could ever live up to these new clothes. Could they turn her into a lady fit for Grayson's world in England?

The rest of the day went by quickly. Mary bustled about, exclaiming over all the new things as she unpacked the boxes and bags. She looked at Sarah who was tiredly watching as she lay on the bed across the room.

"What will you wear to the dinner tomorrow?" Mary asked without noticing that Sarah sat straight up at her question. "All of the gentry and important people are coming. I heard that Governor Bradstreet may even be here," the maid continued excitedly.

"What are you talking about?" Sarah jumped off the bed, walking briskly over to the girl. "What dinner?"

Mary jumped at the urgency in Sarah's voice. "Oh. I hope it wasn't supposed to be a surprise." The little maid's eyes dropped to the floor. "Well, you will need to know anyway," she said more to herself than Sarah.

"Yes, tell me. I do not want to attend any dinner." Sarah said.

"Miss Rose has planned a dinner party tomorrow night. Many people in Boston know Captain Attwood and often she has a small gathering when he is here. It is going to be so exciting. Everyone is busy cleaning and getting the house ready. Cook is planning a wonderful menu." None of Mary's excitement transferred to Sarah, who simply stood staring at the girl.

A short while later Sarah sat at the table beside Rose, picking at the food on the china plate in front of her. "Rose," she began hesitantly, eyes still on the plate. "Mary said something about a dinner party."

Rose quickly responded. "Yes, Dear, I am having a small dinner for some people who want to see Grayson while he is here. Everyone will be very pleased to meet his cousin as well."

Sarah looked into the smiling face of the older woman, informing her, "I really would prefer not to attend. I will not fit with the people coming."

"Nonsense!" Rose exclaimed. "Whyever not? You have nice clothes now. You will be quite stunning in that lovely gown we got."

Sarah gazed into the bright blue eyes across from her, "The clothes are so lovely, Rose. Thank you so much, but I am afraid that even beautiful clothes cannot make me fit for a fancy dinner with important guests. You see, I am used to serving, not sitting, at the table. I have not been trained in how to eat properly at a formal dinner."

Rose covered the small hand that was fidgeting on the table. "Nonsense, Sarah. Your table manners are quite acceptable. I have been observing you and we have nothing to worry about. You have a natural grace and clearly you have learned something about how to behave at the table from your times of serving. We will have a few quick lessons tomorrow to be sure you are ready. I am not at all concerned and you must not be either." Rose leaned close, "Sarah, I would not have you sit at the table if I did not think you could do so without embarrassment. You can rest assured of that. I want you to enjoy the evening. Everything will be fine, my dear."

Sarah felt the confidence Rose had in her and a spark of hope touched her heart. Perhaps she could do it. If Rose believed she could, then she would do her best not to disappoint her. A small smile of agreement touched her lips and Rose responded eagerly. "It will be quite lovely. And you will be even lovelier. I can hardly wait to see Grayson when he sees you in the gown."

Sarah's smile froze on her face. Grayson! Disappointing Rose was one thing. Embarrassing Grayson in front of the Bostonian elite was another. Rose went on talking, but Sarah barely heard. Something about working on hair and manners tomorrow, but nothing registered after the discussion of the dinner and Grayson seeing her. As soon as she possibly could Sarah said she was tired and went to her room. One of the new nightgowns lay out on the bed. It was so soft and clean. She put it on hesitantly and climbed into bed. Her tired body conquered her troubled mind and she fell asleep quickly.

CHAPTER 22

Rose greeted her at the bottom of the stairs in the morning and Sarah was surprised at the stern look on the sweet lady's face. Without a word Rose pulled her over to the small sitting room they had first met in. "Sarah, why are you wearing that," she asked firmly.

Sarah glanced down at the dress Rose had so approved of just yesterday. Perhaps, since they weren't going out today, Rose wanted her to wear her old dress. "I'm sorry, Mistress. I will go and change right away." She started to back away, almost as if she expected a blow to strike her.

Rose was shocked when Sarah called her Mistress and when she saw fear in her eyes as the girl backed away. "Oh, Sarah, I am so sorry. Don't go. You did not do anything wrong. I am sorry I spoke so harshly; I was just surprised. Come back and sit down, Dear." She had walked over to the frightened girl as she spoke and put a gentle hand on her arm, pulling her towards the settee.

When they were seated side by side, Rose spoke kindly, "Sarah, we need to have a little lesson in the ways of fashionable ladies. You will be among many of those when you get to England. More's the pity. The first thing to remember is that you must never wear the same dress two days in a row. In fact, it would be best not to wear the same thing for several days. You have plenty of clothes now to take you even a week without repetition. You can wear a skirt twice but with a new blouse, and no one will notice that it is the same."

Sarah's mouth had fallen open as she listened, her eyes wide. Rose patted her arm. "I know it will take some getting used to. It is not so important over here, but in England what you wear and when you wear it will definitely be noted. I do not mind that you wore the orange again, but you should go and change so that you can get used to the idea. Run along now and change into something else and then, while we have lunch, I will give you a quick lesson in table etiquette and the proper way to greet the guests. After lunch Mary will teach you something about styling your hair since you will not have a lady's maid to help you with that."

"Thank you, Rose. I know I have a great deal to learn," Sarah said as she left quickly to go to her room and change, returning a few minutes later for lunch and her lesson in etiquette. The instruction in table manners and social graces was easy. Indeed, Sarah had attended many similar events as a servant and had learned a great deal simply from observing. Rose told her a few things about the people who would be attending and how to address them properly and she was dismissed to go and learn about styling her hair and get ready for the dinner.

Mary was waiting in the room when Sarah arrived. An array of brushes and hair combs were set out on the bureau. Mary waved Sarah over-enthusiastically. "Oh, here you are, now. Come in and sit down and we'll have a look at what we can do with all that hair." Sarah went over obediently and sat down. She actually was looking forward to learning what she could do with her hair. It was always such a bother.

Mary went right to work pulling out the pins that held the thick bun up and the blonde curls cascaded down Sarah's back. Mary pulled it all together, holding it in a ponytail. "It is very beautiful but there is a great deal of it, isn't there?" For the next couple of hours Sarah had lessons in the proper ways to wear her hair. The hair seemed to obey Mary's every touch and stay wherever she put it. Each time the girl finished a new style she undid it and had Sarah try to do it herself and Sarah found she could manage them quite easily.

"Most often you will want to have your hair up, definitely if you are going out anywhere or having people in," Mary explained. She then demonstrated several different styles where the hair was worn up. These took longer and Sarah secretly thought she would probably just do the simple bun she usually wore.

Her thoughts were interrupted when Mary said, "You will have your bath now and I will do your hair in a more formal style for dinner. I will get the water for you.

Sarah kept practicing with her hair and it wasn't long before Mary had the bath full of steaming water and poured some oil in that smelled lightly of roses. The maid left, promising to return to do Sarah's hair and help her dress for dinner. Sarah felt a little tingle of fear again but sunk down into the warm water and tried to forget about it. The water helped ease the tension and she did almost forget. If only Grayson wasn't going to be there, she would actually look forward to wearing the beautiful gown. She always felt so inadequate around him, afraid she was going to disappoint him.

135

A knock at the door interrupted her thoughts. Mary called from outside, "Sarah, you should finish your bath now and wrap up in the towel I left there. In a few minutes I will come and help wash your hair."

Sarah quickly finished her bath. Stepping out of the tub she reached for the towel, wrapping it around herself. Just as she finished, she heard a quick knock and Mary entered carrying another bucket full of warm water and went to work washing Sarah's hair, shampooing it twice. Sarah was sure her hair had never been this clean before. After wrapping the thick mass in another towel, the two girls went into the bedroom where Mary had laid out Sarah's clothes for the evening. "Sit down here, Sarah," Mary instructed, patting the chair by the bureau. "I'm going to do a few things on your hair while it is wet."

Sarah sat down obediently, and Mary went to work, brushing out the wet hair, explaining, "I'm going to tie your hair in some rag curls so that you can have lovely ringlets. I can use the curling tongs later if we need to. I am going to do a wonderful job of it. I can't wait until Captain Attwood sees you."

"DON'T say that!" The girl jumped at Sarah's sharp cry. "Oh, I'm sorry, Mary. I'd really just rather not talk about him. Let's just get this done."

"Yes, of course," Mary agreed. "We are lucky that your hair is naturally curly. It will be so much easier to style." Mary opened a bag full of long strips of cloth and proceeded to show Sarah how to curl pieces of hair around the rags and tie them together until the hair dried around them. "There now, those will dry while you get dressed. I'm going to go clean up the bathroom and you start getting ready."

Sarah quickly got into her undergarments, marveling at the softness of everything. She had to admit that there was a spark of excitement deep down inside her. Of course she enjoyed getting new clothes and having her hair done. She was a woman, after all.

Mary came in carrying the beautiful blue/green gown. Her eyes were wide as she held it up in front of Sarah. "It's a thing of beauty, it is, Miss. And you are going to be so lovely in it. I will make sure your hair is fit to match it." She laid the dress out on the bed and went to check if Sarah's hair was dry.

"We can start on it now," the little maid announced. "Come, sit down. It should be a surprise for you," the girl declared and pulled the chair away from the bureau so that Sarah could not watch. Mary hummed softly as she worked, occasionally explaining something she was doing. It seemed like a very long time before she stopped and stood in front of Sarah, looking over her work. Sarah waited eagerly to hear how it had turned out, but Mary only smiled and patted the hair here and there.

"We must put the dress on now. I will help you with the corset first." The maid went over to the bed and picked up the stiff garment, bringing it over to Sarah. "You don't really need it; you are so slim. You won't have to wear it all the time, but it is proper to wear it for such an occasion as this. It will make the gown lie straight and keep from wrinkling in front. At least we won't have to lace it very tightly." After getting the corset on, Mary skipped over to the bed, announcing, "It's time for the dress!"

Sarah stepped into the gown so as not to mess her beautifully coiffed head and Mary proceeded to do up the many hooks down the back. The dress fit perfectly; the alterations had successfully made it look as though it had been specifically tailored for Sarah.

Mary just stood back and stared. Sarah nervously clenched the fabric at her side. Why didn't Mary say anything? Softly she enquired, "Is it alright?"

"Ah, Miss, you are a sight to behold. Just beautiful." The maid came over to Sarah and peered at her face carefully. "You don't even need any cheek or lip rouge." Mary surveyed the room and announced, "There is not a mirror in here that is large enough for you to see your whole self. You must come and look in Miss Rose's mirror. You will be able to see all of you in it." She rushed to the door, opening it as she motioned to Sarah, "Come, come!"

Sarah walked to the door. The dress swished around her, and she could feel the ringlets bouncing on her neck and down her back. Looking down she saw the tips of new white slippers peeking out from under the full skirt. She tried to picture what she was going to see in the mirror, but nothing prepared her for the sight of the lady walking towards her, matching her movement for movement. The mirror was at the end of the hallway and Sarah puzzled at each step. How could that be her?

She stopped in front of the reflection and stared into her own green eyes, then down over the heart-shaped neckline and snug bodice to her tiny waist, where the fabric was slightly gathered to accent the gentle curve of her hips. It was as though she had turned into a woman in the span of a few hours. Reaching up she touched the golden ringlets that hung over her shoulder and the little curls that surrounded her face. The mass of curls on top of her head was so beautifully intertwined, the streaks of very light blonde accenting the darker shades. The lovely blue/green of the dress turned her lightly tanned skin to soft cream. Mary was smiling behind her, and she turned, pulling the maid into a big hug. "Mary! However did you do it?"

"Oh Miss, I didn't do much. It is just you, packaged a little differently. You were already beautiful. I can't wait for Captain Att…" Mary stopped quickly at the frown on that beautiful face. Reaching up, she twined a loose ringlet a little tighter. "Now why don't you go back to your room and relax for a while? It will still be at least a half hour before people start to arrive. I will bring you a cup of tea. But don't lie down and mess your hair, mind you."

Sarah's heart had skipped a beat at the mention of Grayson. She was certain she could not walk down the long staircase if he was watching her from below. "I think I'd like to go down now, Mary. I can relax in the sitting room until people arrive."

"Alright, Miss, you go on ahead. I'll go to the kitchen and bring you some tea." She turned to go and then back to Sarah, "Oh Miss, you don't have to worry about anything. There will be no one as beautiful as you are here tonight."

Sarah shook her head and smiled, "Thank you, Mary. I will see you in the sitting room then."

CHAPTER 23

Grayson and Harper stood outside Rose's house almost an hour early waiting for the door to be opened. They had left the ship early in order to stop on the way to check on some last-minute preparations for the voyage and were finished much more quickly than expected. Grayson was sure Rose would not mind if they waited at the house until dinner.

Charles opened the door and greeted the two men. "Come in. Miss Rose is not down yet but you are welcome to wait in the sitting room. I will bring you a glass of claret." He reached to take their coats and hats, but Grayson stopped him, "Thank you, Charles. We can take care of our things. We will wait for you in the sitting room."

They went into the cloak room, a small room off the entry. After hanging up their coats they went to the doorway, where Grayson suddenly stopped, causing Harper to bump into him. "What is going on?" Harper asked. Grayson turned and motioned him to be silent, staying back in the shadow of the room. Peering around the larger man, Harper saw what had transfixed his friend. An incredibly beautiful woman stood at the top of the long, winding staircase in front of them.

Something in the way she held her head and rested her hand on the banister seemed familiar to Grayson. He watched silently as she began her descent, stepping gracefully from stair to stair, her dress swirling around her. The green underskirt shining through the diaphanous blue covering reminded him of the sea he loved so much. Who is this lovely creature? Is she a mermaid? Luring him to disaster? Or maybe to untold pleasure? At this moment, he would willingly go to either. He was captivated by the delicate face, the sweet smile on full pink lips, and the shimmering blonde hair hanging in long curls over soft, creamy shoulders. She had not seen him. He pulled back further into the shadows. As she neared the bottom of the stairs, he saw her more clearly. Emerald eyes shining through dark lashes were visible even at this distance. He was stunned to realize that this woman was Sarah!

It was a shock when Harper slapped him on the back, whispering loudly, "Well, lookee at our little Sarah! Who would've thought that behind that mousy brown skirt, mussy hair and smudged little face there was a bewitching woman. Looks like a beautiful mermaid dancing on the sea, she does,"

Grayson didn't want to admit his similar comparison to himself or to Harper. Tearing his gaze away from Sarah he turned to his old friend, speaking sharply, trying to convince himself, "I wouldn't say she is beautiful and bewitching, but she did clean up better than I expected. I wonder how much that cost me."

The little gasp behind him sent a shudder down his spine. It couldn't be! He turned slowly and saw those remarkable eyes widen in shock, glistening with a hint of tears. The lovely pink from her cheeks and lips had faded away and left a ghost of the sparkling creature he had watched walk down the stairs.

He reached out to her, but she recoiled. "Sarah, I was just surprised to see you," he tried to explain. The words sounded inadequate, even to his own ears. His hand clenched into a fist at his side. Why had he spoken so loudly? Why was she beside the cloak room? Why any of it? And how could he make it right?

Sarah stood, stunned, staring into the familiar deep blue eyes above her. Her mind kept replaying the words, "I wouldn't say she is beautiful, but she cleaned up better than I thought she would." Why does it hurt so much? She never expected him to think she was beautiful, although, maybe, after she saw herself in the mirror, a tiny part of her had secretly hoped he might. How could she have ever let herself think that? He was used to truly beautiful women. Look at him, so elegant in his formal evening wear, his hair tied back to reveal his strikingly handsome face. Why would he ever notice her? More importantly, why did she care?

"Sarah." She heard her name called from what seemed a long distance and turned to the sound. Harper stood with his hands out to her, taking her trembling ones into them. He smiled brightly, also wanting to fix this moment. But how?

Relief flooded over her at the sight of the kindly, older man. She moved to his side, and he gave her a quick hug then stood back looking at her, shaking his head. "Who is this lovely lady giving me a hug? Looks a bit like a servant girl I used to know." His familiar, scratchy laugh rang out in the high-ceilinged foyer. "Sarah, girl, we hardly recognized you. Grayson was just saying that as pretty as you always were, we never realized what a

143

bewitching beauty we had on our hands until right now." He turned to Grayson, "Isn't that what you were saying, Captain?"

Grayson knew Harper's words could not disguise what Sarah had heard him say, but it was at least an opening to making things better and he quickly took it. "Yes, watching you come down those stairs was like watching a lovely sea maiden drifting towards us. You look beautiful tonight, Sarah."

Sarah looked down at the floor, embarrassed at the compliments which rang untrue after the words she had just heard. The hurt and embarrassment collided inside her and she lifted her head, sparks shooting from her eyes. "Thank you, Captain Attwood. I am glad I have cleaned up well enough to meet with your approval. I do not know how much it has cost you, but I will find a way to repay you every cent."

They were all a bit surprised to hear the deep rumbling laugh rolling out from Grayson's chest. "Well, it is good to see the same spirit is there. The cat still has some claws, albeit well-manicured ones. Come now, Sarah. You must allow me my surprise at seeing you. Perhaps even you were surprised. Please excuse my offensive remarks and accept my heartfelt compliment. You are truly lovely." He reached out and took her hand, touching the back briefly to his lips.

A tingle ran up Sarah's arm and she felt the blush rising over her cheeks. She could hear the sincerity in his compliment and replied graciously, "Thank you, Grayson."

"Is there a meeting in the cloakroom I was unaware of?" The soft voice, accompanied by a lilting laugh, came from behind Sarah.

The three turned to see Rose, looking elegant in a deep maroon gown. There was a slight frown on her attractive face. "I see you have all arrived early, and I have missed the opportunity to see the unveiling of Sarah." She reached for Sarah's hand and pulled her towards the center of the foyer. "Let me have a look at you." She stepped back, leaving Sarah to stand alone in the center of the room. After a moment, she declared, "You look absolutely stunning, my dear. Don't you think so, Grayson?"

Grayson joined the older woman, "Yes, Rose. We have all declared Sarah to be a true beauty. I'm sure she is beginning to feel a bit awkward at all the praise." He glanced at Sarah who indeed was looking uncomfortable standing by herself in the middle of the room. "Come, Sarah, let us all go into the sitting room. Charles is bringing some claret."

There was a collective sigh of relief as they all trailed into the sitting room. Things were calm and everyone was relatively happy and ready for the evening to commence.

CHAPTER 24

It was quiet in the sitting room. Sarah and Rose sipped tea and the men drank their wine. Everyone tried to relax and put aside the awkward start to the evening. Sarah sat by herself in one of the large comfortable chairs wishing she could curl her feet up, lay her head back and close her eyes, but of course that wasn't possible in the beautiful gown and with every hair in the correct place. Rose sat on the settee where Harper joined her.

Grayson chose not to sit at all but rather leaned against the wall casually, holding his wine and thinking. Sarah tried not to look at him, but her eyes were drawn of their own volition to him. He was more attractive than she had ever seen him. Light tan jacket and breeches hugged his long, lean frame revealing broad shoulders and muscled thighs. His swarthy skin stood out in contrast to the ruffled white shirt he wore. A brocade vest of dark brown with orange thread was accented by a silk cravat of the same colors tied around his neck. His shiny dark hair was tied back leaving his ruggedly handsome face clearly visible, but unruly strands hung in long waves across his forehead, down past his strong jaw. He truly looked the part of a gentleman of status. Sarah knew she was staring but before she could look away, dark blue eyes met hers. They stared silently at each other for a moment. He nodded in acknowledgment of her, a slight smile on his lips. She returned the nod and they both looked away quickly.

Rose tried to encourage conversation by asking Harper how the preparations for the voyage were going.

Fortunately, it was only a few minutes before Charles returned to announce that the first guests had arrived. Rose immediately got up, waving the others to follow her as she left the room. Sarah prayed silently for strength and peace as she walked slowly towards the front door. Rose had arranged how they should stand to greet the guests. As the hostess, she stood closest to the door with Grayson next to her and Sarah beside him. Sarah nervously shifted her weight from foot to foot, causing her dress to swish around her feet, like gentle rippling waves. Grayson put a calming hand on her arm, "Do not worry, Sarah, you will be fine. I will make sure of that."

His confidence and assurance helped Sarah feel secure, even confident, standing beside him. As people made their way towards them, he made a point of introducing each guest slowly, using any appropriate title she should know. He introduced her to the guests as his stepmother's niece who was returning to England after staying several years with family acquaintances in America. Sarah's eyes widened as she heard the introduction. It sounded so respectable, so plausible, coming from this attractive, accomplished man beside her. She almost believed it herself, almost forgot that she was simply a servant girl, rescued and made over.

As she greeted people the strength and peace she had prayed for began replacing her fear and anxiety. She started greeting each guest with a smile. Before long she found she was actually enjoying meeting everyone and looking forward to the dinner. People gathered in the foyer greeting one another until everyone had arrived. Rose nodded at Charles, who opened the large double doors to the dining room. A long table covered with white linen and set with beautiful china greeted them. Place cards marked each spot and people busily hunted for their seats. Grayson was seated at the head of the table, with Rose at the foot.

Rose had seated Sarah close enough to her so that Sarah could get any cues she might need during the meal, but at the same time far enough away to practice mingling on her own. Harper sat across the table so that she would have another familiar face to look to for support.

Sarah soon discovered that she was able to converse fairly confidently with the people around her. Rose had tutored her in the art of guiding conversation away from herself. "Always end a question with a question. People love to talk about themselves and will quickly forget that they were trying to get information about you," was Rose's wise instruction."

Sarah recalled Rose's advice as the attractive young man she was seated next to engaged her in conversation. Rose had been right. He was eager to tell her about his life and Sarah genuinely found his stories interesting, laughing and talking easily about his situations without having to say much about herself. His easy way and sense of humor soon relaxed her, and she forgot about the tall, dark man at the end of the table.

Grayson heard her laugh and looked towards the lilting sound. Sarah's face was tilted up to the man at her side, the golden ringlets falling back to reveal her slender neck and creamy shoulders. Her smiling mouth was slightly open to let the delicate laugh out and he knew without seeing them that her eyes shone brilliantly into the eyes above her. Even from this distance, Grayson could see that the man was fascinated with the lovely woman beside him. Others around the table turned towards the couple also. Grayson recognized the looks of admiration on their faces. He was surprised at her ease with the guests. Oddly, he felt a tiny twinge of disappointment. He had been sure that she would be uncomfortable, looking to him for help, but she was handling the evening quite well without him.

He turned away, trying to concentrate on the conversation he was having with a portly gentleman on his right. The man had followed Grayson's eyes and watched Sarah appreciatively. He leaned over to Grayson, "Quite a little beauty you have there. Someone said you had never met her until this trip. Must have been a pleasant surprise, eh?" The man elbowed Grayson in the side as he laughed suggestively. Grayson pulled back and grunted in reply, a scowl on his face. He glanced over at Sarah. Indeed, she had been. He had been surprised at her quiet strength, her adaptability, her humility, and, yes, her beauty also. But he wasn't about to talk to this man about Sarah. Henry had been an associate of his father's before moving to Boston and knew too much about their family as it was and didn't keep anything he knew to himself.

"She is lovely, Grayson. Such a shame Bethany never had a chance to meet her." The piercing voice came from the thin woman at Henry's side and a hush fell over the table as heads turned their way. Everything about

149

Lillian was sharp, from her pointed nose and matching chin to her sharp voice and equally sharp tongue. Grayson had almost missed seeing her sitting beside her rotund husband. He would just as soon have missed her altogether. Any friend of Bethany's was to be avoided as far as he was concerned.

Without thinking he answered her, his tone harsh, "If Bethany had wanted to meet Sarah, she should have taken measures to return Sarah to England before she lay on her death bed."

Lillian ignored his comment but threw in a jab of her own, "I wonder what Lydia will think of your Sarah. I would like to be there for that meeting." She laughed gleefully at the picture she envisioned. Grayson knew that everyone was listening. Out of the corner of his eye, he saw Sarah's head snap towards the woman.

"We are ready for dessert now," Rose spoke quickly and loudly to the server and then addressed the table in general. "Ladies, why don't we retire to the parlor for our dessert and tea? The gentlemen can stay here for their brandy and business talk." She rose elegantly and the women trailed after her into the parlor. The moment was forgotten as conversation resumed among the group.

The rest of the evening went by quickly. The women chattered about life and children while having their tea and cakes. Before long the men came to collect them, and everyone began to drift away with well wishes for Grayson and the coming voyage. Finally only Grayson and Harper were left. Grayson was anxious to get back to the ship, "Come along now, Sarah, let's get your things. We should return to the ship so we can get an early start in the morning. The wind is always best in the morning."

Sarah's mouth opened to speak, but Rose spoke first, "Grayson, you must leave Sarah here for the night. She has a great deal more to pack now and is not ready to go yet." At Grayson's frown she touched his arm. "Come now, my boy. I will have her brought to the ship as early as you like. You do not have to return for her. She will sleep better here and be rested for the voyage."

Grayson looked at Harper for support, but the older man simply shrugged his shoulders, not taking sides. With a huff, Grayson resigned himself to defeat and agreed to let Sarah stay the night as long as she was at the ship by first light.

After her first effort to say something, Sarah stood back and simply watched the exchange around her. Grayson gazed at her, standing by herself across the room, looking down at the cup of tea she held. She was remarkably lovely even now, after an evening that must have been very taxing for her. He couldn't help the small feeling of pride he had in her. She had been more than he could have hoped. All the Boston elite had been quite impressed with her. He was drawn to her and softly said her name when he reached her, "Sarah."

She looked up at him, a small smile on her lips that could not disguise her tired eyes, where he saw a faint question mark. He waited for her to speak, ask him whatever it was she had on her mind, but she only said, "Hello, Grayson. Thank you for letting me stay one last night with Rose. I am really somewhat tired, and I would like a chance to say good-bye and express my gratitude without being in a rush."

"It is fine," he acquiesced graciously. "You just get a rest. You've had a strenuous evening and you did a remarkable job. You were beautiful, spoke and acted completely correctly, and charmed the whole bunch. You did me proud."

In fact, it had been a strenuous evening and Sarah responded without thinking, snapping, "I'm glad I didn't disappoint you in front of your important friends. Thank you for the beautiful clothes that made it possible for me to be presentable." There was a hint of sadness in her voice and a slight edge to her words that made Grayson grimace.

He ran a hand through his hair, trying to brush away the thoughts, "You are welcome, Sarah. I'm glad Rose was able to find you something fitting for the occasion, but clothes can only do so much. It is you who people admire, not just your dress. You did *yourself* proud, Sarah, and I was honored to stand beside you and present you to our guests." He gazed into her lovely eyes and reached for her hand, bringing it to his lips for a farewell kiss. He felt the soft, warm skin under his lips and lingered there.

Harper cleared his throat meaningfully and Grayson quickly raised his head, releasing her hand. "It is time for Harper and me to leave and finish a few things for the voyage tomorrow. Good night, Sarah. I will see you in the morning. Sleep well."

"Good night, Grayson. I have some things to finish as well," Sarah replied and turned to walk out of the room, the graceful sway of her hips making her dress shimmer around her, once again making Grayson think of a lovely sea maiden.

He watched her leave, took a deep breath, and turned to Rose. Harper had already said his goodbyes and left to get the carriage. Grayson had a great deal to thank Rose for and they talked quietly for a moment before he pulled her into a hug. He loved this woman like his own mother, and he realized that it would be some time before he would see her again. She stepped back and spoke softly to him, "Grayson, God has brought something very special into your life. This has not happened by accident. There is a reason for everything. Seek His guidance in what you do."

Grayson sighed heavily. They'd had these discussions before. She knew how he felt about God and His reasons for things, for letting his mother die and then his father. A reason for everything, he thought cynically. But he did not want to part badly so he nodded and leaned over to kiss the cheek she offered him, then donned his hat and coat and left the room. Rose walked with him and waved to him as he left.

CHAPTER 25

Sarah stood by the stairs, watching the two say goodbye. There were tears in Rose's eyes when she turned and found Sarah standing there. Sarah went over and put her arms around the older woman and hugged her close. "It must be hard to say good-bye when you know it will be a while before you see him again," Sarah said.

"Yes, it is. I sometimes think of moving back to England. Grayson is family to me. But I have a good life here, with friends I enjoy, and I do get to see Grayson from time to time. So, I just put him in God's hands and pray for his safety and that he will find peace with God somehow."

Sarah looked into Rose's eyes. "Please tell me about Grayson, Rose. What happened to him? How did you become so close to him?"

Rose hesitated, then took Sarah's arm and pulled her back into the sitting room and down onto the settee beside her, smiling affectionately at the girl next to her. "Sarah, although we have only known each other for a few days I have come to care for you deeply and to think of you almost as a daughter. Grayson has been like a son to me for many years and I believe that God has brought you into his life for a reason, and he into yours. There are no accidents with God and so I will tell you my story."

Sarah's eyes glistened as Rose spoke and nodded in agreement, not wanting to interrupt the gentle woman beside her. Rose took a breath and covered Sarah's hand with her own and began as though she was reading a bedtime story.

"Once upon a time two girls met and shared a room at The Greenwood School for Young Ladies. Marion and Rose instantly recognized a kindred spirit in the other and became fast friends. Marion could speak of nothing but a young man back home, Harrison Attwood, and when I met him, I understood why. Harris was elegant, wealthy, and very, very attractive, with slightly curly brown hair and deep blue eyes. Before our final year of school, Mari and Harris were engaged and only months after we finished school I stood beside Marion as she and Harrison were wed."

Rose paused, her eyes looking far away into the past. "Harrison and Marion were very happy, and I was frequently a visitor at their estate. The three of us formed a deep friendship, and I was there with Mari when two years later Grayson was born. Mari and Harris were delighted with their son, and I was as much an aunt as I could be without having a true blood connection. In fact, Mari and Harrison asked me to be Grayson's Godmother, meaning that I would particularly pray for him and help him in his spiritual life, but also that I would agree to look after him in the case of their deaths." Now Rose's eyes glistened and her voice trembled slightly as she continued.

"When Grayson was sixteen, Marion became ill. Despite all their wealth, there was nothing that could be done for her, and Mari died. Grayson was very close to his mother, and it was a difficult time for him to suddenly be without her. During her illness Grayson had

155

gone to church frequently to pray for her, having complete confidence that God would heal his mother. He was bitterly angry at God when she died. Harrison continued to go to church faithfully every week but he could not get through to his son and convince him that God knew best and that they would get through this by drawing closer to Him. Grayson refused to be consoled by God but turned to me for consolation. I continued to visit them often but even when I attended church with Harrison, Grayson refused to come along.

As the first year passed, I realized that Grayson harbored a hope that Harrison and I would marry and he would have a loving mother and father again. I admit that I had grown to love Harris and there was a time when he told me that he couldn't imagine life without me."

Rose stopped, realizing what she had said. She hadn't meant to go this deeply into the story. She stared past Sarah, a far-away look in her eyes. Sarah waited, anxious to hear the rest of the story. What could have happened? It sounded so perfect. She watched Rose, the sadness on her delicate face touching her heart, but she couldn't stop the question that came out of her mouth, "What happened, Rose? Why didn't you and Harrison…"

Rose's gentle voice finished the question, "get married?" She smiled at Sarah, who was nervously biting her lip. "It's alright, Sarah. Harrison met your Aunt Bethany." She swallowed and took a breath, "It simply wasn't God's plan for us, although it did seem to give Grayson one more reason to reject God." Her voice was soft as she said, almost to herself, "I'm not sure why it happened that way, but..." She stopped, looking intently at the little, formerly indentured servant girl sitting across from her, a question growing in her turquoise eyes, "but perhaps God is beginning to show me now. As I said, I don't believe in accidents. God has a plan in you and Grayson's meeting." She stood, saying, "Come along, Dear, I am tired now. I think I will go to bed."

Sarah got up from the settee, her brow furrowed, pondering all the things Rose had just told her. "Yes, Rose, I think it shows that God was hearing my prayers to be free and answering them," she said.

Rose agreed, "Well, yes. We shall see how things unfold when you are back in England. God's plans can often be quite intricate and take time to understand. Whatever God's plans are, I am glad you will be with Grayson now, Sarah. You'll be safe with him. He will take care of you when you get to England. Don't worry about that. He is a good man."

"I know he is, Rose," Sarah answered, continuing somewhat hesitantly, eyes down, "But I am nervous about meeting his friends in England." Lydia – the name came to Sarah's mind immediately. A friend? Or more? Sarah had never thought about women in Grayson's life. Of course, he would have women around him. Look at him. She heard the words of the sharp woman at the end of the table again in her head, "What will Lydia think?" And Rose, when she handed Grayson the letter saying it was from "the beautiful Lydia." Who was this woman? What was she to Grayson?

She couldn't resist asking Rose. "The lady at the table tonight mentioned a woman named Lydia." She glanced up from under thick eyelashes, "Who is she?"

Rose thought for a moment, not anxious to address that question. "Lydia's family and the Attwoods were friends for years. Lydia and Grayson grew up together. They are very good friends." Sarah waited, looking at Rose as if to say, *"And?"*

Without much choice, Rose continued. Sarah might as well know. "For years there has been speculation of a romance between Lydia and Grayson because of the relationship between their families, but nothing has ever come of it. I know they seem to be the perfect match, having the same background and friends, but Grayson has never voiced any intentions to me so I assume the talk is just rumor."

"I see," Sarah said, her furrowed brow clearly indicating otherwise.

She opened her mouth to let the questions spew forth, but Rose stopped that quickly. "You really must go to bed now, Sarah. You will have to leave quite early in the morning. We don't want to start Grayson's day off badly by keeping him waiting."

Sarah couldn't agree more with that and so said goodnight to Rose and walked up the stairs, her mind reeling with the unanswered questions. What is Lydia like? Is she beautiful? That is a ridiculous question, she thought. Of course she is beautiful. What will Lydia think of her? She pushed aside the question that kept coming back – does Grayson love her?

Mary looked up from the dress she was folding when Sarah came in. "Well, hello, Miss. I am just about finished here, and you can get to bed. You must be exhausted."

Sarah stared around the room, puzzled. A new trunk stood open in the middle of the room and Mary placed the dress she had been folding inside. "What are you doing, Mary?" Sarah asked.

"Why, packing your things, Miss. If you are to be leaving first thing in the morning, we have to get you packed tonight. I'm just finishing up. I've left out your night things and clothes for the morning." She placed a neatly folded stack of clothes into the trunk as she spoke.

"Mary, that is not my trunk," Sarah said, puzzled.

"This is a trunk Miss Rose has had stored away in the attic. It hasn't been used in years and is as good as new. Miss Rose said to use it to pack your things. I think there will be plenty of room, but you will also have this case for anything that doesn't fit." The maid pointed at a brown leather suitcase on the floor beside the bed.

"Here, let me help you with your dress," Mary offered. "Such a beautiful thing," she said as she began to undo the long row of hooks down the back. "You were so beautiful tonight, Miss. Everyone was saying how beautiful you are." She noticed Sarah's doubting face and added, "Indeed they were, Miss. I was taking coats and listening to all the conversation, and it was mostly about how lovely you were and how you and Mr. Grayson made such a handsome couple."

Sarah's head snapped up at the words. She and Grayson, a couple? She pictured them standing side by side greeting guests. She had felt good standing beside him, and he seemed to be pleased to introduce her to his friends. He had sounded genuine when he said she was beautiful. What would he think of the picture of them as a couple?

Lydia! The name jumped into her mind again, shattering the picture. Was Lydia the woman who belonged in that picture with Grayson? Lydia - a woman equal to him in wealth and status, sophisticated and beautiful, a woman worthy to be at his side, unlike a servant girl wrapped in new clothes, pretending to be worthy.

She was startled out of her thoughts when Mary yanked on the ties of the corset as she untied it. In a few minutes Sarah was ready for bed, brushing the curls out of her hair as Mary packed away the gown and other final items. "You can have a quick bath in the morning, Miss, and we will fix your hair for traveling." She closed the trunk and explained as she left, "I will wake you early and bring the bath water. Now, lie down and sleep. It won't be long before you will hear me knocking," The maid pulled the door closed behind her.

Sarah blew out the lantern beside her bed and lay down on the soft pillows. Sleep? Was that possible? Tomorrow all this would be gone. She would sleep in her tight cradle as the sea rocked the ship that was taking her to her new life. She closed her eyes and pictured England as she remembered it, visualized her mother's face and her tall, confident father with his arm around her, making her feel so protected and loved. And then they were gone, leaving her alone. A tall, dark figure appeared in the distance as if waiting to take their place beside her. But then she realized that he was standing with his arm around another woman who was smiling up at him.

Her eyes flew open at the knock on the door. Had she really fallen asleep? She shook her head to dislodge the image of the man and woman in her dream and opened the door to a sleepy-eyed Mary carrying two large buckets of water. "Good morning, Mary," Sarah said brightly, reaching for one of the buckets. Mary followed Sarah inside and before long Sarah was bathed and ready, dressed in a new skirt and blouse, her damp hair in a high bun with small curls around the sides of her face. The last items were put in the suitcase and right on time there was a knock at the door and two young men came in to carry her baggage down to the carriage.

Sarah went over to Mary as the men took the cases. "Mary, thank you so much for everything. You have really become a friend to me." Tears threatened to fall, and she tried to lighten the moment a bit, "I wish I could take you with me to do my hair every day." They both put on wavering smiles and hugged each other. Mary gave Sarah a peck on the cheek and a little shove toward the door, "Go now. Captain Attwood will not be happy if you are late." They waved to each other at the door, both turning away quickly.

Rose was waiting in the foyer in a robe, with her beautiful red hair tied loosely down her back. Sarah stopped on the bottom stair, looking at the lovely older woman, and a lump rose in her throat. How had she come to love and admire this woman so much in such a short time? Tears shone in her eyes as Rose walked to her, arms outstretched. Sarah ran into them, and they held each other tightly, tears on the cheeks of both. Rose stepped back first, taking Sarah's arm, still holding her close as they walked to the door. "It really is time to go, Dear."

Charles stood holding the door open but just before going through it, Sarah turned back to Rose and hugged her again, trying to speak, "Rose, I don't know what to say. I can't possibly thank you enough."

"Then don't try, Sarah, dear," Rose swallowed hard, a tear sliding down her cheek. "You have given me a great deal during this time also. I have come to love you and will be praying for you that God will protect and guide you and give you wisdom in the decisions that lie ahead."

The women hugged again and kissed each other on the cheek. Then Sarah turned quickly, almost running down the stairs to the carriage where Charles waited, holding the door open. Sarah looked at the kindly butler, "Thank you, Charles. You have been a great help to me."

"You are welcome, Miss. I hope you will come and visit again. Captain Attwood makes the trip occasionally and perhaps you can accompany him some time." He took her hand to help her into the carriage.

She waved out the window as the carriage began moving but sat back quickly before the tears began to flow too heavily. She tried not to think about the people she was leaving behind. It was hard to imagine that she had tried so hard to avoid staying with Rose and now she could hardly bear to leave. Perhaps Charles was right. Perhaps she could visit sometime.

With that thought, she leaned back and closed her eyes. When the carriage stopped, the door opened, and there was Harper, smiling at her. "Sarah, it's good to see you." The familiar gruff voice made Sarah smile. He reached out his hand to help her down. "Just in time, you are. The ship is set to leave. We'll get you settled on board and then hoist anchor." He started walking to the ship almost pulling Sarah along.

She pulled back and made him stop. "Harper, I have a few things to bring to the ship. We may need some help. I have more than one bag now."

Harper went back to the carriage and inspected the back. "Well, lookee here, you have some real baggage now. I'll send a couple of the lads back for it."

He asked the driver to wait and took Sarah's arm as they moved on towards the ship. Sarah was surprised that she was looking forward to being onboard again. She had been treated well there, made friends, and felt safe. She had lived so many years with the Tompkins but had never thought of that place as home, hardly remembered her little room now.

Harper told a couple of the sailors on the dock to go and retrieve her things and then guided her up the gangplank. She looked around the deck. Sailors were running everywhere, preparing to set sail. Her eyes stopped at the wheelhouse, where a tall man with long

163

dark hair stood looking over his ship. Her heart stopped for a moment, and she couldn't tear her eyes away. Almost as if he felt her watching, he turned toward her and stopped. They stared at each other for a moment, then Grayson nodded to her, and she lifted a small hand to acknowledge his greeting. She was home.

CHAPTER 26

Sarah walked slowly around the deck. It had been several days since they left Boston Harbor, and life onboard the ship was back to normal. Grayson was always busy with the ship as usual. If she was honest with herself, she would have to admit that she had hoped that he might spend a little more time with her after that last night in Boston, where he had been so kind and complimentary. It seemed like they might actually become friends. But everything was right back to the way it had been. If it weren't for the new clothes in the trunk in her room, it would seem as if they had never stopped.

As Grayson was walking around the deck one day, making sure everything was running smoothly, he came across Sarah in a secluded area, looking out at the water thoughtfully. He hadn't spent much time with her since they were back on the ship and stopped, asking, "How are you doing now that we are back on board? You seem deep in thought."

When she looked at him, there was a sheen of tears in her eyes. "Since we left Boston, I realize more and more that there are no more stops before we come to England, and I admit that I feel insecure at that thought. I will not know anyone, and will have no friends to confide in. I will be alone."

Grayson put his hand gently on her shoulder, "You will soon make friends, Sarah. You are an Attwood now. You will meet all the people I know, the people of your own status."

Her eyes accused him when she lifted them to meet his and he heard the concern in her voice when she spoke. "Do you really think that just because you have freed me and dressed me up, your rich friends are going to accept me as their equal? You think they will not feel that I am too far below them? You think they are going to be my friends anyway?" the questions flowed out.

His silence was deafening. What does she want him to say? What does she expect? He wished he could disagree with her, could assure her that, of course, they would accept her as an equal. He shoved his hands through his long hair with a groan. "Sarah, I admit I don't know what it is going to be like in England. You can't just change the way things are. It might take some time, but, yes, I believe some of my friends will be your friend also." He put his hands on her small shoulders, and she gazed into his eyes, tears spilling over. "I will be with you, Sarah. You won't be alone," he promised. Without realizing what he was doing he pulled her into his arms as he spoke and gently held her there.

Sarah gave in to his kind words and let her head fall against his strong chest. Grayson felt her take some deep calming breaths and when she was breathing normally, he couldn't stop himself from saying, "I will be your friend, Sarah."

His deep voice rumbled against her ear, and she looked up at him, her eyes searching his. She could see that he meant it, or at least that he wanted to mean it, but they both knew it would be difficult. They stepped apart at the same time. Neither spoke as Grayson helped her down the stairs where he watched her until she reached her cabin.

He wanted her away from him. If only she didn't feel so right in his arms. Already he was chastising himself for the lovely words of steadfastness he'd just spoken to her – I'll take care of you, stand by you, be your friend. When he said them, they sounded so right that he had even believed them for a minute. But that wasn't in the plan.

CHAPTER 27

The days drifted by like the water under the ship, slow and endless. How long had it been? Three weeks? A month? Sarah was losing track.

She avoided Grayson for the most part, wanting to erase the way she had felt when he had held her on the deck. Of course, he was only doing what anyone would do when they found themselves with someone who was upset, but her heart beat faster when his arms were around her. His strength and confidence made her feel secure, protected, cared for, and something more. And those were exactly the feelings she had to get rid of. Ever since Boston, since hearing about Lydia, she was more and more certain than ever, that even with her new clothes, she would never fit in Grayson's life, never fit in with his friends. That moment of closeness didn't mean anything, didn't change anything. She stood, watching the sea shimmering in the moonlight.

Grayson rounded the corner stopping abruptly, when he saw the girl gazing out to sea, her delicate profile etched against the dusky sky. Long golden curls floated down her back. The wind caught a strand and blew it across her face. She lifted her arm to catch it and her soft feminine form was revealed in the moonlight. Grayson's breath caught in his throat. He had thought he was going to rescue a girl, but Sarah was no girl. She was a lovely woman, a woman he had been thinking about more and more frequently. He couldn't get the way she had felt when he held her out of his mind. Ever since Boston, since seeing her in that green dress, he was more and more certain that with her new clothes, her natural grace and beauty, she would fit easily into his life, even with his friends. With Lydia?

He could not envision that, couldn't think of two women more different from each other. Lydia fits much better with him and his world, and yet he was drawn to the simple unpretentiousness of Sarah. Shaking his head, he moved on, hoping to clear his thoughts.

Sarah's eyes flew open at the movement. The two faced each other, each hoping the other could not read their thoughts. Grayson recovered first, clearing his throat before speaking casually, "Hello Sarah. I'm glad you are out enjoying the evening."

Sarah took a calming breath and smiled brightly, "Hello Grayson. It is a beautiful evening. The breeze is quite warm tonight."

"Come, walk with me for a bit," Grayson said as he moved to her side, putting his arm around her waist to guide her.

It wasn't a command but the thought of refusing never crossed Sarah's mind. In fact, she was finding it difficult to think at all with Grayson walking so close to her, his hand on her waist burning through the fabric of her dress. They walked quietly and slowly, carefully avoiding the ropes scattered across the deck.

"We will be in England in a week or two now, depending on the wind." He stopped walking at the little gasp that came from his partner. "It will be nice to have this long voyage behind us, won't it Sarah? I'm sure you will be glad to feel firm ground under your feet again."

She agreed more confidently than she felt, "Yes, it will be good to finally reach England. I have been waiting for more than six years for that. But, I actually feel a little sad at the idea of leaving the ship. In some ways it feels like home to me now." She laughed, glancing at him, "I could never have imagined I would ever say that when I first saw the ship in Norfolk." She stopped walking, her eyes looking out over the sea, "I am far more familiar with life on this boat than I am with life in England. I keep thinking about my life there before I was indentured. I was 12 when I left, so I do remember some, and yet so much has happened since then that it seems far longer ago than six years." She almost seemed to be talking to herself and Grayson stood quietly beside the small figure, letting her talk. "I so wish that my parents would be there. They would be happy to know that God has taken care of me and brought me safely back."

"If God had been taking such good care of you, you would have been home long ago, and your parents would have been there to welcome you back. Or, you would never have had to leave in the first place." Grayson's voice was bitter.

Sarah turned to him, speaking quietly, "Why are you so bitter at God, Grayson?"

He answered curtly, "Why are you not?"

"I believe there is a reason for everything, even though I may not understand. Rose reminded me of that. I think I ended up staying with her so that God could help me to not be afraid and ever since being in Boston I have been much more confident that everything will be fine." She smiled peacefully.

Before she could continue Grayson said, "Yes, Rose has spoken often enough about that to me." They arrived at the stairwell both lost in thought. "Here you are, Sarah. I will leave you now. Good night." He held her hand until she was safely down the stairs and heard her quiet, "Good night" drift up the stairwell.

CHAPTER 28

The days continued to drift by but soon there was a new excitement in the air. The word "home" could be heard frequently. They would soon be able to see the shores of England. Sarah greeted the news with both excitement and a touch of fear. She prayed constantly for God to give her the strength to face the new life ahead of her. He had brought her this far, seen her through so many changes. She knew that He was with her in this next change in her life, but even so, it was new and unknown.

As she walked across the deck Sarah noticed that there was a particular increase in energy around her. The sailors busily tugged on ropes and yelled at each other. The sails were full, and the ship moved swiftly through the water. The wind tugged at her dress and hair as she pushed against it, slowly making her way to the little alcove where she regularly sat. Everything was calm in her little nook. She stared out at the darkening sky and did not notice the man coming around the corner.

He stopped, looking down at her. "There you are!" he exclaimed.

Sarah was surprised. He hadn't spoken to her in that tone for quite some time. Without thinking, she retorted, "Yes, here I am. I frequently come here. You know that. You have never said that I shouldn't. I didn't mean..."

He interrupted her, "Sarah, stop talking. There is nothing wrong with you coming here but we are heading into some rough weather, and I didn't know where you were." He surprised himself when he admitted, "I was worried when I couldn't find you."

"We have been in rough weather before. I will be fine," she reminded him confidently.

"Not like this." His tone was stern. "I want you to go below and stay in your cabin until it has subsided. The storm we are heading into is not to be taken lightly. I want you out of the way. It is going to be very busy up here. I can't be worrying about you being here. You'll be safer below." He reached down and pulled her up beside him. "I'll walk with you to your cabin." He put his arm around her waist holding her securely against his side.

The sky was dark now with only the occasional stream of light when the moon poked through the rapidly moving clouds. Waves crashed against the side of the ship, salty spray making the deck wet and slippery. Grayson hurried her over to the stairwell, but just before she started down, he took her shoulders and turned her to face him, speaking calmly, "We are going to be alright. This is a sturdy ship. She has weathered fierce storms before. Don't be afraid." His voice was confident, but she could see uncertainty in his eyes. He squeezed her shoulders slightly, "I must go now."

With that he left, his long hair blowing out behind him as he pushed against the wind. A shiver of fear ran down Sarah's back. He was always so in control. She had never seen him this concerned. What if he got hurt? The fear touched her heart and her lips moved in a whispered prayer, "Please don't let him get hurt. Please

173

protect him." She watched until she could not see him anymore and then reluctantly went down the stairwell, making her way to her quarters.

She felt helpless shut away in her cabin listening to the pounding feet on the deck above, the wind howling, the boat creaking. She struggled to make her way across the room, barely able to keep her balance as the boat heaved under her feet, tossing her back and forth. She finally made it to her cradle bed and crawled inside. It was easy to understand now why it was shaped the way it was and securely fastened to the wall. Tucked in the bottom of the cradle she could not fall out although she thought she might have bruises from being tossed violently back and forth against the sides. It seemed like forever that the ship thrashed and rolled but slowly it eased off. Perhaps it hadn't completely subsided, but Sarah convinced herself that it had abated enough that she could go up and see what had happened. She needed to know.

As she was making her way down the hallway, it was clear that the storm was not yet over. She was tossed from side to side, bumping against the walls, but since she had come this far, she decided she could just go up for a minute and see what was happening and then come back down. She would stay close to the wall; she would be safe enough. But was he? Was he alright? If only she could see him, just for a moment, to make sure he was safe.

She stepped up onto the deck. Rather than having subsided, the storm seemed to have increased in intensity again. The ship heaved on waves that rolled towards it like white-capped mountains, crashing against its sides, reaching up over the rails to spill frothy foam on the already soggy deck. Sarah tried to turn back to the stairwell, but the wind slammed against her back, forcing her forward across the deck. The rain slanted in the gale and pricked like needles against her skin while quickly soaking through her clothes. She grabbed for a sturdy post, but her fingertips slid over it as she stumbled on the slippery boards. Fear gripped her as she began to fall.

Grayson saw the small figure struggling against the fierce wind, reaching for safety. He ran and slid across the deck, reaching her just before she fell. His arm whipped out, catching her around the waist, pulling her hard against him. She trembled in his arms, clinging to his neck. She felt so small, so vulnerable with her head pressed against his chest, her womanly softness cradled against him. He held her close, blocking her from the howling wind, steadying her against the thrashing movement of the ship. Fear gripped his heart and turned into tiny pricks of anger. What did she think she was doing, disobeying him and coming topside during a storm like this!? She could have been badly hurt, or worse. Or worse! Suddenly it didn't matter that she had disobeyed him. Keeping her safe was all that mattered.

How had this happened? When had she ceased to be a nuisance and become a lovely, spirited woman? When had he begun to care for her, her gentleness, goodness, and quiet strength? Care for her so much that it touched his heart. He should release her; the wind had abated enough that she could stand alone, but he liked the way she felt there.

He looked down at her, his chin grazing her hair. She automatically lifted her face to his. Their eyes locked, gray looking into green, like the sky and waves around them. The desire to kiss her seemed irresistible. His pulse was racing, and he felt her breathing fast against him. His need for more of her was almost unbearable. He took a shuddering breath. *This could not happen now. He corrected himself quickly. This could not happen ever!* He released his hold on her slowly and she stepped back, her eyes still on his.

Sarah was having feelings of her own. Feeling things she had never felt before. She wanted more from this man. This man who was generally so distant and cold, now so close, and warm, the heat of his body searing through their wet clothes, burning her skin everywhere they touched. She stepped back when his arms loosened. She should not have left her cabin. She should have listened to him and none of this would ever have happened. Is that what she really wanted? For none of this to have happened? She took a quivering breath before saying, "Thank you, Grayson. I should have listened to you. I am sorry."

He was moved by her apology. It was somewhat uncharacteristic of her. He smiled down at her and replied gently, "It is alright, Sarah. I am glad I was close by and could help. It is done now. You are safe. The storm has ended."

They both looked up to see the last, wispy dark clouds blowing away. The storm above them had ended, but the storm between them was boiling beneath the surface.

CHAPTER 29

In the morning, the sun was out, the sky blue, the sea calm. The storm had done little damage to the ship; small tears in the sails were already being stitched, and a few boards that had been ripped off were being replaced. None of the masts had been broken and, although they had been blown somewhat off course, it was not enough to make much of a difference in their time of arrival in England. Grayson rubbed his hand over the rail affectionately as he walked around his ship inspecting the damage. She had weathered the storm well. She was a fine vessel and had proven it once again. He patted the rail fondly as he stopped to gaze out at the now-calm sea. He was most thankful that no one had been hurt, not even Sarah, maybe especially Sarah.

He took a deep breath. What was he going to do about her? He felt that same catch in his heart when he thought about her now, as he had last night when he held her. But his eyes were troubled. Sarah still thought of him as a noble, honest man. Should he tell her about the will? He pounded the rail. He had sensed her trust in the way she rested her head against his chest and clasped her arms around his neck. He had seen her gratitude in her lovely eyes when she looked up at him. No! It would hurt her too much to try and explain it to her now, and there was no reason for her to learn about it at home. The will was not common knowledge among his crowd. He would get his inheritance and provide a more than comfortable living for her. He would marry Lydia, proud, willful Lydia. She was his match. She belonged in his life. It would be enough. He moved on, walking around his ship confidently, reassuring the men that they would be home soon, and that the storm had not set them back. Anything to keep his mind off Sarah.

Sarah emerged from the stairwell, happy to see the sun. It was already high in the sky, meaning she had slept late. But then, she had gone to bed late and slept restlessly. She tried to convince herself that it was because the ship was still rocking and creaking in the aftermath of the storm, but she knew what it really was that kept her awake. So many emotions had been brought to the surface in those minutes the night before. Yes, she had been afraid, but that wasn't anything new to her. She had been as afraid many times before. But what she had not felt in a very long time was someone caring for her, worrying about her, protecting her.

She had always been so alone at the Tompkins. No one cared when she got hurt; no one cared when she was sad or lonely. Several times in the early days she had gone to the Mistress hoping for comfort but all she got were orders to get back to work and stop blubbering about missing her parents and home. Each time that happened, another sliver of hope that she would ever feel kindness and love again was sliced off her heart, until slowly, she had come to believe that she simply was not loveable.

Last night, held in Grayson's arms, saved from falling, protected from the storm, a tiny spark of hope that maybe she *was* worth something had returned. She had felt so comforted, so protected, so lov.... No, a small, wry smile touched her lips. She was still a bother to him, but there had been kindness in the way he held her, making her wonder if maybe someday, someone would find something loveable in her again. But despite what she had felt last night, she did not belong in Grayson's life, did not fit with him. She would find a position in England and take care of herself. It would be enough. Her smile was real when she lifted her face to the sun feeling its warmth run through her.

Grayson saw the smile as she lifted her head and couldn't stop himself from going over to her. "Good morning, Sarah. I trust you are feeling well after the storm last night."

She turned her smile to him, "Yes, thank you. I am fine. It is so nice to see the sun out." Her face turned serious as she asked, "How did the ship fare? Is everyone alright? How is Harper? And Clarence?"

"She's a strong vessel, Sarah, and suffered very little damage. We did not lose any crew members and only a few were injured. Harper and Clarence are fine. In fact, I think you will find them both in the galley if you are on your way for something to eat. You will also be happy to hear that we weren't blown off course to any degree, and so will be arriving in England in a few days as planned."

"Oh," Sarah clasped her hands, "I'm so glad to hear that no one was hurt. God is so good."

Grayson could hardly disagree with her. A storm at sea has a way of making a man realize that some things are beyond his control. Nothing made him feel so small, so powerless, as when he saw the dark sky overhead when the mountainous waves tossed his ship like a twig on a raging river. There was nothing but God to turn to at a time like that, no other power able to calm the storm and bring them through to the other side. He was sincere when he agreed, "Indeed, Sarah, God was good to us last night. There is no denying that."

Grayson saw the surprise in her eyes and said, "Don't be so surprised, Sarah. There are times when any man knows that it is only through God's providence that he has been spared. A storm at sea is one of those times. Last night God chose to spare us, unlike other times when, for no good reason, He chooses not to."

The bitterness had crept back into his tone and Sarah decided it was best to leave it at that for now. She nodded and changed the subject, "I think I will go and get something to eat. I would like to see Harper."

"And I must continue my inspection of the ship." They both turned to leave. Sarah was stopped by Grayson's deep voice, "Sarah, I would like you to dine with me tonight. There are things we should discuss about England."

Sarah was surprised but agreed without hesitation. She would be glad to know more about what would happen when they arrived at his home.

"I will come for you at 7:00," Grayson informed her, "Try and stay awake."

Sarah saw his smile before he turned away. She smiled also, her eyes following the tall figure as he strode across the deck. There was little chance that she would fall asleep waiting for him now. She already felt like something was missing when he disappeared around the corner. She tossed her mane of hair back over her shoulder as if she could toss him out of her mind as easily. Talking to Harper and Clarence would help clear her thoughts. She left for the galley, unaware that the smile was still on her lips.

Clarence and Harper were sitting at one of the tables talking about the storm when she came in. They were pleased to have Sarah join them and the three shared their stories. At a break in the conversation, Clarence said, "I have to put things out for lunch and then work on dinner. The captain is having a special dinner tonight so I need to see if we have any chickens still living, and hopefully, if I find one it won't be the last hen or we will be out of fresh eggs. It is good that home will be in sight soon."

Clarence left for his kitchen, and Sarah leaned toward Harper, with a grin, "I think I may be responsible for the chicken's life if there is one left." At Harper's quizzical look she explained, "Grayson asked me to dine with him tonight." She paused, "I thought you would be there also."

There was a question in her voice and Harper hid his smile behind a yawn, "No, Sarah, Grayson has said nothing to me about dinner. I guess I won't be having chicken tonight, just hard tack and some moldy cheese I expect."

"Perhaps Grayson intends to invite you the next time he sees you. He only just now mentioned it to me."

181

Harper's smile was out right now, "Sarah, girl, he is not going to invite me. It appears our Captain would like the pleasure of only your company tonight."

"He wants to talk about England. He said he would tell me more about it, and I'll be glad to hear it." She knew she was talking too quickly and felt the blush on her cheeks.

Harper patted her hand on the table, "Certainly, dear. You will want to know, and it is a good opportunity for that. We are only a few days away now and Grayson will get busier as we get closer. I am sure he feels that it will be difficult to talk to you out on the deck. A dinner will be much better. Very practical of him." Harper chuckled.

Sarah frowned back at him. She could hear the teasing lilt in his voice and answered tartly. "Yes, Harper, he is obviously thinking ahead, wanting to prepare me for the arrival. It is good of him to make time. I don't know why you are laughing."

Harper cleared his throat, "Right you are, Sarah. I am just enjoying the pleasure of your company." He watched the fresh-faced girl across from him, so sweet and naïve, untouched by the superficiality of the society she was about to enter into. How would she survive? She accepted everything at face value, never questioning underlying motives. But she sat straight-backed before him, a firm set to her delicate chin and a spark of determination in her brilliant eyes. She was strong despite her delicacy, and her sensitivity was tempered by a degree of confidence. She had never had anyone to lean on or trust except God, and she was going to need Him more than she maybe knew when she was thrown into Grayson's world.

He covered her hand again, speaking sincerely, "Indeed, Sarah, it is good of Grayson to take time to tell you of his home and answer your questions.

"Thank you, Harper. I do wish you could dine with us, though. Maybe I will talk to Grayson and tell him I would like to ask you."

"No, no." Harper spoke quickly, "That isn't necessary. I'm sure I will be needed on deck to supervise if Grayson will be gone. We will all have dinner together another time, perhaps in London." He got up, "I must go now. I hope you have a pleasant dinner and learn all about life at Grayson's estate." He turned to go and then stopped, "Oh, Sarah, I wanted to tell you that we collected a lot of fresh water during the storm last night and I put a barrel aside for you. Since we are so close to shore there is enough to spare. I thought you might like to wash your clothes and maybe that hair of yours in freshwater before we land. I know you've had to wash mostly in salt water for the last while since we had to save the fresh for drinkin'."

Sarah jumped up and threw her arms around the old man's neck, "Thank you, Harper! You are always so thoughtful."

Harper patted her back, "There, there, Girlie, when you are ready for it just tell old Harper and I'll get one of the boys to bring it to you." He helped her up the steps while she continued to thank him. When they were on deck, they said goodbye and went their separate ways, he to his duties, she for a brisk walk around the deck and some time sitting in the sun in her favorite nook.

She thought about the things she would like to ask Grayson at dinner; things she would like to know about where he lived, what she would do there, what he did when he was away from the ship, who his friends were, and what about Lydia. No, she would not ask Grayson about Lydia. His relationship with Lydia was none of her business. Why did she even care? It wasn't that she cared really. She was just interested. Anyone would be.

CHAPTER 30

The afternoon passed and when a tinge of gray began to spread across the blue sky, Sarah decided it was time to get ready for dinner. The ship's bell gonged six o'clock as she walked to her room. That was more than enough time, but she wanted to be sure to be ready when Grayson arrived.

Maybe she would do something a little special with her hair. Harper was right about the salt water; it had left it dull and heavy. She only wore it up now, hiding it in a bun, but she would do something a little more creative with it for this special occasion. She certainly didn't have to worry so much about what she would wear. She smiled as she recalled how she had fretted about not having anything nice to wear at that first dinner. Now she had so many choices.

After looking quickly through her trunk, Sarah pulled out a soft blue dress with white lace lining the V-neck and the cuffs of full sleeves that ended just below her elbow. Dainty white piping accented delicate tucks from the neck down to her tiny waist, which was circled by a white satin ribbon. After slipping it on she fashioned her hair into a thick twist at the back of her head with a high pompadour over her forehead. She looked in the mirror and was satisfied with her reflection.

Sarah sat down but was careful not to relax too much. She was not going to fall asleep this time! The knock came just as that thought crossed her mind. She opened the door to Grayson and was startled again at how impressive this man was. He stood framed in the doorway, his head almost touching the top, while his shoulders grazed the sides of the narrow opening. "Hello Grayson. I am ready," she greeted him.

He smiled at her. "Yes, Sarah, I see. Come, let's go then."

Once on the deck Grayson took her hand and tucked it in the crook of his elbow. "I don't want you falling and hurting yourself after surviving that storm." Her soft laughter floated up to him.

The dining room was as warm and rich-looking as Sarah remembered. The candles in the sconces around the room were lit, giving the same soft golden glow to the room. The long table in the middle of the room was set at just one end with a white linen cloth and two place settings across from each other. Grayson ushered her to the table and pulled one of the chairs out for her to be seated. He then pulled on a tasseled cord hanging from the ceiling. Even now, weeks from when she had left the Tompkins, Sarah could almost hear the bell ringing far below in the kitchen.

She was deep in thought, a faraway look in her eyes, when Grayson returned to the table. "Sarah," He said quietly, "What are you thinking about?"

Sarah blinked and her eyes cleared. "Oh," She explained, "I was just remembering how the Tompkins used to ring for me like that. It seems so long ago now. Sometimes it seems like another life."

"It was another life. A life you will never know again. When we are home you will not be answering bells or taking orders from anyone," he assured her.

Just then a young man entered the room carrying a couple of large trays. The aroma of the food preceded him and by the time he got to the table Sarah's mouth was watering. It had been some time since there had been any fresh meat or vegetables served in the galley. Grayson told the server to leave the food and they would serve themselves which the young man seemed relieved to hear, quickly placing the dishes on the table before saluting his Captain and being dismissed.

When Grayson lifted the cover off the dish, Sarah saw the lovely golden roast chicken. With a smile and humorous lilt in her voice she commented, "So, I am responsible for the chicken's life." Grayson appeared confused and she explained, "When I was in the galley earlier Clarence mentioned that he was going to cook the last chicken because the captain was having a special dinner. I feel a little guilty, but it looks and smells so delicious I will try not to let it bother me."

Grayson chuckled with her but then asked her with concern, "Have you been going hungry, Sarah? I know rations have been a little sparse lately, but I hope you have been getting enough to eat. "

"Oh yes, I am fine. I think everyone has been a little hungry at times just lately. I was often hungry at the Tompkins." Her eyes were getting that faraway look again.

Grayson's fist balled up on the table when he answered. "As I was saying earlier, Sarah, nothing like that is ever going to happen to you again. When we are at home you will have the position and status of an Attwood."

"But I am not an Attwood. I am a former indentured servant and the daughter of a simple clergyman," the contemplative girl answered.

"You are the niece of an Attwood and hence will be considered as one." There was a finality in his tone that brooked no discussion.

They ate slowly as Grayson began talking, "Sarah, I wanted to tell you what to expect once we dock. We will be arriving in the afternoon the day after tomorrow." Grayson did not hesitate at the little gasp that came from the woman across from him, but answered her unasked question, "Yes, we will be arriving that soon."

He gave her a moment to digest that thought and then continued. "We are not going to dock in London as originally planned. If we dock in Bristol, we will be able to be at Attwood Manor by that evening. Attwood Manor is in the country, near the town of Burford. When we dock, you and I will disembark. Harper is perfectly capable of taking the ship on to London and getting her unloaded and looked after. We will go by carriage to my estate. It will be about a four-hour trip. You won't have to worry about meeting anyone except some of the servants when we arrive. We will be greeted by my housekeeper, Mrs. Walters. She has been with the

Attwood family for many years. She is a bit possessive and protective of everything there, including me, but she is a dear old thing, and I don't know what I would do without her. She will help you get acquainted with the place and all the staff. You will like her."

"I'm sure I shall. Maybe she will find something I can help her with, a job for me to do," Sarah answered eagerly. "I can do almost anything around a house."

Grayson could see she was about to chatter about all the things she would like to do to help and quickly stopped her. "Sarah, there is something you need to understand. You will not be doing household work! As I said, you are an Attwood now. Mrs. Walters is looking forward to serving you. You are not to inquire about what you can do to help. Do I make myself clear?"

Sarah was surprised at his stern voice and look. "Grayson, I understand what you are saying, but not why. I have been a servant for the past six years. I do not know why I shouldn't help if there is something for me to do."

"Sarah, this is precisely why I thought we should have a little talk before we arrive home. You have to understand that my set, the people I see socially, think of servants as…, well…, as servants. They do not associate with them on an equal level. My friends know that I am bringing my cousin back from America with me. They will expect you to be as you are now, a woman of style and equal status, not a servant in an old brown skirt. I want you to be accepted by my friends, Sarah. It will be much easier for you if you do as I say and try to fit in

189

with them. They know you are Bethany's niece and not my blood cousin, but even so they consider you my family. I have told them that you went to America with some family acquaintances. That is enough said. They do not need to know the details of your situation there."

"Grayson!" Sarah's voice was loud and firm. "I will not lie! I went to America as an indentured servant with people I did not know and worked for them for six years before you came for me. I worked hard and never had a really stylish dress until Boston."

"And there is no reason to go into all of that." Grayson did not raise his voice, but each word was punctuated. "You will not be lying. Remember how it was at the dinner in Boston? I introduced you as my stepmother's niece and said that you had gone to America with some family acquaintances for a few years and were returning home. This is no different. You didn't make such a fuss then."

Sarah frowned thoughtfully. "Yes, it seemed alright then. You must admit it was a very different situation to what we have here. For one evening, with a group of people I will probably never see again, it seemed sufficient." She paused, thinking it through. "I suppose it was a bit deceptive. Everything was such a blur back then. I only remember thinking how respectable I sounded when you introduced me."

"And that was nice, wasn't it? Why make it worse than it has to be, Sarah? We can just as easily say the same thing now. You will feel comfortable and respectable, and they will be happy to accept you as an equal and include you in all our activities. It will be best for everyone." His voice was cajoling, almost pleading.

"But Grayson, I am going to be living there! How can I avoid speaking of my time in America? They are sure to ask questions and how will I answer without talking about the true situation? It is wrong to lie, or hide the truth, even if it is for a good reason. Yes, it would make it easier for me, and it would make it easier for you, but ultimately the truth will come out and then it will be much worse for us. Telling the truth is always better."

Grayson stared at her closely as she talked. If he didn't know better, he would think she knew that he was hiding something from her, that he was not telling the whole truth. He pushed his hair back, hoping to push the thought out of his mind along with it. Leaning down, putting his face close to hers, eye to eye, he asked, "What would you like to do, Sarah? How would you like to introduce yourself?"

The question startled Sarah. She wasn't used to deciding how to do things. He always had everything under control. She thought for a moment before speaking, "I am not really sure exactly how I would like to explain my situation. Perhaps we could just say that due to some unfortunate circumstances at my home six years ago, I went to America to work for some people who were recommended by friends of the family, and I am very happy to be back home in England now."

Sarah watched Grayson for any reaction. Finally, he responded, "That seems to cover it simply enough. It doesn't go into details about your work, but at the same time it is clear that you went as hired help. I don't know how everyone will react to it but if you are more comfortable with saying that, then so be it."

With that settled they both leaned back in their chairs. The conversation had so occupied them that they had not noticed that there was still a small custard left on the tray. Sarah spooned some into two bowls and gave one to Grayson. Before they started to eat Sarah said, "Tell me about your friends, Grayson. Who are they? What are they like? What do you do? Do they come to your house often?"

Grayson took a spoon of custard, thinking about his friends. What were they like? He enjoyed being with them, mostly. They did all the things privileged men and women did - spent a lot of time having fun, spending money, and not accomplishing much. Wasn't that what they were supposed to do?

He studied Sarah, the planes of her face highlighted by the flickering candlelight, the clear eyes that held no secrets, a soft contented smile on her lips. She was as beautiful as any of them, but she had worked hard all her life, had no luxuries, little love or fun and yet she was more contented than all of them put together. How could he explain to her what his life and friends were like?

"My friends all come from neighboring estates. My best friend is Charles Fredrick Farnsworth. I have known Freddy all my life. He is a good chap. Most of the men in my circle are involved in some type of business and have offices in London with managers there to run things, so they work from their homes, meet with other businessmen, and travel for business and pleasure. I also have offices in London. My father owned the Attwood Shipyards and shipping line and now I own them." *At least he left that to me*, he thought. "I have a business manager at the shipyards, and Harper stays there to keep an eye on things as well. I like to be directly involved in the business, so I go to London quite frequently. I captain a vessel now and then because I love the sea and the adventure."

Sarah had listened carefully as he talked, but she ended up still confused about what any of Grayson's friends really did. It seemed that they all had people who ran things for them. It was hard to understand a life with so few responsibilities and so much freedom. "And what do you do when you get together?" she asked.

"We do the things most of the gentry do: hunt, ride, go to parties and dances, because the ladies insist we must, play tennis and cards." He paused, shifting in his chair. "Really Sarah, I don't think there is any more I can tell you about it. It will be easier when you are there and can see what life is like for yourself."

Sarah nodded but asked, "And the women?"

Grayson stretched and groaned. He really had not intended to go into detail about his life. He had simply wanted her to understand that it would be best not to discuss her life as a servant, that he, and now she, were part of a different class of society and she would be expected to play the part. "Sarah, the women do what women do – go shopping, sometimes to Burford or Bath, sometimes into London, have tea and outings together to talk about the men and each other. They compete with each other over who can put on the best party and have the best dress. You know… the things women do." He knew he sounded a bit irritated and stopped speaking.

Sarah reminded him. "I haven't had much opportunity to know a whole lot about what ladies of society do."

Grayson got up, "We should go now, Sarah." He held her chair as she stood. They walked out of the dining room and stepped into the night, stopping to gaze around them. The black sky was studded with thousands of brilliant stars, a warm breeze blew softly over them, and the ship rolled gently under their feet. Sarah glanced over at Grayson, "I will miss this, the sea, the movement of the ship, the quiet. It is hard to imagine that in a couple of days this life will be done. Life is about to change quite drastically. I hope I won't embarrass you, Grayson."

He put his hands on her small shoulders, turning her to face him. She looked up at him, her eyes catching the light of the shining moon. His breath caught for a moment and without thinking he spoke the words he had thought earlier, "Sarah, you are as beautiful as any of the women I know. You have never embarrassed me, and I look forward to introducing you to my friends. You have nothing to worry about."

Sarah couldn't answer for a moment and then said quietly, "Thank you, Grayson."

He tucked her hand into the crook of his elbow and guided her across the deck and down to her room. Neither of them spoke as they walked, both lost in thought about the changes ahead of them. At her door they said a simple good night and parted company.

CHAPTER 31

The next day Sarah took Harper up on his offer of fresh water for washing her clothes. The weather was nice so they would dry quickly, and she could start packing. It was hard to believe that this was the last full day of the voyage. By afternoon, the distant coastline could be seen. The deck was buzzing with activity and excitement.

Sarah saw Grayson standing in the wheelhouse a few times during the day but never had a chance to talk to him. She was glad that they had had dinner the night before because she was sure she would not get a chance to talk to him again before they docked. She went about the day doing little things that came to her mind. Often the thought would come to her that this was the last time she would do that particular thing or see that particular person or place. It was with a little sadness that she crawled into her cradle bed for the last time, but she was tired enough to fall asleep quickly.

She woke with the same thought still on her mind: this was the last time she would wake up in her little cradle. She sighed deeply; everything was changing once again. But she was glad it was finally here. This was it! She would soon be back on her native soil, a new life, a new beginning. She deliberately ignored the little niggle of fear that tried to push its way up inside of her. NO! She was not going to let fear conquer her. God had been with her through all the changes in her life. He was with her now.

Things were busy on deck when she climbed out of her stairwell. The little sailor monkeys scampered about on the lines high overhead. Sarah remembered how strange they had seemed when she first came on board. Now they were all familiar to her.

"Good morning, Sarah."

The deep voice behind her made her jump. "Good morning, Grayson."

"We should be arriving at Bristol in a few hours," he informed her. "Have you got your things ready?"

"I have a few things left to do. I will finish them now and be on deck in three hours," Sarah assured him.

"I will look for you then." Grayson glanced back over his shoulder as he left to go captain his ship.

Sarah waved briefly and left for her quarters to finish her packing and get ready to leave the ship. Before putting the last things in her trunk, she changed her clothes, realizing that what she put on now would be what she would arrive at Grayson's home wearing. She decided on the burnt orange dress that accented her healthy tanned skin and hair color. After she had washed her hair the night before, she had put it in the rag curls Mary had shown her in Boston and now it fell in thick, shiny curls around her. She pulled half of it up and clipped it at the back of her head.

When everything was done, she went up on deck to watch as they came closer and closer to shore. A tap on her shoulder startled her and she turned to find Harper standing there. He opened his arms to her, and

197

she walked into them, burying her face in the old man's shoulder. A sob shook her, and he patted her back. This girl had become like a daughter to him, and he would miss her greatly. "Don't cry, Sarah, me girl. Yer off to a new life, a good life. God is looking after you, so you have nothing to worry about."

He cleared his throat gruffly.

Sarah sniffed and gave him a shaky smile, "Thank you, Harper. I was thinking that same thing this morning, but I will miss you very much."

"Aye. But we will see each other again, Sarah, girl."

Sarah found a place out of the way to watch as the ship was maneuvered into port and docked. Later, as she was walking around the deck, she saw Grayson approaching. Her heart brightened at the sight of him. At least he would be with her. She had come to rely on him, anticipated seeing him, spending time with him. At least she would still have that. Her mind paused. Would she? Would she still see him and spend time with him? She stared down at the deck, the niggles of fear pushing in around her. She was so used to being able to see Grayson whenever she wanted to, knowing he was taking care of things, taking care of her. He was such a big part of her life here. But this wasn't the real world; this was the ship, a place where nothing else existed. Now, there would be other things in his life, other responsibilities, other people to care for. Her throat ached, and she swallowed hard. It felt like she was saying goodbye to him also. She was part of his life on the ship, not of the life he was going to.

"Sarah, are you ready?" He came straight to the point, obviously still busy and preoccupied with the landing. Slowly she lifted her head. He leaned down to look into her eyes. "Are you alright?" he asked.

Sarah answered quickly, "Yes. I am fine. I just finished saying goodbye to Harper."

Grayson nodded, that explained the tears he could see in her eyes. "I understand. But you will likely see him again before long. The old man often comes out to the house to bring work to me."

His consolation was awarded by a shaky smile. "That would be nice. Yes, I am ready. I left my trunk in my room. Could one of the men bring it up for me?"

"Of course. I'll send someone while we go ashore. I am expecting a carriage to be ready for us to leave right away." He stopped a sailor walking by and gave him instructions about the trunk. "Come along now, Sarah. He will bring your trunk down to the station house." With that, he turned and began walking away, knowing she would follow.

Sarah quickly picked up her little worn bag and trotted after him, down the gangplank and onto the platform below. Immediately she missed the gentle movement of the deck beneath her. It would take a while to get her land legs. She walked with Grayson into the station house and waited at the window while he went to speak to the clerk. She stared out at the ship; this really would be the last time she saw it. The journey had been good. It had given her time to experience life away from the Tompkins, a life where she made her own decisions and was responsible for her own choices. For the most part she was comfortable with herself now. She couldn't really say that she was looking forward to going to Grayson's home and meeting his friends, but she was confident that with God's help she would manage it.

"It's hard to see her leave without us, isn't it?"

Sarah had been so lost in thought that she hadn't heard Grayson come up and join her at the window, watching the ship.

"Yes, it seems strange." Her voice was quiet.

"But we will soon be home and have plenty to occupy us and won't have time to miss her at all." He spoke with a somewhat forced enthusiasm. He loved life at sea and really there was little that he looked forward to at home. He stared out at his ship, remembering when he was a child how he and his mother would watch eagerly from the upstairs window for the sight of his father's carriage coming down the road to the house after a voyage. They would hurry to the front door and wait to run into his arms when he jumped out of the carriage. Grayson tried to picture someone waiting for him like that, but the empty house was all he saw.

Part 3
England

CHAPTER 32

The dark-haired beauty stood at the window, watching the road below for any sign of his arrival - dust rising in the air or the flash of a black carriage coming down the drive. She knew he would be arriving today. One of the maids at Attwood Manor was the niece of her own housemaid and passed any important news regarding Grayson on to her aunt, who then informed her. Not that she really needed to be told. Somehow, she knew in her heart when he was about to return, but it never hurt to be certain.

She had waited for him at Attwood Manor only once before. She scowled at the memory, the look marring the smooth perfection of her pale skin. He had been in a foul mood, unappreciative of her surprise welcome, barely giving her a peck on the cheek when she threw her arms around his neck. A Cheshire smile replaced the frown. He had not been so unreceptive the next evening after the gathering of their friends. But still he held back. Still, she waited for the proposal. Slowly the frown returned. He knew he would make it as well as she did and she was tired of this tomfoolery, constant delays without any explanation, possibly at Christmas. It was only three months away now and he was done with this annoying expedition he had to go on to fetch this child back from America.

The thought of the child made her think of Bethany. What had the woman been thinking? She was usually so clever, but what good was this going to accomplish? Why bring the girl here when she, herself, would be dead and gone? Obviously, she had not been thinking clearly because of the illness. No matter how much she had tried to tell the woman that there was no need to feel guilty about the girl, Bethany would only moan, "My sister's child, my sister's child. How could I?"

And now it was done. The child would be arriving with Grayson any time now. Lydia grimaced. She would have to welcome the girl and then quickly find some way to get rid of her. Perhaps she would convince Grayson to send her away to a girl's school somewhere. She smoothed the perfectly fitted bodice of the deep yellow dress she wore. She would convince Grayson easily enough. The new dress had turned out very well and he could not help but appreciate it. The rounded neckline was possibly slightly more revealing than completely proper, but then, she wasn't one to worry about being completely proper. Her narrow waist was accented by the soft flare of the full skirt, giving her the perfect female silhouette.

She wore yellow well, as few women did, she thought. Blonde women looked ridiculous in the color, so much yellow all blending together into total obscurity. But yellow accented her own thick auburn hair, bringing out the red sheen, intensifying the rich darkness of her brown eyes. The yellow fabric gave a glow to her perfectly pale skin and with the right touch of cheek and lip rouge her beauty was undeniable and unmatched. Even Grayson could not resist forever. She smiled, her full red lips parting to reveal perfectly straight, brilliantly white teeth. She had been so angry at her mother, God rest her soul, for insisting that she brush them three times every day, but now she was thankful for the persistent nagging – brush your hair 100 strokes every night, brush your teeth three times a day, buttermilk your skin, lemon rinse your hair, use your parasol. She sighed. Mother had been good for something after all. There were even times she missed her, albeit seldom.

Opening the glassed-in French doors she had been looking through, Lydia stepped out on a small balcony, leaning over the rail to see the road better, eager for his arrival. Only a few minutes later she was rewarded with the sight of dust swirling above the trees in the distance. The coach! It had to be. She almost ran the few steps back inside and immediately went over to the wall mirror, smoothing her hair, which was perfectly styled in a bun on top of her head with dainty ringlets at her temples and framing her face. Not one hair dared be out of place. After a quick inspection, she went downstairs to be certain everything was ready as she had ordered.

"Mrs. Walters," she called out, then put dainty fingers to her lips, reminding herself to remain dignified at all times. She picked up a bell on the side table and rang it just as the housekeeper came around the corner.

"Yes, Miss Barker. Can I help you?" Mrs. Walters inquired, barely disguising the irritation in her voice.

"The carriage is coming down the driveway. Is everything ready as I instructed?" she snapped.

"Tea and cool lemonade are prepared as well as some cakes. Dinner will be served later unless Mr. Attwood requests it now."

"That is fine. You may go. I will ring for you when you are needed." Lydia dismissed the housekeeper curtly.

"Begging your pardon, Miss; Mr. Attwood will be expecting me to be here to greet the new Miss. I am always at the door when he returns from his journeys."

"And today you will not be! I will be! You will be waiting in the kitchen until I ring for you." Lydia rang the bell to emphasize her point. "You are dismissed."

The older woman could barely contain herself. She answered to Mr. Attwood, and everyone else around here answered to her. Miss Lydia Barker was not the Mistress of Attwood Manor yet and had better wait to start giving orders until she was. May it never be! How had she known that Mr. Attwood was arriving today? Mrs. Walters wondered as she walked to the kitchen, doing the only thing she could – obey.

Lydia set the bell down, watching the servant leave. Impudent! That would change. Mrs. Walters best watch herself or she will find herself in search of another position. Well, never mind that for now. Grayson would soon be here. Lydia went to stand by the parlor window, watching the driveway intently and was finally rewarded with the sight of a black dot in the distance, getting larger and closer every second. The carriage! Her heart beat faster. He was here! She watched until the carriage came around the brick-paved circle at the front of the house to stop under a high archway that stretched across the drive. She ran to the door, forcing herself to wait a few minutes before she opened it with an eager smile on her face.

205

CHAPTER 33

Sarah watched nervously as the carriage went down a long driveway, the imposing structure of Grayson's home getting closer until finally the carriage stopped in front of the house.

Grayson had just stepped out and was reaching back to help Sarah when he saw movement out of the corner of his eye. He turned and there was Lydia coming towards him, her arms outstretched. "Grayson! Welcome home, Darling."

What?! Grayson was stunned and quickly shut the carriage door. She should not be here, and yet he smiled at her enthusiastic welcome. If only she had not presumed to come to the house without an invitation. But then, Lydia tended to do what Lydia wanted to do. In some ways, it was part of her charm. He opened his arms for her hug, holding her briefly but stepping back quickly when he felt her head turn to kiss him. He would not encourage her until he had decided what he was going to do about their relationship, and yet he did keep his arm around her. She felt good there, familiar. Maybe he had missed her more than he realized. However, he had not wanted her here when he arrived home, and his greeting was somewhat cool, "Hello, Lydia, I am surprised to see you here."

"Pleasantly, I hope," she said sweetly with a pout on her pretty, painted lips, looking up at him from under thick dark lashes.

"Of course," Grayson answered politely, but without enthusiasm. He then looked past her, scanning the front of the house expectantly. "Where is Mrs. Walters?" he asked, puzzled.

"Oh," Lydia laughed and answered off-handedly, motioning toward the house, "She is inside preparing tea and cakes. Now, come, Grayson, give me a proper hello." She smiled beguilingly, reaching out to him again.

Grayson stepped back, turning toward the carriage. Sarah! To his surprise he had forgotten that she was waiting there. What must she be thinking? He had assured her that only Mrs. Walters would be at the house. There was concern in his eyes when he stepped over to the vehicle.

Lydia followed him, "Oh, my! I forgot about the child!"

Lydia waited to meet the girl, still pouting at Grayson's lack of enthusiasm at seeing her. Of course, he was tired from the journey and preoccupied with the child, she consoled herself. She would say hello and then shuffle the child off to get some flavored ice in the kitchen. Then she would have Grayson's full attention and get a proper greeting! She watched as one dainty foot reached for the first step of the carriage, momentarily revealing a trim ankle and shapely calf. Lydia frowned. That was not the leg of a young girl. Ah, perhaps a governess.

Sarah watched her feet as she maneuvered the three steps from the carriage to the ground, gripping Grayson's hand tightly. Her full skirts were covering the steps and when she leaned forward for a better view her hair fell over her shoulder swinging in her face. Without thinking, she let go of Grayson's hand to flip it back out of her way. Her foot missed the step and she started to fall when strong hands gripped her waist and lifted her easily out of the vehicle. Her laugh was soft as she grabbed Grayson's arms for support, "Oh Grayson, I'm sorry. I am still so clumsy in these full skirts. You always seem to be rescuing me from something. Thank you."

Lydia was puzzled and angry, watching the interlude. Who was this woman? She was far too familiar with Grayson to be a governess, standing so close and gazing into his eyes. Where was the child? She stepped over to the couple, "Well, what have we here?" Sarcasm and barely disguised anger dripped from her voice.

Sarah jumped, quickly letting go of Grayson's arms, a long-forgotten fear gripping her. She had so wanted to make a good impression on the head housekeeper and instead had already upset her. She never could do anything right; the old feeling rushed over her, and she dropped her head, looking down at the smooth bricks beneath her feet. Grayson had assured her that Mrs. Walters was a kind woman but the tone in her voice did not reflect that. Sarah forced a smile on her lips, lifted her head and turned to meet the woman who ran Grayson's home.

The women stood face to face; their eyes locked – deep rich brown with brilliant emerald green. Lydia turned away first, glancing back at the carriage and then over to Grayson, waiting for an explanation. Sarah also turned to him, a question mark in her eyes.

Grayson felt trapped and he did not like it. This was not supposed to happen like this. The meeting between these two should have been at a different time and a different place, not alone in the middle of the driveway before Sarah had any chance to acclimate to her new home. But he had to do something. Lydia was standing taller, straighter. He knew she would soon take things into her own hands.

Sarah, on the other hand, was wilting. After one uncertain glance at him her eyes were turned down to her shoes, thin shoulders starting to droop. He felt like a betrayer. He had promised her a simple, kindly reception. Without thinking, he moved closer to her.

"Grayson!" The voice was sharp and commanding. He stopped short, turning to face the woman who just minutes earlier had sweetly called him "Darling".

Before he could say anything, Lydia began moving towards him, each step confident and purposeful, her expression changing as she came closer until she reached him with an assumed smile on her face. Placing a delicate hand on his arm and standing close to him, she said softly, "Grayson, Dear, I believe there are some introductions that need to be made." Her face hardened as she turned her eyes on the spiritless little blonde thing beside the coach, who seemed to have a fascination for her own shoes.

Sarah felt the look like a hot poker touching her head. It irritated her. If this was Grayson's housekeeper, it would be best to let her know that, as Grayson's cousin, she was due a certain amount of respect. If the woman was not the housekeeper, who was she? Regardless, now was not the time to let Grayson down by being timid, no matter how intimidating the woman might be. She lifted her head, squaring her shoulders, looking first at Grayson and then over at the vibrant beauty standing beside him. Again, green eyes clashed with brown.

Grayson moved away from Lydia to stand between the two women. He would rather be at sea facing two pirate ships than here. However, here or at sea, he was the captain. He stood tall and commanding. Things did not just happen around him; he made things happen. Looking from one woman to the other, he requested, in his most gentlemanly fashion, "Ladies, please pardon my oversight." He strode to Sarah's side, his boots tapping against the brick road. He put his arm around her waist, urging her forward to stand beside him. "Sarah, this is Miss Lydia Barker, a longtime friend."

Lydia had followed Grayson and looked at him, raising perfectly arched brows at his description. She laughed lightly and switched her gaze to Sarah, an affected smile on her beautiful face, expanding on Grayson's introduction, "a long time, *very close* friend," she said pointedly.

Sarah was completely out of her element. Her mind had stopped when Grayson said, "This is Lydia." She gazed at the stunning woman in front of her. Lydia. Grayson's Lydia. That thought startled her, and she quickly smiled and dropped a small curtsey to the woman, acknowledging the introduction, "Pleased to meet you, Miss Barker."

Lydia nodded somewhat condescendingly. Grayson quickly introduced Sarah, "Lydia, I am pleased to present to you Bethany's niece, Sarah Blake."

Sarah's open smile met with Lydia's startled and almost militant stare. Without any acknowledgement, Lydia turned to Grayson, her voice rising as she questioned, "This is the child? This is the girl you went to rescue? Impossible." She scrutinized Sarah, taking in the honey-smooth skin, the startling eyes in a delicately beautiful face, and the thick, shiny blonde curls that almost touched her narrow waist. She was slim but not so much to detract from her femininity, especially in that deep orange dress that accented all the right places. There was no doubt that this was a woman standing before her. "She is not twelve," Lydia declared.

Grayson could feel Sarah quivering beside him and immediately felt protective. She was no match for Lydia, but he knew how to handle his old friend. His voice was deep and gruff, "Be careful, Lydia. Sarah is indeed Bethany's niece and my cousin. Be mindful of that. She was twelve when she left England six years ago."

"Oh Grayson, don't be upset with me," Lydia cajoled, reaching over to lay her hand on his arm, looking into his deep blue eyes. "I didn't know. I was just so surprised. You can understand that."

She could tell that he was softening and with an effort, forced any gloating out of her voice when she spoke to Sarah, "Hello, Sarah. I am happy to meet you.

211

You certainly are a lucky girl to have had Grayson come all the way to America to rescue you and bring you home."

Sarah had no trouble agreeing with that even though the tone was somewhat sarcastic, "Yes, I certainly am, Miss Barker."

Enough of this, Grayson thought, speaking quickly, "Now where is Mrs. Walters? I think we are ready for some refreshments. Come, Sarah," he took her hand and started walking to the house.

Lydia trailed behind, all pretext of kindness gone from her face. Getting rid of this girl was not going to be as easy as she had thought. She was too old to usher off to a girl's school, and Grayson seemed quite attached to her. But there would be a way. There always was. If she couldn't find one, she would make one. She had waited too long for Grayson to take any chances now. She hurried past the two and into the house first, picking up the bell to ring for Mrs. Walters, looking every bit the mistress of the house. "Why don't you take Sarah into the drawing room, Grayson, and I will have Mrs. Walters bring the tea there."

"Thank you, Lydia. I will do that. Oh, and ask Mrs. Walters to have Jeffery see to the carriage and horses." He tucked Sarah's hand in his arm and guided her across the tiled entry.

CHAPTER 34

The drawing room floor was a gleaming honey-colored wood, while the walls were pale green. A beautifully framed tapestry depicting the English countryside hung over a large fireplace surrounded by a gleaming wood mantle against the main wall. Two camel-backed settees were upholstered in brogade with various shades of green and several armchairs with gracefully curved legs were covered in plain light green damask. Delicate lace curtains covered a large window with a deep hunter-green valance scalloped across the top. On either side of the window, long tapestries of gold, green and orange hung on the wall. It was a lovely room, at once both elegant and comfortable.

Grayson and Sarah were standing by the window looking out at the yard when Mrs. Walters came in. "Mr. Attwood, welcome home!" she called cheerfully as she set the tray she carried down on a table by the door.

They both turned, and Grayson walked quickly to the jolly woman smiling happily at her, "Hello, Mrs. Walters. It is very good to be home, thank you." He put one arm around the woman's shoulders, giving her a quick hug and directing her towards the window. "Come meet Sarah."

Sarah watched the two approach, the matronly, round woman with apple cheeks and the tall, handsome captain smiling down at her. They obviously had affection for each other, and Sarah couldn't help but smile. What would that be like? To have a master who treated you so kindly, like a person, not just a servant. She took a step toward the two.

Suddenly a flash of yellow appeared at Grayson's side. Lydia took his free arm and said, "Yes, Mrs. Walters, come and meet Bethany's niece. It is so nice to have her here finally, back with family and new friends."

Her smile was sweet and her voice sounded genuine. Grayson smiled down at her. Maybe she would help Sarah fit into society here after all, he thought hopefully.

The older woman huffed. *There she goes again, acting like she's the mistress.* When they reached Sarah, Mrs. Walters did not wait for any more introduction but stepped close with the warmest smile on her face, "Welcome, Sarah, my dear. I am so glad you are here safely."

Before Sarah could say anything, she found herself pulled into the woman's arms and hugged tightly against her ample bosom. It felt so wonderful, and she hugged the woman back.

Grayson intervened with a smile, "Apparently introductions are not necessary so why don't we have our refreshments now."

Mrs. Walters was quickly all business, bustling over to the table where the tea tray was. "Yes, of course. It is past teatime and I am sure you are ready for some cakes and a cup'a. Sit down, sit down."

Sarah joined the housekeeper at the serving table while Lydia settled in beside Grayson on the settee. "I will deliver the tea after you pour," Sarah told the housekeeper who would have none of it and told her firmly to have a seat. Sarah obeyed meekly, sitting in one of the armchairs. She looked over at the settee and met Grayson's disapproving look. She nodded to indicate that she understood why he was frowning. She was an Attwood now and must behave as one.

Shortly Mrs. Walters came over with the tea tray tittering while she delivered the cups and cakes, "My, my, not a child, is she? But a lovely young woman."

Lydia's face hardened but she quickly looked down at her tea. When she lifted her head a moment later, she was smiling, looking kindly at Sarah, "She is a lovely surprise isn't she?"

Sarah squirmed a little further back into the soft chair, uncomfortable with the attention. Grayson didn't say anything and when she finally did look up, he had his arm around the back of Lydia's seat and was patting her shoulder. Sarah's small gasp was not audible. It was unsettling to see Grayson like this, comfortably sitting in his drawing room, his arm around a beautiful woman. They were so perfect together, fit so well in this world which was so different from the ship. For a moment she longed for her little cabin, so cozy and secure, and for the captain who cared for nothing but his boat and the people on it.

Mrs. Walters began to comment when Lydia snapped, "You may leave. I will ring for you if we require anything else".

"Yes, thank you, Mrs. Walters. This is quite fine. Sarah and I will have dinner later," Grayson added kindly.

The housekeeper ignored Lydia, addressing Grayson, "Yes, Sir. I will make sure things are ready." She picked up the tray and left.

"You really must be careful, Grayson," Lydia said sternly. "That woman sometimes acts like she thinks she is part of the family, not just a servant. You need to be firm with her. Make sure she knows her place."

Sarah gasped at Lydia's insolent comment and Grayson removed his arm from around the shoulder of the woman beside him, stating, "I will deal with her as I see fit, Lydia. My mother loved her, and she was like a grandmother to me when Mother died." An awkward silence immediately filled the room, broken occasionally by a brief comment from one of the three.

"Oh!" Lydia suddenly exclaimed, turning to Grayson, her face bright and animated. "I almost forgot. I am having a little party at my house the day after tomorrow. Everyone was happy to hear you were back after this long voyage and anxious to get together as soon as possible." She looked over at Sarah and back to Grayson, putting her hand on his arm, "And you must bring Sarah, of course. She will be such a surprise." Her crisp laugh held a note of excitement as she silently thought of introducing the timid little thing to their group.

Sarah's face flushed, a nervous look coming over her face, which Lydia did not miss. She got up and went over to her patting her head, "Don't worry, dear. You will be fine. It will be very casual, just a little after-dinner gathering."

Grayson got up and the two women listened when he spoke, "Sarah, I'm sure you are anxious to get settled. Your things have already been delivered to your room. Lydia, I will see you to the door." Sarah hopped up, indeed eager to get away, and Lydia took the arm Grayson offered her as he escorted her out of the room.

Sarah followed the maid up the stairs and stopped suddenly at the top, awed by the scene before her. There were long hallways on the right and left and a lovely sitting room directly ahead with a domed ceiling from which hung a large chandelier holding ten candles on the bottom tier and eight above. The front of the room was curved with several windows and a door leading out to a matching curved balcony. It was breathtaking.

Sarah's room was down the left hallway and consisted of far more than a single room. She had her own sitting room with a fireplace and lovely furniture. In the bedroom there was a large four-poster bed piled high with comforters and pillows and covered with a deep blue coverlet. The windows in the far wall were hung with heavy, deep blue velvet curtains that matched the coverlet. A door between the windows led out to her own balcony and a private bathing room could be accessed from the bedroom. Her trunk and bag were on a pale blue carpet beside the bed. The maid showed her everything including tasseled ropes that could be pulled to ring for assistance at any time. The luxury was quite overwhelming. In fact, the whole day had been somewhat overwhelming, and Sarah was glad it was coming to an end.

CHAPTER 35

Two nights later Sarah stood in front of the intricately carved armoire, fingering through the clothes hanging inside. Maybe it was better to have only one black skirt, one brown skirt, and one faded dress to choose from, she thought. Looking at the variety of colors and styles in front of her she sighed heavily. What was she going to wear? Tonight, she would go to Lydia's house with Grayson and meet his friends. Her heart thumped in her chest, and she breathed in deeply. "*Lord, give me strength and help me make the right decision.*" She was glad that God didn't mind if she asked for something so trivial. But right now, it didn't seem trivial. With another loud sigh, she shut the armoire doors and walked back across the room. Perhaps starting fresh in a few minutes would make the decision easier.

She stopped pacing at the knock on her door. Delicate brows drew together in puzzlement. She had not rung for anything but when she opened the door the maid who had originally shown her to her rooms stood there.

"I had some time and thought I would see if there was anything you needed." The girl bobbed a little curtsy, smiling cheerfully.

"No, I don't think so, Sadie. I am just deciding what to wear tonight. Thank you for checking.

She started to close the door, but the girl moved forward peering inside. "Maybe I could help you, Miss," she offered.

Sarah was uncertain but decided it might be nice to get another opinion. She opened the door to the girl, "Come in, Sadie. I just don't know. Miss Barker said it would be a casual after-dinner gathering but I am not quite sure what that means." She pulled a dress out of the armoire, "I have almost decided on this one. What do you think?"

The girl looked from the deep maroon dress to Sarah. There was no doubt Sarah would look lovely in the dress. Quickly, Sadie said, "Oh no, Miss. I don't think that will do for tonight. It is a bit too fancy. Perhaps a nice skirt."

Sarah was disappointed at the reaction and examined the dress again as the maid started moving things around inside the armoire. Before long she emerged with a dark blue skirt. Sarah was surprised. It was a nice enough skirt, but she had thought she would wear it for going to town or the market, not to a party, no matter how casual. She took the skirt from the girl, "Thank you, Sadie. I will consider your suggestion. You may go now."

"I could help you get dressed, Miss. Perhaps help with your hair."

"No, thank you. I can do it myself." Sarah walked to the door and held it open while the girl reluctantly left.

Sarah contemplated the maroon dress lying on the bed. It felt right. With the weather being cooler and fall-like, the color was perfect and the long sleeves were just right. Suddenly she was eager to put it on. She changed quickly, slipping the dress over her head. It fell into place with a swish around her feet. Sarah hooked the row of hooks up the front of the fitted bodice. The high neckline was circled with a ruffle of cream lace and the sleeves ended with a matching ruffle. The skirt was only slightly gathered, flaring softly over one stiff petticoat to stand out in a small circle around her feet. The dress suited Sarah perfectly; the high neckline brought the deep maroon color close to her face giving her skin a soft pink glow, and accented the gold fleck in her eyes, turning them an intriguing shade of olive green.

After pulling her long ringlets up on top of her head she pinned them in place with loose tendrils curling around her forehead and face. She looked in the full-length mirror inside the armoire and was once again surprised when she saw herself. How had Rose turned her into this fashionable woman? She smiled, thinking of the dear lady. If only she was here now to help her meet Grayson's friends correctly. Sarah smoothed the front of the dress. With a whispered prayer and deep breath, she closed the armoire doors and left the room.

Grayson waited in the entryway for her. He glanced up when he heard the tap of her feet on the stairs. His heart stopped for a moment when he saw her. He had not seen her looking this beautiful since the dinner at Rose's. As she gracefully descended, he thought how much she had changed from the little brown mouse he had first met in Norfolk. And yet, when she walked up to him, a sweet timid smile on her soft pink lips and her gold-green cat eyes gazing at him with trust and confidence, he couldn't help but think how much the same she still was, still kind and gentle, needing to be protected and cared for. He took her hands when she reached him, guiding her to the door and the waiting carriage.

It seemed like a very long twenty-minute drive to the Barker residence. Sarah wasn't sure if she was relieved when they finally arrived or if she wished the ride would last forever. It didn't matter now; she could not put off the inevitable. She took a deep breath and reached for the hand Grayson held out to help her down. The Barker house was as large and stately as the Attwood's, if not more so. Although it was only dusk, large lamps were lit at the front door and the main entry was bright and welcoming with a white tile floor and a huge crystal chandelier hanging from the high ceiling. The light from the burning candles danced off the sparkling crystals shining around the room.

The sound of laughter and conversation came from one of the side rooms. Just after the butler had taken their coats a group of men and women came rushing in, led by a tall, slim man, with Lydia close behind. Grayson walked eagerly towards the man. As they grasped each other's shoulders they exclaimed as one, "Grayson!" "Freddy!" Then there was a loud exchange of 'how are you' and 'good to see you old chap'.

Lydia soon insinuated herself between the two men. Putting her arm around Grayson's waist she smiled up at him sweetly while pushing Freddy away, "Freddy, stop hogging him. All the others want to greet him also." She pulled Grayson towards the group behind them and stayed right by his side while he greeted everyone.

Sarah stood back, watching, shrinking closer to the wall. She was glad she had worn the maroon dress as it did not appear to be as casual a gathering as she had been told. The women all wore party dresses with ruffles and lace, their hair styled fashionably.

She jumped when she heard a voice beside her. "Well, what have we here? You must be Grayson's cousin." She turned to meet a pair of lively hazel eyes and a cheerful smile. The man paused, brushing back the blonde hair that fell over his eye. Crossing his arms, his lips pursed, he quickly perused Sarah, taking in her lovely face, and glancing appreciatively over her shapely form. "But wait, you can't be the cousin. Grayson's cousin is a child and you," he declared, "You certainly are not." His laugh was a pleasant boyish sound and Sarah was immediately put at ease.

He bowed to her, "Hello, I am Charles…" was all he got out before a deep voice interrupted, finishing the introduction for him, "Charles Frederick Farnsworth, the third."

Sarah looked over at Grayson, relief in her eyes. She was so glad to see him! He immediately came to her side and put an arm around her shoulder.

The attractive stranger bowed extravagantly, "And you, my dear, may call me Freddy," he said with a cheerful grin and a barely hidden wink.

"Freddy, behave yourself," Grayson said, a warning note in his tone as he elbowed his friend. "Let me present to you my cousin, Miss Sarah Blake."

Before Sarah or Freddy could reply, Lydia's sharp voice intruded, "Yes, everyone, this is Bethany's niece." The whole group had gathered around to watch the exchange and Sarah shrank closer to Grayson's side when all eyes turned to her. Lydia moved in, taking Sarah's arm and pulling her forward, away from Grayson. "Come Sarah, let me introduce you to everyone."

Sarah pulled back slightly, looking over her shoulder at Grayson. He saw the fear in her eyes and moved quickly to stand in front of Lydia, "Thank you, Lydia but I will introduce Sarah around".

"Oh, of course, Grayson, here you are." She gave a little laugh and pulled Sarah forward, handing her over to Grayson.

Grayson took Sarah's arm, tucking it securely in his and guided her over to the waiting audience. It was all done quite quickly and even painlessly. Everyone was friendly and welcoming. As they were finishing all the introductions, Lydia instructed everyone to go back to the drawing room for refreshments. While they were getting their confections and drinks Lydia announced, "Everyone get a partner and sit down. We're going to play whist. I will get the cards." People began milling about, laughing, and talking. Everyone stopped when Lydia spoke loudly, "OH! You do know how to play Whist, don't you, Sarah?"

Everyone watched the newcomer who was looking flustered but with a deep breath collected herself and answered quietly, "I am sorry, I do not. But please go ahead."

"Oh dear, that is a shame," Lydia consoled, barely hiding the smile that twitched on her painted-red lips. "That's alright, you can just watch this time. I am sure you will understand it quickly."

Sarah knew her cheeks were bright red. She looked across the room at Grayson who immediately started making his way over to her. He should have stayed with her, he thought. Of course she was overwhelmed by all of this.

Lydia reached out as he passed and put her hand on his arm, stopping him. "You can be my partner, Grayson."

Grayson watched her, forcing the irritation out of his eyes and his voice, "Thank you, Lydia, but I think it is time for Sarah and I to leave."

"No, no," Freddy spoke up from where he stood at Sarah's side. "You go ahead and play. I cannot abide the game myself. I will be happy to show Sarah around while you play." He had moved closer to Sarah as he spoke and she smiled at him, thankful for his intervention. She did not notice the deep blue eyes turning hard gray steel as Grayson moved across the room.

"Sarah!" She jumped when she heard his deep voice boom behind her. "We are leaving now."

Lydia glided across the room, a little pout on her lips. "I am sorry you have to leave. Maybe next time we can play something Sarah knows."

The room was silent, and Sarah was sure everyone could hear her little gasp. She looked down at the floor avoiding all the eyes watching her.

Grayson glared at Lydia then put his arm around Sarah's waist and leaned down to say softly, "It is alright, Sarah. We will just say goodbye and go home." He urged her forward and they said goodbye to people as they left the room.

One of the women Sarah had met, Gwendolyn something, she couldn't quite recall, was waiting in the hall and took Sarah's hand, whispering, "Don't worry about her. Maybe sometime you and I can go into town together." At Sarah's little nod, Gwen said, "I'll get a message to you. It was very nice meeting you."

Sarah was touched and smiled at the girl. "Thank you. It was nice meeting you also, Gwen."

When Sarah came out of the cloakroom, she saw Grayson at the door talking with Lydia. She stood back in the shadows not sure what to do. Grayson's face was stern, and Lydia grasped both of his arms as she pled with him, "Grayson, darling, I only meant that I would plan things better next time. I did not want her to be uncomfortable. You understand, don't you?"

Grayson felt a firm slap on his back and turned to see Freddy. "Good to have you back old chap!" Lydia moved away, thankful for the interruption.

Grayson grabbed his friend's shoulder, shaking him. "Good to see you, Freddy. For the most part, anyway." The friends laughed and shook hands.

Sarah left the shadows and went over to the men. Grayson took her arm and Freddy did a snappy little bow, "It was nice to meet you, beautiful Sarah. I hope to see you again, soon."

Sarah gave a little shy laugh, "Thank you, Freddy."

Grayson's rumbling laugh surprised her. He gave his friend a punch on the arm, "Always the same Freddy. I will see you soon."

He ushered Sarah out the door and into the waiting carriage. As the vehicle rolled away from the house, Grayson turned to the silent girl beside him, "I am sorry, Sarah. Lydia is sometimes not the most considerate."

"It's alright. I don't think she meant any harm by it," Sarah answered graciously. "Naturally, she expected that you all would play a game that you enjoy. You should have played, Grayson. I wouldn't have minded watching."

Grayson was silent, then said firmly, "We won't speak of it anymore. I will make sure nothing like that happens again."

Sarah changed the subject, "I did enjoy meeting your friends. Gwendolyn…. Oh! I can't remember her last name; is very kind. She said she would take me into town sometime. I look forward to that. And Freddy is awfully nice."

Grayson laughed, "I cannot argue with you on that. Freddy is a good chap." After a moment, he said,

"Martens." Sarah looked at him blankly, and he explained, "Gwendolyn Martens."

They did not talk anymore until they reached the house and went inside. They walked up the stairs together and stopped at the top. A few candles burned low in wall sconces down both hallways. They gazed at each other in the dim light. Grayson, regretting that he had not stayed closer to her, protected her from that pain; Sarah wondered if it would ever be possible for her to fit into his world. They joined hands almost unconsciously as though they felt each other's thoughts. Together they spoke, "Good night, Sarah," "Good night, Grayson," and went down their separate hallways.

CHAPTER 36

The following evening Sarah stood outside of Grayson's study, her hand poised at the door, ready to knock. She didn't want to disturb him, but she really must speak to him. She took a deep breath and knocked briskly on the door dropping her hand quickly to fidget with the cloth of her long gray skirt.

When the door opened, Grayson looked surprised, "Sarah. I was expecting Mrs. Walters with tea." He looked down the hall and back to Sarah, "What can I do for you?"

"I need to talk to you for just a moment. I won't take much of your time."

"Certainly. Come in. It will be a good excuse to take a break from these tedious books. And look, here is Mrs. Walters now. How convenient. Would you join me, Sarah?"

Sarah was delighted to see that Grayson was in a good mood, considering what she wanted to ask him. She replied without hesitation, "I would be happy to join you."

"We will need another cup, Mrs. Walters," Grayson instructed the older woman as she brought the tea tray into the study.

"Certainly, Sir. I won't be a moment." She dropped a quick curtsey and hurried down the hall.

Grayson stepped back and gestured for Sarah to enter. She hesitated a moment, feeling like she was entering the lion's den but went in slowly. The room was very masculine with dark wood paneling and heavy wood furniture. Bookcases of lighter-colored wood lined one wall, and a matching desk faced a large window that let in enough light to bring out the rich tones in the room. It was a room that fit Grayson perfectly, imposing, exuding confidence and strength but accented with softer, warmer shades.

By the time Sarah was done looking around the room, Grayson was seated in a large leather chair behind the desk strewn with papers and a large ledger. "Sit down, Sarah," he invited, indicating a smaller chair across from him.

Just then a maid came rushing into the room carrying a teacup and saucer. "Here you are Miss." She handed Sarah the cup, curtsied and left as quickly as she had come.

Sarah poured tea for Grayson and herself, bringing it to the desk and then sitting on the chair across from him. Grayson watched her, raising one eyebrow quizzically.

"Oh!" Sarah startled herself with the exclamation. The way he raised that eyebrow was so distracting that she had almost forgotten that she had asked to speak with him, and he was waiting for her to begin. With a quick breath, she began, "I have just learned that tomorrow is Sunday. I had completely lost track of the days but heard Mrs. Walters saying that she was going to church tomorrow, and I would like to go also."

Grayson frowned, took a gulp of his tea and then replied, "Is it really Sunday already? We have just so recently arrived back, and I have so many things to get done, I do not think we will go tomorrow. Perhaps another time."

"I would like to go tomorrow," Sarah said firmly. She was not asking or pleading. She was simply stating a fact.

Grayson folded his hands on the desk and leaned towards her, looking directly into her eyes. "I believe I have told you, Sarah, that I do not attend church on a regular basis anymore. We will go at Christmas."

"I understand, Grayson, and you are free to make your choice. I, however, have just now become free to make my choice and I would like to attend church on a regular basis. Perhaps I can go with Mrs. Walters."

Grayson almost smiled when he saw the little sparks in the cat eyes looking at him. There was something he liked about her when she was like this, but not enough to go along with what she was asking. "Mrs. Walters goes to a different church and would not be comfortable having you go with her."

Sarah frowned, "I understand. I will send Gwendolyn a message then and see if she can take me with her."

"And how will you do that?"

"I am sure Mrs. Walters will help me find a way."

Grayson pushed his chair back, standing up, clearly frustrated. "Sarah! For heaven's sake! I will not

231

have you running around begging the neighbors for rides." He paced across the room and stood by the window gazing out at the smooth green grass.

Sarah watched him. Perhaps he had not been in such a good mood after all. She got up and went to stand beside him, looking out the window. "Grayson," she said softly, "I wish you could understand." She felt him turning towards her and turned to face him but dropped her head when she met his stern look.

Grayson focused on the intricate braiding covering the top of her head, trying to distract himself from her soft voice when she continued, "I have waited so long to sit in church, to remember my father when he used to preach. There must be some way I can go."

Without thinking Grayson reached out and put a hand on her shoulder. His voice was sincere, "I had not thought about how you might like to remember your father in church, but I do understand, you know. There are places I like to go because they remind me of my mother." He paused. Thinking about his mother was his undoing. Knowing that she would want him to, he said, "I will take you to church tomorrow."

Sarah looked up at him, her eyes glistening, a smile wavering on her lips, "Thank you, Grayson."

He wanted to embrace her, comfort her but instead, he took his hand off her shoulder and stepped back, clearing his throat. "You are welcome. Actually, it will be a good time for me to reacquaint myself with some of the local people I have not seen in some time."

He walked back across the room to his desk and sat down.

Sarah was at the door when his voice stopped her, "Sarah, come sit down for a minute. Since you are here, I have something I would like to talk to you about."

Sarah moved slowly to the desk, her brows drawn together in thought. What could he mean? She sat down looking across at him curiously.

He opened the desk drawer and pulled out some money, holding it out to her. "I realize that you do not have any money and I want you to take this."

Without thinking Sarah reached up to take it, then dropped her hand down on the desk, shaking her head. "I don't want any money, Grayson."

"Take it, Sarah," he commanded. "I will not have you going about penniless. I am going to give you a weekly allowance. Now take this and every Sunday, I will give you the same amount."

Sarah hesitated, beginning to protest again, "I really can't take your money."

He stood up and came around the desk, taking her arm and pulling her up. He put the money in her palm and closed her hand around it. "It is done, Sarah. Now, I must get back to my work. Apparently, I have other things that will occupy my time tomorrow. We will leave here at 9:00 tomorrow morning."

CHAPTER 37

Sarah watched excitedly as the carriage entered the town of Burford, coming to a stop in front of a large brick building with a tall steeple holding a large bronze bell. People were milling around the front enjoying the sunshine which was coming out less and less frequently in these September days. Grayson got out and turned to help Sarah. When she reached the bottom step, she realized that it had gotten very quiet and, looking up, met a sea of eyes, openly staring at the two of them with surprise and curiosity. It was only a moment before the silence turned into a low buzz as people turned to each other, talking in low tones about the couple standing by the carriage.

Sarah's excitement had turned to nerves, and she was glad when Grayson held his arm out for her. She put her hand in the crook of his elbow, suddenly feeling more comfortable and stronger. He was the captain again, confident, and capable. As they moved forward through the crowd, she saw welcoming smiles spread over their faces and smiled happily back. Grayson's posture remained stiff and straight but he nodded to people and occasionally greeted someone by name. He moved ahead purposefully, anxious to get inside the building and get this done.

"Grayson, here you are!" All heads turned to the door of the church where Lydia stood, a happy smile on her lovely face. The auburn-haired beauty stood directly in the sun as though a spotlight was shining on her, and clearly, she belonged in the spotlight this morning. She wore a deep autumn-green dress with a full skirt held out by layers of petticoats making her waist look impossibly tiny. The deep square neckline was bordered by a wide ruffle that was just high enough to be appropriate while still drawing eyes. A small, matching hat was perched perfectly on her hair which was done in elaborate ringlets, the red highlights shimmering in the sun accenting her perfect porcelain skin. She skipped gracefully down the stairs, the crowd parting for her automatically. She took Grayson's arm before he offered it and gazed up at him, her smile dazzling.

Grayson smiled down at the vivacious beauty, catching her enthusiasm. "Hello, Lydia. I am surprised to see you here. I thought you attended the church in Bath," he said, puzzled at her appearance.

A lilting laugh floated out of Lydia's perfectly painted lips, "Oh, I would much rather attend church with you, here."

The crowd stared at the trio before them, the tall, handsome captain with a woman on each arm. The contrast between the two was striking, Lydia on one side and the demure, shy newcomer on the other. She was beautiful in her simplicity, her blonde hair done in a conservative bun high on her head revealing the classic structure of her face and a long, delicate throat. Her lilac dress had a high rounded neckline and long sleeves, the bodice adorned only by three rows of small ruffles from neck to waist.

Sarah smiled sweetly at the faces around her fighting feelings of inadequacy, determined to keep her focus on the joy of worshipping God in the church. This time was not about her or Lydia or Grayson. It was all about Him. She took a step forward, unconsciously pulling on Grayson's arm.

Grayson felt the gentle tug and turned to look at Sarah, but Lydia tugged on his other arm, announcing, "Grayson, I have seats for us." Sarah stopped and Lydia glanced over at her, eyes widening, appearing bewildered. "Oh Sarah, I forgot about you," she said apologetically, quickly adding, "Never mind, there is room for you also."

Grayson moved ahead up the stairs, seemingly having missed the exchange between the two women. Inside the building Lydia directed them to the front pew, shooing people down to make enough room for Sarah. Once settled Sarah hid her flaming cheeks by looking down at her hands, tightly gripping her Bible. She prayed silently, the peace of God slowly engulfing her and setting her heart at rest. The booming voice from the pulpit made her jump and she raised her joyful face to see the minister standing before them, the sleeves of his robe hanging down from outstretched arms.

Sarah tried to listen attentively but often her mind took her back to her childhood, sitting by her mother in the pew, listening to her tall, handsome father as he preached. She closed her eyes, and it was really like being with them. She could feel her mother's warmth beside her and the minister's voice became her father's. When she opened her eyes the realization that it was not them hit her hard and a tear splashed on the worn cover of the Bible they had given her.

Grayson saw the tear fall and knew she was thinking of her parents. He too was having mixed emotions being in the church, thinking about his youth. He sensed his mother's presence strongly and tried to pull up his feelings of anger at God but all he could sense was his mother's joy at seeing him there. And there was a certain peace in this place that crept over him unbidden. He glanced at Sarah and could see that peace on her face also, even though the tear streak still showed on her cheek.

After the service the trio made their way to the back of the building. Grayson and Sarah were still contemplative and quiet while Lydia busily talked to people as they left. Once outside they found friends to talk with. Many from the gathering at Lydia's house were there. Gwendolyn and Sarah talked for some time and Freddy made sure to say hello.

It wasn't long before Grayson announced, "Sarah and I will be leaving now. It was good to see you all." With that he took Sarah's arm and helped her down the stairs to the waiting carriage. Lydia followed them down the steps, calling Grayson, but Grayson was in no mood for more idle chatter and simply said a firm "Goodbye Lydia" and climbed into the carriage after Sarah.

It was quiet as they drove home, both occupants thinking about the morning. When they arrived at the house Mrs. Walters was there to tell them that lunch was ready whenever they were. "I will go change my clothes and then be down," Sarah said, already on her way to the stairs.

"We will be ready in half an hour, Mrs. Walters," Grayson told the smiling woman.

"Quite right, Sir," Mrs. Walter said with a quick curtsey before leaving.

A half hour later Grayson and Sarah sat across from each other at the table eating cold meats and fresh bread.

"Thank you for taking me to church, Grayson," Sarah said. "It meant a lot to me. I really enjoyed the message, and it was nice to see some of the people from the other night."

"You are welcome," Grayson replied, and not wanting to talk further about the service quickly added, "I noticed you talking with Miss Martens. It looks like you two are becoming friends."

Sarah smiled, "Yes, she is very nice. She has offered to take me to market in town on Tuesday."

"It's good I gave you some money then. I can't think of a woman who would go to town without wanting to buy something." His smile took away any note of sarcasm.

"It might take a while for me to become comfortable with having money to spend," Sarah said.

"You will find it quite an enjoyable pastime, I expect," he responded with a laugh.

"I cannot think of anything I need but it will be nice to look around and spend time with a friend. I have not had one of those in a while," Sarah said.

Grayson answered, trying to sound reassuring, "Gwendolyn Martens will be a good friend for you. She comes from a good family and is of equal standing with us."

Sarah gasped, "I don't care about her standing or background! She is kind to me and pleasant to be with. That is what matters. You cannot choose my friends for me, Grayson."

"I am sorry if I offended you, Sarah. I did not choose Miss Martens as a friend for you; I was simply offering my approval." He pushed away from the table, standing up to leave.

Sarah stood up, saying quietly, "And I am sorry I snapped back when you talked about Gwen. I know you only meant that she would make a good friend. I think I am still sensitive about my time as a servant, feeling that I was not worthy to be a friend to anyone who was not in the same position as I."

She stood like the Sarah he had first met at the Tompkins, like a wilting flower, head bent on a neck too delicate to hold it up, eyes downcast, shoulders drooping. She always made him think when she talked like that, wonder how his servants felt, how he made them feel. He realized he needed to be more careful about that. He put his hand on Sarah's delicate shoulder. "Sarah, you are, and always have been, as worthy as anyone."

She lifted her beautiful eyes to him, and he smiled that slow smile that made her heart skip a beat. "I will try not to choose your friends, but I might offer a suggestion or two along the way?" he raised one eyebrow, making it a question.

Sarah nodded, replying, "I will take your advice into consideration."

His deep chuckle made her smile. They walked to the entryway together where Grayson went to the stairway, saying, "I must go to my study now. I still need to finish those things that I put off this morning."

Sarah stopped him on the first stair, "Thank you again for taking me to church."

He cleared his throat, "You are welcome. We caused quite a stir, didn't we? Perhaps next time we should arrive a bit late so we can sneak in the back without being noticed."

Her eyes widened in surprise and joy. He was puzzled for a moment before his own widened. Next time? It seemed he had just offered to take her to church again. It was getting harder and harder to deny her anything.

CHAPTER 38

When Tuesday arrived, Sarah waited anxiously at the window for Gwen. The money Grayson had given her was tucked safely away in a little cloth purse she had gotten in Boston. She still felt a bit guilty about the money and had really never intended to use it, but it was nice to know that she would be able to buy a cup of tea or lunch with her own money. Her heart beat fast at the thought. Freedom and independence. She couldn't have imagined those feelings three months ago.

"You are ready to go, I see," Grayson spoke from behind her.

"Yes. They are coming down the lane now. I thought I would meet them outside," she said eagerly.

"I will wait with you." Excitement exuded from her, and he couldn't help the deep chuckle that came from his chest. "I don't think I have ever seen anyone quite this excited about going into Burford before."

The carriage was just arriving when they stepped outside. Grayson opened the door for her, greeting Gwendolyn as he helped Sarah in. "You ladies have a good time in town today," he said as he shut the door, and the carriage immediately pulled away.

Gwen chattered the whole way into town, but Sarah only half listened as she watched out the window, waiting for the town to appear. The carriage jolted to a stop in front of the market, and the driver jumped down to open the door for the two girls.

The market was noisy and crowded, filled with a variety of vendors selling everything from tomatoes to jewelry and shoppers browsing through their wares. Gwen seemed to know almost everyone and introduced Sarah as they made their way through. Sarah quickly felt overwhelmed and pulled Gwen aside, "Gwen, I cannot possibly remember all these names. I am not used to meeting so many people."

Gwen smiled and linked arms with Sarah, pulling her along, "Don't worry about remembering them. They probably will not remember either. Come on, we only have an hour before lunchtime. We should go into town now and come back to the market before we leave." She led the way to her favorite shops, showing Sarah the best places to have clothes and shoes made or ordered from a catalogue.

They wandered slowly down the street looking in the shop windows. Sarah suddenly stopped, grabbing Gwen's arm. Her voice was excited as she pulled Gwen over beside her, pointing at a window. "Look! Look at that painting, Gwen." Sarah pointed to a large painting standing on an easel in the window. It was a painting of a storm at sea with a ship at partial sail being tossed on angry waves. Sarah stood transfixed, gripping Gwen's arm.

"It is a lovely painting, Sarah," she agreed hesitantly. "Let's go get some lunch now."

She pulled her arm to loosen Sarah's grip but to no avail. "Sarah! What is it?" she asked loudly.

Sarah blinked, her eyes losing that faraway look. "Oh, Gwen, I was in that storm! On the ship coming here. It was exactly like that." She stared at the painting, "When I see that painting, I can actually feel the deck heaving beneath my feet and the wind raging about my head. It is amazing! I must go inside and look at it more closely."

"Certainly, Sarah. Maybe the artist is here, and you can talk to him about it. An artist loves to hear that his painting has affected someone so strongly."

They went inside and were greeted by an older gentleman with a well-trimmed, long, gray beard and long gray hair in complete disarray. His nose was quite long and topped by a pair of wire-rimmed spectacles that magnified his pale blue eyes. "Hello, ladies. How may I help you this fine day?" He nodded several times, and his smile was cheerful.

Sarah quickly answered, "Sir, I would like to see the picture in the window. Would that be possible?"

"Of course, of course," he said as he made his way to the window, carefully picking up the picture and bringing it over to the women. "Ah, The Storm. You like it? It is one of my favorites."

"I like it very much. It makes me feel like I am in the middle of the storm again. It is so real." Sarah explained.

"Thank you so much. An artist could not ask for anything more than to have his painting make someone feel like they are in the picture."

"Could you paint another one like it?" Sarah asked hesitantly.

The man seemed surprised at the question and answered her, "Possibly, but this one is available. I am willing to discuss the price with you."

"Oh, it is not so much the price, although I will need to consider that. It is that I would like the ship to have a name painted on it to personalize it. Perhaps you could add it to this one? Would that be possible?" Sarah asked.

The man leaned close to the painting, squinting at the ship. "I suppose it is possible. The writing would be quite small, but I think I could do it so that it would be readable. I will have to charge you a little more for that, of course."

Sarah was smiling, although there was a note of concern in her voice when she asked, "Could you give me some idea of what it would cost?"

The man cleared his throat and named a figure somewhat hesitantly. Sarah was not used to the value of money yet, so glanced at Gwen for an indication, but Gwen just lifted her shoulders slightly, and Sarah knew they would need to talk about it. "Thank you so much, Sir. I will consider it and return later."

"Certainly. That is quite fine. I look forward to talking to you later." The man opened the door for them and bid them goodbye.

"Lunchtime," Gwen said. "We can talk about it then." She led the way to a little tearoom and greeted the woman at the door by name. The woman took them directly to a table across the room, leaving menus with them when she left. Gwen ordered sandwiches and tea for both of them.

While they ate Gwen explained the cost of the painting. Sarah told her how much money Grayson was giving her each week to see how long it would take her to save enough for the painting. "I want to give it to Grayson for a Christmas gift, but I want the ship to have the name of the one we sailed on. I have enough time before Christmas to save the money. I wonder if the man would keep it for me and let me pay him something each week until it is paid for."

Gwendolyn shrugged, "I don't see why he wouldn't. He seemed very pleased that you liked the painting and if he paints the name of the ship on it then it would only make sense to hold it for you. As soon as we are done eating, we will go back."

Sarah smiled happily and clasped her hands together. "It is so perfect. I think Grayson will really like it."

Gwen caught her excitement, "Of course he will, and it will be such a surprise. I do love a good surprise. Hurry and eat, and we'll go talk to the artist!"

The lunch was delightful even though they ate it so quickly. The door had just closed behind them when a pleasant voice called out, "Well, isn't this my lucky day!" Both women turned to see Freedy smiling at them. "Hello, ladies. Are you going in for lunch?

"Why, hello, Freddy. We are actually just done and going to do some shopping. I am showing Sarah around town." Gwen answered.

"I don't suppose I could convince you to postpone the shopping for a bit and join me for some tea while I have lunch?" His smile was charming, and his lively brown eyes sparkled. "It is very nice to see you again, Sarah. It is good of Gwen to show you around but if I can be of any assistance do not hesitate to call."

Sarah opened her mouth but couldn't get a word out before Gwen gave Freddy's arm a playful slap, "She does not need any assistance, Fred. She is in perfectly capable, and far safer, hands with me." She took Sarah's arm and pulled her down the street, calling back over her shoulder, "Enjoy your lunch. The cucumber sandwiches are delicious."

Gwen laughed as they walked down the boardwalk, but Sarah was concerned, "I hope we weren't rude. Perhaps we should have stayed. I don't want him to feel bad."

"Freddy?! He won't feel bad," Gwen assured her. "Come on, you want to go get the painting, don't you? And then we have the market to see."

At the store the artist greeted them with a smile, "Here you are! I was not sure that you would return. Come in, sit down and we will talk." He led them to a large desk with two chairs in front where he had them sit and then went to the other side to sit down opposite them. After some time of discussion, he said he thought he could put the name on the ship, and they agreed on a price that Sarah could pay in installments and have the painting a few weeks before Christmas. She gave him some of the money she had in her purse, and they parted company happily.

At the market the girls walked around, stopping at different stalls that caught Gwen's eye. She had already purchased some earrings, a purse, and a shawl, but eagerly continued to browse.

Sarah was standing beside her while she examined some jewelry and suddenly exclaimed, "Look at that beautiful scarf hanging there." Sarah pointed at an emerald green scarf blowing in the breeze a few stalls down.

"Let's go have a look," Gwen said excitedly, pulling Sarah over to the stall.

Sarah pulled back, "But I can't buy anything else. I just bought the painting. I don't want to spend all the money."

"It's just a scarf, Sarah. You still have lots of money left. Let's just have a look." After looking at the scarf, Gwen said quietly to Sarah, "Watch this," a twinkle in her eyes.

She went to the owner and said seriously, "I would like this scarf, but this is too much." She pointed at the price tag. After a few minutes of dickering back and forth Gwendolyn called Sarah over, giving her a price much lower than the tag said. Sarah could easily make the purchase and still have some money left, so with just a little twinge of guilt, she bought it.

Gwen eagerly put the scarf around Sarah's neck, "Here, wear it home. It looks so lovely on you, makes your eyes the exact same color."

"Yes, it does." Both girls looked up and there stood Freddy, smiling his boyish grin. "I am glad to have found you. In honor of your first trip to our fair city I would like to present you with these, Sarah." He pulled a large bouquet of fresh flowers from behind his back.

Sarah was uncertain about taking them, but Gwen smiled and nodded. Sarah took the flowers, smiling shyly, feeling the blush spread over her cheeks. "Thank you, Freddy. You did not need to do that. They are beautiful. I will share them with Gwen."

"You don't need to do that, Sarah," he said, pulling another bouquet from behind his back, "because I have these for Gwen," and with an elegant bow, he presented them to Gwendolyn.

"Why thank you, Fred. So thoughtful of you." Gwen seemed genuinely surprised and smiled fondly at her old friend. "Oh, here is our carriage. We must be off."

"Goodbye then, fair ladies," Freddy said and, with another elegant bow and a broad grin, helped them into the carriage.

"Goodbye Freddy," the girls called in unison as the carriage pulled away. Gwen laughed again, "That Freddy. Always good for a laugh. He better watch out for Grayson, though." She looked pointedly at the flowers Sarah held.

"Oh," Sarah gasped. "Is it alright to take the flowers?"

"Yes, of course. I wasn't being serious. Grayson and Freddy have been friends forever. Grayson knows what Fred is like. He won't mind."

They were still talking when the carriage stopped in front of the house. The door opened and Grayson stood there, his hand held out to help them down. "Hello, ladies. So, you are finally home. Let me help you." Sarah moved to the door and two strong hands circled her waist, lifting her out of the carriage, and setting her down on the ground beside him.

He reached back for Gwen, but she declined, "Thank you, but I really should be getting home now." Looking past Grayson she called, "Oh, Sarah, you almost forgot these." She held out the bouquet of flowers. Grayson reached in and took them from her, stepping aside while the two girls said goodbye and the carriage pulled away.

Grayson handed Sarah the bouquet as they went inside the house. He immediately rang the bell to summon the housekeeper. "Mrs. Walters can put these in some water for you. I am happy to see that you bought yourself some flowers, Sarah," he said, glad that he had given her the money to take shopping.

Sarah stammered and then said, "Actually I did not buy the flowers. We bumped into Freddy after lunch and later he came to the market with the flowers."

"Oh, really," Grayson said, a frown in his voice. "And how did Gwen feel about that?"

"Oh, he gave flowers to Gwen as well," Sarah quickly answered, surprised at Grayson's tone. "It was really very nice of him," she said, clearly impressed by Fred's apparent good deed.

Grayson frowned. He might need to have a word with Fred. Fred was a good chap, but a notorious flirt. Their crowd enjoyed his antics, but he did not understand Sarah's naiveté and Grayson was not going to have him toying with her heart.

Mrs. Walters appeared from around the corner, answering the bell he had rung, "Hello," the smiling woman greeted them. "Did you have a good time shopping, Miss? What can I do for you?"

"Sarah has some flowers she needs put in a vase," Grayson answered.

Mrs. Walters took the flowers from Sarah, exclaiming, "Oh, and aren't they lovely! Where did you get them, Grayson? I did not realize you had been out."

Sarah opened her mouth to explain but Grayson growled, "Please take them and put them in some water. When will dinner be ready?"

In half an hour, Sir." She answered quickly, uncertain why the master seemed upset. With the flowers in hand, she scurried from the room.

Sarah was anxious to get away and walked to the stairs as she said, "I will go get ready for dinner now."

Grayson watched the two women leave, wishing that he and Sarah were back on the ship where there were no flowers, and no one did anything without his permission first. But what he really wished was that the flowers had been from him. Pushing that fleeting thought out of his mind he stomped up the stairs to his study.

CHAPTER 39

By dinnertime Sarah and Grayson had put the flowers out of their minds, until they encountered them in a lovely vase on the dining room table. Grayson considered asking Mrs. Walters to remove them but thought better of it. That would only serve to bring more attention to them.

Dinner was a quiet affair. Sarah attempted to make conversation by commenting on some of the things she had seen in Burford, while Grayson mentioned that he had received word that the ship had arrived safely in London.

"Oh! I'm so glad. How is everyone?" Sarah was anxious to hear all the news and several minutes were spent talking about the ship. Memories of the voyage flooded both their minds. How long ago it seemed that they were in the isolated world of the ship. The room was quiet as they both thought of those days.

When the last of the dinner dishes had been removed Grayson stopped the maid, "We will have dessert and tea in the parlor in fifteen minutes." The maid curtsied and left. Grayson turned to Sarah, "Please excuse me. I will meet you in the parlor shortly." With that he left the room.

Sarah opened the French doors and stepped out onto the patio. The cool night air touched her warm skin, and a quick shiver ran over her. It was refreshing and she breathed in, smelling the far-off scent of roses from the garden across the yard. Walking over to the low stone wall that surrounded the patio she rested her hands against it and stared up at the night sky, diamond stars blinking back. The moonlight gave her skin a soft glow and shimmered in her golden hair.

Grayson stopped in the doorway watching her, different emotions tugging at his heart. She had come to mean so much to him in so many different ways. He was drawn to her like the tide to the moon and moved quietly to stand behind her.

"Out here alone?" The voice was familiar, but intimately deep. She turned around to see his broad shoulders, touched by the wavy brown hair that drifted back from his face in the gentle breeze. Her eyes moved up over the chiseled jaw, full lips, and straight nose to at last meet his eyes, dark like the night, deep as the bottomless sea. She felt herself drowning in them.

When she turned to him his breath caught. The smell of roses in the air mingled with the lilac on her skin, drawing him closer. The wide neck of the deep blue blouse she wore left her neck bare almost to her shoulders. Her skin shone like smooth, spun honey in the pale moonlight. He wanted to taste it, to put his lips to the pulse that was throbbing at the base of her throat. His eyes moved up across her full pink lips, parted slightly to reveal small white teeth. He shuddered when her tongue slipped out to nervously run over her lips, leaving them smooth and glistening. Reaching out, his hands gently circled her arms. Her skin was warm and soft. He pulled her one step closer to him, leaving the smallest space between them. She stepped easily to him, almost into his arms. He looked down at the same moment she looked up and their eyes collided.

A small gasp escaped them both. Grayson dropped his arms and turned away to break the spell.

Sarah moved back to the wall, her arms sizzling where his hands had been. She nervously twisted the emerald, green cloth she held, waiting for her heartbeat to return to normal.

It was just a moment before Grayson spoke quietly, "It is a beautiful evening, although there is a bit of fall chill in the air."

Sarah moved away from the wall to stand by him but kept her eyes on the cloth she twisted in her hands. He reached to take it from her. "Here Sarah, let me have that." His hand touched hers and she quickly released the scarf. He shook it out and reached around to drape it over her shoulders.

"I don't believe I have seen this before. It is a beautiful color."

"I bought it at the market today," Sarah explained.

There was a smile in his voice when he replied, "I am glad you found something to purchase with your money. Spending time at the market seems to be something the ladies enjoy a great deal."

The voice from inside the room startled the couple. "Oh, there you are," Mrs. Walters said from the door. "I have just brought the dessert and tea in. Would you like me to pour for you?"

Grayson smiled, relieved to have the moment broken. "No, thank you Mrs. Walters, we will take care of it."

The housekeeper dropped a quick curtsey, "Right you are then. I will be going to my room now. Good night."

"Good night," Grayson and Sarah said together and followed the woman inside.

When she had left, Sarah quickly said, "I think I would like to retire also. I do not need any tea just now."

"That would be fine," Grayson agreed. "It has been a long day for you, and I am weary from all my bookwork also. Come along then." He held the door open for her.

Sarah stopped just before the door, picking up the tray Mrs. Walters had left. "I will take these things back first. Then I will put out the candles."

"Leave it for the maid, Sarah," he ordered.

"I don't mind. Remember, I was the maid not so long ago."

She said it with a smile and once again he marveled at her lack of bitterness, trying to picture Lydia, or any of the women he knew, picking up after the maid without complaining, let alone happily. He followed her out the door and walked with her across the hall to the staircase, where he stopped and said simply, "Good night, Sarah."

"Good night, Grayson," she answered quietly turning away quickly when the blush touched her cheeks again.

CHAPTER 40

Once in his room, Grayson plopped down in his favorite chair leaning forward with his elbows on his knees, his head resting heavily in his hands. He needed to think, but not about her. It seemed like he had been thinking about her forever, first all those weeks on the ship on the journey out to get her, angry that he had to go, that Bethany could withhold his inheritance until he came back with the girl. And then after meeting her and seeing her fear, thinking about what she had been through, about protecting her, taking care of her, even making her happy. And now, having her in his home, down the hall, thinking about her as a woman.

He stood up quickly and paced across the room. He needed to get away. He was planning to go to London on business in a week; he would move the trip up and go now. That decision seemed to energize him; he yanked a bag down out of the closet and began throwing clothes in it. He would go at first light, before anyone was up. He finished packing and stretched out on top of the bed to wait for dawn, his hands behind his head, long legs with boots still on, crossed at the ankle. The minute his eyes closed, blonde hair and green eyes appeared behind them. He forced the image away with thoughts of business. Jumping up at the sound of the first bird chirping he grabbed his bag and quietly left his room. At the entryway he left a note on the table for Mrs. Walters, letting her know where he would be. As he turned to go the maid, Sadie, came around the corner. She dropped a quick curtsey; he nodded and left for the stable.

257

Sadie watched him leave, puzzled to see the master up at such an early hour. As she walked past the foyer table, she noticed a white sheet of paper. She glanced around, making sure she was alone, opened the note and read it quickly. After putting it back where she had found it, Sadie rushed down the hall to her room, grabbed her coat and slipped out the back door. If she ran both ways through the shortcut, she should be able to get to the Barker mansion, give her aunt the information and be back before Mrs. Walters missed her. Then her aunt could tell Miss Lydia that Master Attwood would be gone to London for quite some time.

In the stable Grayson had the groom prepare his horse. Riding would be good for him; perhaps the wind blowing in his face would blow her out of his mind and the pounding of the hoofs might jolt him back to his senses. He patted the smooth skin on the neck of his favorite horse. With such an early start he would be in London by mid-afternoon. He mounted the steed in one fluid movement, doffed his hat in appreciation to the groom and disappeared down the lane.

He was more than glad when he arrived at his flat in London. Even though he hadn't ridden hard and had stopped a few times along the way, he was exhausted and saddle-sore. It had been quite some time since he'd spent that much time riding. He kept a flat in the city because he was frequently here on business, and it was convenient to have his own place waiting. It was near the shipyards, and he opened the window, breathing in the salt sea air. That in itself would help, being near the sea, thinking about his ships. He lay down, listening to the sounds of men yelling and seagulls screeching. Soon, he drifted off to sleep. It was dusk when he awoke, and he was hungry. After splashing cold water on his face, he left to find some dinner.

He ate at a public house nearby but didn't stay long after it began to fill up with sailors who were drinking too much and talking too loudly. He'd learned a long time ago that alcohol wasn't a good way to deal with his problems. He had given it a good try after his mother died but soon realized that he always felt the same when it wore off. Work was a better answer for him - go on a voyage, design a new ship, sell some cargo. He thought about these things as he strode back to the flat and worked late into the night on some fresh plans for the future. He lay down on the bed with those things still going around in his head and woke late the next morning, surprised to find that he had slept well and felt refreshed. This was what he needed: time in his own world. He walked briskly down to the docks taking in the sights and sounds and smells, occasionally meeting someone he knew and stopping to talk about life and business.

He was standing at the end of the dock, gazing out at the sea when a ship in full sail moved by. Seeing the white sails against the blue sky brought her instantly to his mind, wearing that dress of the same colors, standing by the rail, uncaring that the wind was blowing her long curls into disarray, raising her face to the sun, uncaring that it might darken her skin. He heard her laughter floating on the breeze. She loved the sea, loved the ship. Somehow, she fit into this world too. He turned

259

away, his boots knocking loudly against the wood dock
as he walked.

CHAPTER 41

Back in his room he went to the desk pulling out some business papers, settling down to do some work. The soft knock on his door made him scowl. He did not want to be interrupted. Ignoring it, he turned back to his papers when the sound came again, a little firmer this time. Grayson pushed his chair back, the legs screeching against the wood floor. He strode over to the door and yanked it open, prepared to tell whomever to leave him alone.

Lydia stood with her hand in the air, poised to knock again. When he appeared, her face brightened into a happy smile and she opened her hand to lay it against his chest as she stepped closer to him, "Hello Grayson, darling."

"Lydia?" Grayson was confused, startled to see her standing there.

She laughed up at him and pushed softly on his chest, following him into the room. "Yes, of course it's me." She slid her arms up around his neck.

Grayson found himself embracing her without even thinking about it. He stood back after a moment and she dropped her arms, turning to shut the door behind them.

"Lydia," Grayson said again, moving across the room, "What are you doing here?"

She followed him, "Why, I heard you were going to be here, and I thought this would be the perfect opportunity for us to catch up." She stood close to him again, smiling up at him, her topaz eyes shining. "We haven't had a chance to spend any time together since you got home." Her lips came together in a little pout.

He couldn't stop the deep laugh that rolled out, "Ah, poor Lydia. I suppose we haven't, but perhaps a simple invitation to dinner would have sufficed."

She stepped away from him, fluffing out her skirts to draw his attention. "Why thank you, Grayson, dear. I would love to have the pleasure of dining with you tonight," she said, deliberately misinterpreting his comment.

Grayson couldn't help smiling at the lady before him. She was perfect, from the top of her shiny auburn hair, every strand exactly where it should be, to the tip of her dainty pointed brown patent boots that perfectly matched the satin flounce at the bottom of her deep pink dress. A wide satin ribbon of the same rich brown circled her small waist. The low heart-shaped neckline of the fitted, pink bodice was designed to be eye-catching and Grayson had to admit that it did a remarkably good job as he pulled his eyes away. She wore a brown satin ribbon around her white throat, the deep color making her perfect porcelain skin shine. Her lips and cheeks were artfully painted to appear to naturally match the pink dress. She smiled brightly when his eyes met hers, unabashed by his perusal.

He returned the smile, complimenting her, "You look lovely, my dear. It would indeed be a pleasure to dine with you, but not tonight. Perhaps back at home we can go into town for dinner one night."

Her face immediately fell, "Oh pooh! I don't want to wait until then to see you. Here we are, both in London where there are so many things to see and do." She moved over to him and took his arm. "Let's at least go for a carriage ride, get away from this noise and that awful smell! I certainly hope it doesn't stick to my new dress and ruin it. I don't want to smell like the ocean every time I wear it." She turned up her pretty little nose with a look of disgust.

"I like the smell of the sea," Grayson answered sharply.

Lydia tittered, "I know you do. We will have to add a new wing on the house for you to keep your ship clothes in so they don't smell up anything else. Oh, come on, let's go for a ride," she took his arm and pulled him towards the door.

Grayson pulled his arm away. "I really do have some things I need to get done and you should not be here in my room."

She moved close to him, a seductive smile on her face, reminding him, "It's not as though we have never been alone before, Darling."

Grayson moved away quickly. What could he say? "Lydia, that was a long time ago. We were young and we both know that you were never completely compromised."

263

Her laugh was mocking, "Not completely compromised? But not completely innocent either." She walked slowly over to him again, her voice sweet, beguiling, "It is alright, Darling. I don't mind and everyone knows we are going to be married anyway."

"That has not been decided. I am sorry. Things are different now," he said firmly.

Now it was her turn to move away, her face set. "Because of HER?!" She spat out the words, glaring at the man in front of her, daring him to deny it.

And he did, "No, it is not because of Sarah. I have just had too much going on. First there was Father, then Bethany and her damn will, the trip to America." He paused, looking across at the beautiful woman before him. "I have not had time to think." He could not help but go over to her. "Lydia, I know you deserve a decision, but I want to make the right one. I care about you too much to do anything more until I am sure."

Lydia responded more gently than she felt, "These have been trying years for you, Darling, but think carefully now. We belong together! With our combined fortunes, we can have anything we want. You can go into politics, even become Governor one day. Between the two of us, we know ALL the right people to get us wherever we want to go!" She became more animated as she spoke, trying to transfer her enthusiasm to him.

Grayson had to admit that he felt a surge of power at her words and enjoyed the picture of himself standing in the Governor's mansion, making important decisions, influencing the course of his country. And then he pictured Sarah, in her shabby clothes and bruises on her face, but a smile of contentment on her lips and trust and forgiveness shining in her eyes. She had more peace and joy with nothing than he had with all his fortune. He spoke quietly, "I have come to realize that there is more to happiness than wealth and power."

Lydia laughed and answered as though she knew what he was thinking, "Oh, so you have forgotten that it was wealth and power that made you go out and get that girl in the first place? Come now, Grayson, you know that you would not have gone for her except for the money."

Grayson's face blanched. Lydia's eyes narrowed as she watched him, seeing the guilt and pain wash over him. Her eyes widened, "She doesn't know!!" She sidled over to him putting her face close to his, her quiet voice sinister, "She doesn't know about the will, does she, Grayson? She thinks you were doing a good deed, sacrificing to carry out a woman's dying wish." Her laughter was triumphant.

Grayson walked slowly across the room, his shoulders bent. "That doesn't matter anymore. I do not care about the will or the money. Whatever my motivation was for going, all I care about now is that she is free and safe. She believes God sent me to free her. I don't know. Perhaps she is right."

He jumped when Lydia leaned against him, her head resting on his back, her hand on his shoulder rubbing gently. "Grayson, Grayson, she has got you thinking crazy things. God didn't have anything to do with you going to America. It was Bethany. I am quite sure you would not get the two confused."

He felt the soft laugh vibrate against his back and her words tugged at his mind. God and Bethany? No, he would not confuse the two. He had gone to America because of Bethany but who was he to say that God had nothing to do with it? Rose's words mingled with his mother's and Sarah's in his mind until he could not distinguish who was speaking, "Everything happens for a reason."

He shook his head to clear his mind. What was he thinking? He did not want to think about this. Lydia was right. He was deceiving Sarah, had been all this time. He turned around and Lydia was there, so close her perfumed hair touched his chin. Without thinking, he put his arms around her and hers slid up around his shoulders. He felt all her curves pressing against him, got lost in her dark topaz eyes. When she reached up to touch his lips he lingered there, tasting their softness, before suddenly breaking the contact. "Lydia, you must go now," he choked the words out, pulling her arms from his neck and stepping back.

Lydia could see that she had lost. Pleading would do no good. She snapped her head up and walked sharply to the door, the click of her heels punctuating each step. At the door she turned, glaring across at him, anger flashing in her eyes, "This is not the end of it, Grayson. You belong to me! Since we were children, it has been the plan and it WILL happen. No little slip of a servant girl is going to change that! You will never get anywhere

266

with a servant on your arm!" She reeled and yanked the door open.

Grayson closed the door, leaning back against it. He had come here to try and clear up his confusion, and now he was more confused than ever. He walked to the bed, slumping down on it, holding his head in his hands. He suddenly longed for Sarah, for her quiet confidence, assuring him that everything would be fine. He longed for her sweet smile and tender touch. "Sarah!" he called out, hearing his own voice echo in the room. He lay down on the bed, his turmoil easing slightly. He knew what she would say, but was it possible? Could he learn to trust God again?

CHAPTER 42

Lydia left Grayson's room, got the first cab she saw and snapped out the name of her hotel to the driver, letting out an unladylike word when the horse jumped forward before she was settled. This had not gone at all as she had planned. What was the matter with Grayson?! Did he really think she had waited all these years to let that little slip of a servant girl steal him away? Somehow the girl had worked her way into his affections, but if she could think of a way to get rid of her for a while, Grayson would soon forget about her and come to his senses. Hadn't he just proven that? She could change his mind easily enough.

At the hotel, she ordered a carriage. It only took a minute to get her things together and she was waiting when the bell boy arrived. The whole ride home she alternated between crying brokenheartedly, calling Grayson names that would normally never cross her lips, and plotting different ways to get rid of Sarah. It was dark when she arrived home and she went immediately to her room and finally, content with the plan she had devised, fell asleep.

She woke up late and quickly sent a message over to Attwood Manor inviting Sarah to a small gathering that evening. She sent similar messages to the rest of the group and then spent time with the housekeeper, giving her instructions for the evening.

Sarah was surprised when Mrs. Walters gave her the note. After reading the invitation, she asked the older woman, her heart pounding, "Did Grayson say when he would be back?"

"No, Miss, he did not say, only that he would be gone for a while. May I ask what the message is?" The kindly woman could see the tension moving over Sarah.

"It is from Lydia. She is having a gathering at her house tonight and has invited me to attend." Her eyes were wide and her face pale as she explained. "I wish Grayson was here. I really would prefer not to go without him, but I don't know how to refuse."

The housekeeper frowned. "Yes, I wish he was here also. I do not trust Lydia Barker, but I don't see how you can refuse either. Miss Gwendolyn will be there." Her face brightened. "She will stay by you. You will be fine." The woman tried to sound reassuring but they both knew she was trying to convince herself as much as Sarah

It was early afternoon when the invitation arrived, so Sarah did not have long to worry and pray and worry and pray some more. She decided not to spend a lot of time thinking about what she would wear and quickly chose a simple ivy green dress with long sleeves. After rolling her hair into a shiny blonde rope, she wrapped it around her head, finishing with a high pompadour over her forehead. It was all very simple, and Sarah hoped she could just blend into the background without anyone paying attention to her.

When she arrived at the Barker home, there were already several carriages waiting outside the house. Sarah knew that she had left herself more than enough time to arrive on time but when the butler showed her into the parlor, a hush fell over the already crowded room and all eyes turned to her. She smiled nervously as she scanned the faces until she came to Gwen's. Relief flooded her when her new friend smiled back and began to make her way over.

"Oh, Sarah, here you are." Lydia's loud voice chimed out as she quickly stepped to the front to take Sarah's hands as if greeting a good friend. "I was worried that you weren't coming when it got so late."

"I'm sorry. I was sure the invitation said 7:30," Sarah explained, puzzled. Everyone was staring at her, and she felt her neck and face getting hot.

Lydia put an arm around Sarah's shoulders and reassured her, "It was 7:00 my dear, but don't worry about that now. Come on in and get something to eat at the buffet table."

People began talking again as Lydia guided Sarah to the table laden with a large variety of delicacies. "Grayson isn't home from London yet?" she asked, handing Sarah a plate.

Sarah's eyes widened in surprise. *Lydia knew that Grayson was in London?*

Lydia saw the surprise in those ridiculous eyes and, with a Cheshire smile, patted Sarah's shoulder consolingly, "Come join us after you get some food."

Sarah had no appetite, but she put a few things on her plate to be polite. She glanced around the room hoping to find a seat open beside Gwendolyn. "Come sit

270

with me, Sweet Sarah." She turned to see Freddy at her side, smiling charmingly down at her.

"Hello, Freddy." Relief was in her voice and face as she greeted him. "It is nice to see you again."

He settled her in a seat next to his and then went to get her some punch. Sarah began to relax with Freddy beside her and Gwen just a few seats away. She listened to the conversation around her, entering in occasionally. After a while the room began getting quieter and it was clear that people were beginning to think about leaving.

"Sarah," Lydia's voice rang out through the room. Everyone stopped talking and looked from Lydia to Sarah.

"Sarah," Lydia began again, "We really have not had much opportunity to get to know you yet. Why don't you tell us about America? What was it you were doing there again? Why would you leave England to go over to that wild land?"

The color left Sarah's face. Her eyes were like two huge emeralds on a white satin cloth. Her mind was frantic. *Grayson, where are you? I need you. Please God, help me.*

"Sarah, it's alright. We are all your friends now," Lydia said sweetly. "We just want to get to know you better. It's quite exciting to have someone who has been to America right here. Now, tell us, what were you doing there?"

There were murmurs throughout the room encouraging her to talk. With a deep breath and another

271

quick prayer Sarah started speaking, moving her eyes from Gwen to Fred and back, trying to imagine that she was just talking to the two of them. "Some people my parents had been introduced to were going to America and wanted to take someone along to help them as they settled there. My parents and I decided it would be a good opportunity for me, so I went with them."

She breathed a sigh of relief when she sensed that people were content with that. Freddy put his arm around her shoulders and gave her a comforting squeeze and Gwen smiled encouragingly at her. Sarah was surprised that she could give a genuine smile back.

Some people at the back of the room got up preparing to leave when the voice chimed out again. "You went to HELP these people?" Lydia paused slightly, not wanting an answer but waiting for the question to take root. "So, you worked for them?" She waited.

Sarah had just said, "Yes," when Lydia began again. "You worked for them. You were a servant then?"

Sarah heard the intake of breaths around the room. She swallowed hard before answering, "Yes. I was a servant." There was a sense of relief at having said it. It was over. She had said it straight out and now no one had to wonder about it anymore. She was so relieved that she stood up, saying, "I think I will go home now. Thank you for inviting me, Lydia."

Lydia stood also, protesting, "But you haven't really told us anything yet. We knew that you had gone to help some people, but I am surprised that your parents would let you go all the way to America. How could they do that?"

Wanting to defend her parents, Sarah spoke without thinking, "My mother was very ill and the church my father pastored was about to be closed. We would have no place to go. In order to keep me out of the workhouse, my father and I decided it would be best for me to take the position with these people for a few years. We hoped the money they got for my service would help to send my mother to Bath for medical treatment."

The room was completely quiet when Sarah stopped speaking. Lydia broke the silence, "Your parents received money for your service? What do you mean?"

There was nothing else to do so Sarah simply stated factually, "I was an indentured servant. I was to work for the Tompkins for eight years and then be free to come home. My parents received the money for my years of service when I left."

"Indentured? Isn't that kind of like being a slave? Your parents sold you to these people?" Lydia's voice rose, reflecting the shock of all the people in the room and there was a general movement away from Sarah. Even Gwen seemed to lean away from her.

All the blood left Sarah's head. She started to sway and sat down quickly. Hot tears pricked behind her eyes and when she closed them, she felt the tears overflow and run down her face.

Freddy was touched by the tears he saw streaking down her cheeks. He touched her arm and quietly said, "Come, Sarah, I will take you home now."

Her eyes shimmered with tears when she choked out, "It's not how it sounds. I can explain."

"Not now, Sarah." He took her hands and stood up with her, putting an arm around her waist to help her walk to the door.

Neither of them spoke during the ride. Freddy heard the soft noises that told him she was still crying. He understood how the others felt. He was also surprised to hear about Sarah's situation, but he was quite well-traveled and understood the indenture process. Having met people in all types of situations he had come to realize that people are people regardless of where life has landed them.

He was hesitant to comfort her too much because Grayson was his best friend, but hearing her crying in the corner of the carriage tore at his heart, and he reached out to lightly touch her shoulder, trying to reassure her, "It was just a surprise, Sarah. They will get over it. I've known most of them all my life and they really are good people. Give them a little time."

She nodded and took a shuddering breath before speaking so quietly he had to lean over to hear, "Thank you, Freddy."

He squeezed her shoulder and, placing a tender kiss on her hair, and whispered, "You are welcome, Sweet Sarah."

At the house, he took her inside and, after a brief word with Mrs. Walters came back to her, gently lifting her chin to look up at him. When she opened her eyes, he smiled at her and was rewarded with a wavering smile back. "Chin up, my dear. Goodbye for now." He nodded to Mrs. Walters, who came and put an arm around the girl, and then he left.

CHAPTER 43

Mrs. Walters helped Sarah up the stairs to her room. Mr. Farnsworth had only told her that Lydia had made a spectacle about Sarah being a servant and all. The housekeeper could imagine the rest. Lydia was difficult at her best and quite awful at her worst. That woman was unhappy about Grayson's interest in Sarah she suspected. Miss Lydia wanted to marry Grayson and what Lydia wanted, Lydia usually made sure she got. Mrs. Walters looked over at the quiet little miss walking beside her as if in a daze. She took her into the room and undid all the buttons at the back of her dress, helping her to get into her nightgown and take down her hair.

It was while the kindly woman was brushing her hair that Sarah spoke, quietly, almost as though talking to herself, "I am a shame to him. They will never accept me. He should never have come for me."

"Now, you don't mean that, Miss. I'm sure you were treated much worse over there than what Lydia has done tonight."

Sarah sat, staring ahead, memories of the Tompkins flooding her mind. "But it was just me over there! It did not matter what they thought about me or did to me. It did not affect anyone but me. But what Grayson's friends think about me will affect him. I am so glad I am not really related to him. I should not be part of his life or his friends at all. He only came for me because he wanted to carry out Bethany's last wish. He was doing a good deed. He wanted to care about me because we were family, but we were not really family.

He should not feel that he has to include me in his life. I am nothing to him." She paused, and fresh tears ran down her cheeks.

"That is not true, my dear," Mrs. Walters said as she put the brush down and started braiding the golden strands into a long, thick braid. "I have known Grayson all his life. I can tell how he feels almost better than he can. He cares for you a great deal."

Sarah shook her head, "I am an embarrassment to him. They were all staring at me, pulling away, afraid they might accidentally touch me. They were so shocked to hear that I was an indentured servant. I think even Gwen leaned away from me." She covered her face, moaning. "I do not know what to do."

The older woman pulled her up, walking with her to the bed. "We are not going to do anything more tonight. You need to get a good sleep. Remember that God has been with you through all these years. Trust Him now. It will be alright." She pulled the comforter over the girl.

Just as the older woman was about to blow out the lamp on the side table Sarah reached up and touched her hand. "I would like to get my Bible out of the drawer and read for a while. I can blow out the light."

"Certainly," Mrs. Walters agreed, reaching down to get the little Bible for the girl. "Good night, my dear. Everything will be alright."

"Thank you," Sarah said quietly. "Good night, Mrs. Walters." By the time the door had closed, Sarah was busy reading her favorite passages, but it was not long before her eyes were drooping closed, the emotion of the evening having taken its toll. She closed the precious book, blew out the lamp and settled down, clutching it to herself. How she wished her parents were here. She longed for her mother's gentle assurance and her father's quiet strength. It seemed he could always fix everything when she was a girl. But she remembered him the day she left, saying, "I can't fix this, Sarah". Tears ran down onto her pillow. He couldn't fix this either. But she heard a voice, not her father's, clearly saying, *"I am with you, Sarah."* She knew it was true and slowly, her sobs eased and she fell asleep.

Sarah tried to find things to keep herself busy over the next few days. She talked with Mrs. Walters about some things she had noticed around the house that needed to be cleaned more thoroughly. Mrs. Walters gave her full authority to do whatever she liked and sent her a group of house servants she could supervise. Sarah quickly made a list of the things she wanted done and gave out assignments. Overseeing the workers kept her busy and gave her a sense of accomplishment. She went through the house room by room making sure every shelf was dusted and every corner cleaned. The crystals on all the chandeliers were taken down and washed and put back sparkling bright. As each room passed her inspection, she rewarded the servants with a special tea.

Freddy came by several times and brought flowers. He made her smile and feel hopeful. Gwen also came by and assured her that she had not pulled away and that she would always be her friend and stand by her.

The days went by and slowly, the events of that awful night came less and less frequently to her mind. But another thought came often – where was Grayson? The thought of him came to her mind that day as she was inspecting the front entry. She couldn't hold it back. Thoughts of him flooded over her. When was he coming back? She felt like something was missing inside of her. He had become such a big part of her life over these months of being near him all the time. On the ship, there was the constant, comforting knowledge that he was there, in control, taking care of things, taking care of her. And he was the same captain here, at his home, his essence everywhere. Just knowing he was there made her feel safe and happy.

The lack of his presence left a hole in everything, even in her. She longed to see him, ached to see him, to hear his voice. He had been gone more than a week now! It seemed like forever. And it was in his absence that she finally admitted to herself what she would not allow herself to admit when he was present – I love him. The thought shocked her for a moment. She stopped what she was doing and stood completely still, letting it wash over her. I love him. It took a few moments before she realized that she was smiling. She felt so free, finally allowing herself to put the word to all the emotions, all the feelings she had for this man, the good and the bad. They all added up to this one thing – love. I love him.

The rap of the large door knocker on the front door startled her. She waited a minute for George to come and answer it, but the rap came again, and he still did not appear. She went to the door and opened it,

279

gasping when she saw Lydia standing there. She looked beautiful, perfect. She wore a long, navy blue, velvet cape and matching hat with a lighter blue ribbon tied in a big bow under her delicate chin.

"Hello Sarah, aren't you going to invite me in?" The saccharine sweet voice was as cold as the November night.

CHAPTER 44

The sweet voice sent a shiver through Sarah. She took a deep breath trying to still her pounding heart. She looked behind her hoping that George or Mrs. Walters would appear.

"I believe your housekeeper and butler are occupied at the moment," Lydia announced, her voice, no longer sweet. She stepped forward, pushing Sarah aside as she came into the house. "Really, Sarah, don't you have any manners? You shouldn't leave a guest standing on the doorstep without so much as a greeting."

Sarah was slowly recovering from the shock of seeing Lydia there. She shut the door and turned to face the woman who was pulling off her gloves and then untying the ribbon of her hat. When she had them off, she held them out to Sarah, simply waiting until Sarah came over and took the hat and gloves from her. Immediately Lydia slid off her cape and draped it over the arm that Sarah automatically extended.

Snapping out of her daze, Sarah finally greeted the woman, trying desperately to sound polite and controlled. "Hello, Lydia. What a surprise to see you here. Please come into the parlor. I will ring for some tea." She led the way into the room across the entryway. After placing Lydia's things on one of the chairs she rang the bell on the table. It was a silent and uncomfortable minute before Sadie appeared at the door.

Sarah was puzzled, "Sadie, where is Mrs. Walters?" she asked.

"Oh, she received a message that she was needed at her sister's place. She had to leave immediately," the maid explained, a small smile hovering on her lips as she glanced at Lydia.

Sarah's brow furrowed, "I am surprised she didn't tell me." She paused for a moment and then, realizing the maid, and Lydia were staring at her, instructed, "Sadie, please bring tea for Miss Barker and me."

"Yes, Ma'am," Sadie said, dropping a quick curtsey as she left.

Sarah swallowed hard. She wasn't comfortable being alone with Lydia. What was she doing here? If only Mrs. Walters were in the house. She took a deep breath and looked Lydia directly in the eye hoping that she appeared more composed than she felt. "Please have a seat, Lydia. I must say I am surprised to see you. I don't recall inviting you here. Did we have an appointment?" She felt stronger having said that. Perhaps Lydia could intimidate her at her own house, but not here. Sarah squared her shoulders and lifted her chin, waiting for an answer.

Lydia laughed, mocking her. "Oh Sarah, really! I do not need an invitation to come to Grayson's home, especially from the help. I have come to ask you to return these to Grayson when he gets home." She held out her hand and Sarah had no recourse but to go over and open hers to receive whatever Lydia held.

Lydia dropped two gold cufflinks with diamond studs into Sarah's small hand. Sarah recognized them immediately. She had seen Grayson wear them on several occasions – at the dinner at Rose's house, at dinner on the ship, to church, to the party at Lydia's.

While Sarah stared down at the cufflinks, Lydia said, "He left them in my room in London. They are his favorite so I am sure he will want them back right away."

Sarah's hand was shaking so she closed it quickly and walked back across the room, her heart beating so hard she was sure Lydia could hear it. She turned around to meet the condescending smile on Lydia's brightly painted lips.

The woman walked towards her stopping at the couch, "Sarah, I am going to do you a favor and help you understand something. Perhaps we should sit down." She gracefully positioned herself on the settee, motioning to the chair across from her for Sarah to sit.

Sadie appeared at the door with a tray of tea things and Sarah went quickly over to the tea table, relieved to see the little maid. "Oh Sadie, thank you. Has Mrs. Walters returned by any chance?" she asked.

"No Ma'am. I think she may not return tonight as her sister lives some distance away."

The girl turned to leave, and Sarah quickly asked, "Is George here? Perhaps he can take care of Miss Barker's carriage."

"Mr. George is not here Ma'am. He drove Mrs. Walters to her sister's as no one else was available."

"I see. Well, please let me know when Mrs. Walters returns and stay near so you can hear the bell if I need anything else."

"Yes Ma'am," the little maid said and bobbed the faintest of curtsys as she left.

"You should not let her get away with that, Sarah. I suppose that is the problem with a servant directing a servant, the blind leading the blind, as they say." Lydia laughed at her own cleverness and once again indicated for Sarah to sit in the chair across from her.

Sarah was stunned by the comment and went docilely to the chair sitting down and staring at the woman across from her.

"What just happened with that impudent maid is partly why I came, Sarah, besides bringing Grayson's cufflinks, of course. He is such a careless man. I gave those to him as a gift, you know, but I have had to bring them back to him several times." She tittered.

"I will give them to him." Sarah's voice was quiet, emotionless.

"That is fine, but back to what I was saying. I really hope this isn't too harsh, but I see the way you look at Grayson and I don't want you to make a fool of yourself. And I am sure you want the best for him after all he has done for you."

Sarah nodded and Lydia continued, "First of all, you must understand that Grayson and I intend to announce our engagement at the Christmas ball next month." At Sarah's little intake of breath, Lydia smiled,

"That should not be a surprise to you, Dear. Everyone knows that Grayson and I have been intended for many years. He just had to get this trip to get you out of the way before we could make it formal. And now, here you are, and that poses quite a problem for Grayson. Of course, he would never tell you this because he fancies himself to have feelings for you, maybe even be in love with you, but that would be disastrous for him, Sarah." She paused when she saw the surprise and denial on Sarah's face, waiting for her words to soak in.

"Grayson does not have feelings like that for me. He would never love me," Sarah stammered. "I know that you and Grayson belong together."

"Yes, we do, but I am afraid that Grayson might be getting a little distracted by having to take care of you." She leaned forward, looking seriously into Sarah's eyes. "Grayson is an important man, Sarah. He has aspirations of getting into politics and running for Governor someday soon and has a very good chance of succeeding, as of now, that is. If you care about him at all you must know that having you, a servant, almost a slave, at his side would be a great handicap to his ability to accomplish that goal. The word is already spreading through the township of his situation, and I am sure people are beginning to wonder if they would want to vote for him in this case. Even if you never become Mrs. Attwood, which you won't," She didn't even try to prevent the sneer in her voice or on her face, but said it again for effect, "Even if you never become Mrs. Attwood, just having you around, reminding people that he is related to a servant, will destroy his chances of becoming anything more than he is now, the head of a shipbuilding company and a ship's captain."

Sarah's heart felt like it would burst. Hot needles of pain pricked behind her eyes, and her throat hurt so badly from holding back the tears she could hardly breathe. Everything Lydia said was true. She was nothing but a liability to Grayson in every way.

Lydia watched her and knew the moment when victory came. She laughed triumphantly and got up to walk over and sit down beside the devastated girl. "Sarah, do you really think that Grayson came to free you because he cared? Because he cared about Bethany's wish?" Her laugh was loud and harsh. "Grayson hated Bethany. He would never voluntarily carry out any wish of hers. He would never care about any servant's plight. Grayson does not care about servants!" She spat the word out. "Grayson cares about money. That is all he cares about. And I have money to offer him, and Bethany had money to offer him."

She waited until the question formed in Sarah's eyes. "Yes, Bethany had money to offer him and put it in her will. Foolish woman got soft in her old age and started worrying about her sister's child. I kept telling her not to bother about it but, oh no, she couldn't die in peace unless she knew you were going to be set free. So, she put it in her will. That, at least, was very clever. She would leave all the money and property to charity, and Grayson would not inherit his father's estate unless he went and brought you back to England. Not only that, he had to make sure you were settled here or could get a position where you would be able to take care of yourself in comfort. That is all he cared about, my dear, his inheritance! Not you, not Bethany. Money!"

Sarah could hold it back no longer and the sob tore from her throat. It had all been a lie! All this time he had let her believe that he was doing it because she was family, even if not blood-related, family, nonetheless. How many times had he said that she was an Attwood now? And she had so wanted to have some family left, someone who was somehow connected to her parents, even if it was only through a stepmother.

She remembered so clearly when Mrs. Tompkin had scornfully asked him why he would want to take her back to England, saying, "She isn't even strong enough to be a good servant." And Grayson had answered so quickly and strongly, "She is family. I do not need another reason." But he did have another reason. He did not care that she was family at all.

Lydia could see all the thoughts going through that little head. "Sarah, he never wanted you, doesn't want you now. You are just an obligation to be fulfilled until he can get rid of you and finalize his inheritance. I am here to offer you a solution. I have the name of a family far away in Scotland who need a maid. They are friends of my family. I know they will not be cruel, and they will pay you well. They already know the situation and are willing to take you without an interview. I have a carriage waiting now to take you there."

Sarah's eyes were huge. Tears ran down her white cheeks. She could not think but she knew she had to leave. She would never be good enough for Grayson. She could only cause him trouble. But she had just realized that she loved him. The burning in her chest threatened to consume her. But he was not the man she had come to love, and yet, when she pictured him so tenderly caring for Rose and when she felt his strong arms holding her, protecting her from the storm, it seemed impossible to believe it was all about money. But so many other things finally made sense. She was so confused and didn't know what to believe. She had to leave. She could never see him again. "I will go," she choked out the words to Lydia.

Lydia was smiling but Sarah couldn't see through her tears. Lydia said urgently, "You are doing the right thing, but you must hurry. Go! Pack your things and come back immediately. I will make sure the carriage is ready and the driver knows where to take you. GO!"

CHAPTER 45

Sarah ran up the stairs to her room, swiping at the tears still running down her face. Once inside she threw herself on the bed, taking deep breaths, trying to calm herself. Lydia's hard voice kept ringing in her ears, "He only cares about money!" Tears started flowing again and Sarah sat up, swinging her feet off the bed. All this time she had been wondering when Grayson would be getting home, looking forward to seeing him; now she wondered when he would get home, knowing that she had to be gone before he did, before she saw him again. She could not face him, knowing that he had been lying to her, knowing that he did not care about her, and especially, knowing that she loved him.

What was it that Lydia had said? Sarah's forehead wrinkled and she closed her eyes trying to remember. He had to keep her here until she found a position and could take care of herself. Yes, that was it. He could finalize his inheritance and be free of her if she left now and took the position Lydia offered. She would not stay here and be an obligation he had to fulfill. She would set him free to start the life he wanted with Lydia at his side. She waited, her eyes still closed, listening quietly for that still small voice that guided her. She couldn't hear it. She had too many of her own thoughts confusing her, but she felt sure this was the right thing to do for Grayson.

She stood up and went to the closet to pack her things. When she opened the door, she gasped at the array of clothes before her. Were these really all hers? No. Grayson had bought them for her so that she would not embarrass him in front of his friends. He wouldn't have to worry about that now. She wouldn't be here to embarrass him, and she wouldn't need these clothes where she was going. She rummaged around in the closet for a minute, looking for her old carpet bag, and then remembered that she had thrown it away after Rose gave her the trunk and new bags. She missed it now, something that was really hers.

She could not take the trunk, but she pulled out one of the other bags and stood back, staring at the clothes again, uncertain where to begin. She had left the Tompkins with two skirts and a dress and that is what she would take now. She quickly picked out a couple of simple skirts and a few shirtwaists, then chose the burnt orange dress. She had always liked it, since Rose had picked it out at the shop in Boston. Tears pricked at her eyes again as she remembered that time. Rose had been so wonderful; had reminded her of what it was like to have someone care about her, what it might have been like if her mother were still alive. Oh Rose, if only you were here to help me. But she would never see Rose again, just like she would never see Grayson again.

She shook herself and took a deep breath, wiping at her tears. She packed the things into the case. As she went to close the closet doors, she saw a blue/green swish at the bottom. She couldn't look away and slowly reached for the dress, pulling it out and holding it against her. Wearing this dress was the first time she had ever really felt beautiful. She could exactly picture Grayson's expression when he saw her in it. Could she bear to leave it behind? It was a gift from Rose, she rationalized, then quickly tossed the dress onto her bed. Those days were gone! After packing a few personal things, she snapped the case shut. She wanted to leave a note for Mrs. Walters but what could she say? At least she could tell the dear lady not to worry. After finding a piece of paper she wrote a short note: *Dear Mrs. Walters, It is time for me to go. Please do not worry. I am safe. Thank you for all your kindness. Please tell Mr. Attwood that I appreciate everything he has done for me very much and that I have only taken the number of clothes that I had when he found me at the Tompkins. That is all I need.* A tear splashed on the page, and she quickly signed. *Love, Sarah.*

As she took one last look around the room, she noticed the painting she had gotten for Grayson in the corner. She decided to leave it in his study for him to find and picked it and her bag up, then left the room, closing the door on another chapter of her ever-changing life.

Lydia was in the foyer waiting for her. Sadie was there also, which puzzled Sarah but she had no time to think about it as Lydia rushed her out to the waiting coach. "Get in, Sarah," she ordered. "The driver knows where to take you. I am sure you will find the position suitable. I hope you haven't forgotten how to be a good servant!" With that final thought she shut the door behind Sarah.

Sadie came forward, holding up a little bundle to the coach window, "A little lunch for you, Miss."

Sarah was surprised, "Why, thank you, Sadie. That was very thoughtful." The little maid flushed guiltily as she left.

Sarah could not resist watching out the window as the coach pulled away and the house got smaller and smaller until it disappeared in the distance. Gone! She had only just begun to think of it as home, but it wasn't. Perhaps she would never have a place that was really home for her, a place full of love and trust. She leaned back and shut her eyes, letting the tears flow. The one thing that comforted her was the knowledge that no matter where she went, God went with her and He loved her and was completely trustworthy.

She slept after a while, the gentle rocking of the carriage lulling her. It was light when she opened her eyes and she wanted to get out and stretch her legs. Maybe the sunshine would energize her somehow. She felt so drained. She reached for the stick by the door and rapped it against the ceiling. Immediately the carriage slowed. When it stopped the driver came to the door. "Is there something you need, Miss?"

"Yes, I would like to get out for a while and walk around."

"We will be passing an Inn up the way in just a few minutes. We can stop there for a while, and get something to eat if you like."

Sarah's face brightened, "Yes, thank you."

Ten minutes later the driver pulled into the yard of an Inn and helped Sarah out. Ahhh, it felt good to stretch. She walked slowly to the Inn and found a dining area inside. The money Grayson had given her was in her purse, but she really didn't want to spend it; after all, it was so important to him, she thought with uncharacteristic sarcasm. She should have left it in her room. She would eat the lunch Sadie had given her and send the money back with the driver. After walking around in the yard for a while she climbed back in the coach and they were on their way once again.

They stopped twice more for short breaks. Sarah fell asleep in the afternoon and woke when the carriage came to a stop. Her eyes were still hazy when the door was opened by a tall, middle-aged man with a friendly smile on his face. He was dressed in a uniform, and after handing her down from the carriage introduced himself, "Welcome, Miss Blake. I am Winston, the chief butler."

"Hello, Winston. Please call me Sarah," she greeted the man while glancing around at the house behind him. It was large, with lots of stone and brick, similar in some ways to Attwood Manor. Her heart caught at the thought and her throat tightened. She had nothing to do with the Attwoods anymore.

"Right this way, Sarah," the butler's voice intruded. "I will take you to meet Matilda. She will give you your instructions." The butler was already leading the way and Sarah followed behind. They entered the house through the kitchen, which was busy with what Sarah presumed would be dinner preparations.

They were immediately greeted by a rosy cheeked woman with a big smile and cheerful voice, "Ah, this must be Sarah." Before Sarah could reply the woman continued, "Welcome, my dear. I am Matilda. I will show you around and help you get settled."

"First I will take you to your room." They turned into a long hall with seven doors facing out. "These are the house servants' quarters. You won't have a room to yourself I'm afraid, but you will only have one roommate. You will get three shillings a week plus room and board."

Sarah's mouth fell open. She had never thought about getting paid. Of course, she knew that many servants got wages, like the servants at Attwood Manor, but somehow, she had never thought that she would actually get a salary for working. Her heart beat faster. She would be an independent woman! She bumped into Matilda's back when the woman stopped to open one of the doors in the hall.

The room had a small window through which the sun was shining. The walls were whitewashed, which made the room look bright and probably bigger than it actually was. There was a bed, a small bureau, and a chair on each side of the room. Sarah had been envisioning her tiny, dark space at the Tompkins and was amazed. She smiled at Matilda, hardly able to speak, but stammered out "Thank you. This is very nice."

Matilda bustled over to one of the bureaus, talking as she pulled something out of one of the drawers. Sarah went closer to look. "These are your uniforms." Matilda snapped open the dress she held which was an exact replica of the one she was wearing. It was a non-descript gray-blue color, with elbow-length sleeves and a button-down collar. After laying the dress on the bed, the woman pulled out a long navy blue apron, where her own was white. The navy was more practical for the maids; it didn't show the dirt so quickly. "You have two dresses, three aprons, and two caps, and you'll be getting some shoes right off. We just have to find some that fit," she explained to the girl in front of her.

It was all very organized and sensible and for a moment, Sarah wondered if she could institute something like it at Attwood Manor. Her heart gripped at the thought, realizing that she would never be doing anything there again.

Matilda noticed the pain on her face immediately and consoled, "I know it can be difficult to leave a place and people you are familiar with and come somewhere new, but you will be happy here. You have come to a good situation and before long you will hardly remember your former place at all."

Sarah nodded, but her heart didn't agree. She would never forget Attwood Manor or its owner. A picture of Grayson standing on the ship, his loose white shirt billowing in the wind, long dark hair blowing back from his handsome face, flashed into her mind. He was unforgettable, and his home also. But she didn't fit there. This was where she fit, in the simple sparse room, wearing the practical maid uniform, not pretty dresses.

However, she did not feel resentful or upset when she thought of that. There was no shame in being a maid. She liked working hard and took pride in doing a good job even when she wasn't being paid. She didn't even mind taking orders. What she found difficult was never having a loving person in her life, someone to give her a kind word and encourage her. And just when she thought she had found that, it turned out to be a lie. When someone does something kind for you, or acts lovingly to you, for his own gain, it isn't really love at all. Sarah felt her throat burning again, her eyes stinging with salty tears.

"Oh, my dear, poor girl." Large arms encircled her pulling her against an ample bosom. "Don't you worry now? No one is going to hurt you here." Sarah leaned against the kind woman and let her tears flow for a minute while Matilda stroked her head.

"Thank you, Matilda," she said. "I'm fine. Really, I am." She managed a wavering smile. If the rest of the people here were even half as kind as Matilda, maybe Lydia really had done her a favor. Maybe she would be able to forget Grayson here.

CHAPTER 46

Grayson remained in London for another three weeks, working hard and distracting himself. The shipyard and the sea were great distractors, but at times she intruded even there. He could see her standing on deck gazing out at the waves, laughing into the wind, her hair glistening in the sun. How often had he imagined running his fingers through those long golden curls, standing behind her, brushing them, separating the silky strands until they lay in a smooth, wavy curtain down her back? He dragged his hand over his own dark curls, forcing the image out. Why had she not been like the typical female, sick all the time, complaining about all the hardships of the voyage? That would have been so much simpler. Instead, she had fit perfectly into his world at sea and now was fitting into his world at his home. He saw Harper several times, but the old sea dog was no help in getting Sarah out of his mind, constantly telling him what a great girl she was and urging him to tell her the truth, to make sure he didn't lose her.

Finally, Grayson found himself running out of things to do and wondering more and more about what was happening at home. How was she doing? Was she lonely? Was Mrs. Walters taking good care of her? Did she miss him? It was useless! He might as well just go back. What he needed to do was to get her set up in the guest house with a better allowance. She could take care of herself, and he wouldn't have her underfoot all the time. But the truth was, he would still worry about her, wonder if she had everything she needed, if she was lonely or afraid. He pounded his fist on the desk! It might take some time, but life would get back to normal, and he would forget about her. Really? He refused to acknowledge the question. He was a man who made things happen and he would make that happen; he would forget about her. He should get back home and see to getting the guest house ready for her. It was December now and she could be settled before Christmas.

With that decision urging him on, he finished off his final tasks and packed for home. It was a cold, gray day when he mounted his horse. He rode hard, his need to get back to her now as great as his need to get away from her had been then. When he turned into the lane, he found himself looking at the windows, looking for a hint of yellow hair, wondering if green eyes were watching for him, waiting. He jumped off the horse at the front door and ran inside. The foyer was empty; she was not there to greet him. The catch in his throat and disappointment in his heart irritated him. He stomped across the room to ring the bell for Mrs. Walters.

The housekeeper appeared immediately. Her eyes widened when she saw the tall, dark figure in the entry. "Master Grayson!" The woman beamed, her smile pushing her apple cheeks so high that her eyes were almost squinted shut. She ran to him, arms outstretched, and he opened his arms to accept her embrace, patting her plump shoulder.

It was an enthusiastic greeting, albeit perhaps not from the one he had hoped for. He stepped back out of her hug, smiling fondly down at her, "Hello, Mrs. Walters. It is good to be home. I will take my things to my room, and then perhaps we can have some refreshments and talk." He picked up his bag and turned to leave, then stopped, adding, "Could you please call someone to take care of my horse? And have Sarah come down to join us."

The woman's face instantly fell, eyes dropping to the floor, shoulders drooping. "Oh, Grayson, my boy, I forgot. You don't know." Her voice was quiet, and Grayson stepped closer, waiting for her to look up at him. When she did her eyes were sad and filled with tears. There was something ominous in her tone, in her look.

A shiver ran down Grayson's spine. Was it something about Sarah? Had there been an accident? Different scenarios started running through his mind, none of them good. His voice was deep and gruff, "Don't know what? Please tell me. What is it?" He entreated.

"Sarah is not here," the woman said softly.

"What do you mean, she is not here? Is she at the market? Out with Gwen?" He asked.

Mrs. Walters shook her head, "She is gone. She has been gone these past three weeks now."

Grayson was baffled but could not deny the fear that was rising over him. His voice rose along with it. "Gone? Gone where?"

The housekeeper took another deep breath and spoke calmly, "Grayson, dear, I think you should take your things upstairs now. I will prepare some refreshments and have Jeffrey come for your horse. Then we will talk."

Grayson opened his mouth to protest, but she made sense. He needed to calm down. Picking up his bag, he stated firmly, "I will be down soon. I expect some answers then." He turned and walked up the stairs slowly, his mind trying to grasp what he had just heard. At the top of the stairs, he stopped, looking to the left, down the dark hallway where her room was. Even in the short time she had been here he had become used to seeing the candles lit, to knowing she was there. The emptiness of it reached out to him echoing in his heart. He was drawn down the hall, wanting to find her there. What would it be like if the hall was never lit again if she was never there to brighten it with her presence, her smile, her laugh? Somehow, since he had met her, he had never really thought of a life without her in it.

He knocked on the door, waited, then knocked again more loudly. After waiting another moment, he turned the handle on the door and it opened. He went in. "Sarah?" he called, knowing there would be no answer. There was a deep emptiness in the room, no sense of her presence, no hint of the rose fragrance she always wore. There were no personal items on her bureau or on the night table by her bed, but that didn't mean anything, he told himself. He had never been inside her room. Perhaps this was how it always was. He went to the nightstand and opened the drawer. Her Bible was gone. For a moment, real fear gripped him but he took a breath and reminded himself that she would take her

Bible with her whether she was going away for a few days or forever. It didn't mean anything.

When he went to the closet relief flooded him. The trunk Rose had given her sat beside it and when he opened the doors, he saw her clothes still there. Wherever she was, she was not 'gone'. She was just away, perhaps visiting someone. She was clearly going to come back. She would not leave her clothes if she were not. He was relieved and turned, eager to tell Mrs. Walters that there was no need for concern.

When he turned, he noticed the green/blue dress tossed carelessly on the bed. A stab of fear touched his heart again. He went to the bed and fingered the soft fabric. He could see her walking down the stairs at Rose's, looking like a lovely sea maiden in the dress, so simple and natural and yet so surprisingly beautiful. His breath caught at the image in his mind. What would it be like to never see her again? Somehow on the voyage he had come to care for her and admire her more than he could have ever imagined. And at that moment he acknowledged, for the first time, that he had come to more than admire and care for her; he had come to love her. Maybe he had loved her from that first moment when she looked up at him with those blazing green eyes after crashing into him on the staircase. The feeling overwhelmed him. I love her, he thought. He said it out loud, "I love her".

Why had he refused to admit it before? Something about the will? About his position? He didn't know but acknowledging it made him feel free and despite his fear he smiled. Surely if he could admit it to himself, he could make her understand. What was she thinking when she tossed the dress onto the bed? Was she tossing him aside as well? Fear gripped him again and he groaned, "I love you, Sarah." He shook his head, scolding himself, don't tell it to the empty room and a dress! Go find her, wherever she is, tell her and bring her home. Why ever, it was that she had left, he would make her understand, he assured himself as he left the room.

In the drawing room he paced, waiting for Mrs. Walters to bring the refreshments. He still could not block those words out of his mind, "She is gone." Where would she go for three weeks? Why would she go? They had been getting along quite well. She seemed to have been settling in, making friends. What had changed? The questions went on and on. What he wanted were answers!

"Here we are, then." The housekeeper's voice interrupted his thoughts. She bustled into the room carrying a tray and quickly poured two cups of tea, handing one to the tall man who was hovering at her shoulder.

"Tea? I think I need something stronger than tea," he said.

"Tea is soothing," Mrs. Walters answered. "You can have something stronger later. Right now, you need a clear head. Do sit down and have a cake as well. I am so glad that you are finally home."

The woman was surprised to see a hint of a smile on Grayson's handsome face when he came over to her. "She is not 'gone', Mrs. Walters. Her clothes are still here. I don't know where she is, but she is not gone. She will be back."

He expected Mrs. Walters to join him in his relief but she shook her head sadly and pulled a piece of paper out of her apron, handing it to him. He opened it slowly. It was addressed to the housekeeper and said simply not to worry, she was safe and thank you for everything. It was the last line that made his heart sink. "*Please tell Mr. Attwood that I only took the number of clothes I had when he found me at the Tompkins. That is all I need.*"

Grayson sat down heavily in one of the upholstered chairs saying slowly, "Mrs. Walters, you know how to reach me in London if there is an emergency. You could have sent me a message."

The housekeeper stammered to explain, "I considered sending a message but there really wasn't much I could tell you, Sir. At first, I thought she would be back right away. Her note said that she was fine and not to worry. After a week went by I did begin to worry and Freddy was constantly after me to do something but I just didn't know. I didn't want to bother you for no real reason. I thought I would wait a while longer." The poor woman was twisting her hands, her voice quivering as she spoke.

Grayson covered her hands with one of his, stilling them. "Mrs. Walters, the last line in the note makes it clear that it was more than NOTHING". He couldn't stop the irritation in his voice but felt sorry for the dear old woman who was like family to him. He added, more gently, "It is alright. You should have informed me, but we will discuss that later. Right now, I want to know everything - when she left, what happened before she left, what she said, who she talked to, and what does Fred had to do with any of it."

There was silence while Mrs. Walters collected her thoughts. "It was after that awful night when Mr. Farnsworth brought Sarah back from Miss Barker's party. Of course, she was upset after that but…"

She paused for a breath, and Grayson spoke immediately, "What party? Why was she upset?"

"Oh, I'm sorry. You have been gone a long time, indeed. A few days after you left, Sarah received an invitation to one of Miss Barker's gatherings. I remember she asked when you were going to be back because she was afraid to go without you. But she thought it was the right thing to do so she went, brave little thing. Later that night, Mr. Farnsworth brought her home, white as a sheet and weak as a kitten from shedding so many tears, she was."

The blood drained from Grayson's face. He should have been here. He pounded the arm of the chair, "Just tell me what happened! What did Lydia do?"

"Grayson, dear, I am doing the best I can. Mr. Farnsworth did not say much, only that Miss Lydia had shamed poor Sarah in front of everyone about being a servant and all. Later when I talked to her, Sarah said that she was a shame to you, that you should never have come for her. She said that you were doing a good deed for her and now she was an embarrassment to you. She was convinced that your friends could never accept her. Poor dear. I tried to tell her it was not so, but she was distraught. After a few days she seemed to be doing better. She wanted something to keep her busy, so I let her take charge of some of the girls. She got them to work cleaning every corner of this house. She enjoyed that and Mr. Farnsworth came by with flowers regularly to cheer her up, and Miss Martens too. It seemed like everything was getting better." The woman stopped, shaking her head, her brow furrowed as she tried to remember, to figure it out.

"If things were getting better, what happened? Why did she leave? Something had to have happened," Grayson demanded.

Mrs. Walters shook her head, at a loss for an explanation. "I have tried to figure it out. I just don't know. The last time I saw her was the morning of the day she left. She was busy with some cleaning inspections, and I greeted her on my way to the kitchen. Then Sadie came and told me that my sister in the next village had sent a message that she needed help." The woman's eyes pled for Grayson to understand. "I had to go, of course. I had nothing pressing here, and she is my sister after all. Sadie said she would get George to drive me. I didn't even see Sarah before we left. I thought I would see her later that evening and I knew Sadie could tell her where I'd gone if she asked."

Before the woman could continue, Grayson bellowed out, "SADIE!!" He got up and went to the door yanking it open and yelling again, "SADIE!!"

Mrs. Walters hurried to his side, pulling on his arm, "Grayson, Grayson. What is it?"

He whirled around, reaching out to grip her shoulders but dropped his arms and stalked across the room. "Do you not hear the common denominator in your story, Woman?" The housekeeper stared blankly at him. He took a deep breath, speaking more calmly, "Sadie! Sadie told you your sister needed you. Sadie got George to drive you. Sadie was here, alone with Sarah. And why did your sister need you so badly?"

Mrs. Walters's pale eyes filled with tears, and her voice was quiet when she answered, "She had no need of me, was surprised to see me in fact."

"And you didn't think that odd?" His voice boomed in the room. "Did you question Sadie about it?"

"Oh, of course, Grayson. I called her right away when I got home and asked her why she thought my sister needed me. She said a messenger had dropped off a note. She had the note to show me. We were both puzzled about it. When I asked Sadie about Sarah later, she assured me that she had not seen or heard anything. She was as surprised and concerned as I when we discovered it."

"Yes, I'm sure," Grayson said sarcastically. Something was odd about it. That maid always seemed to be skulking around. His boots pounded the floor as he went out into the entryway, yelling for Sadie once again.

This time the little maid appeared from behind the staircase, timidly looking out. She walked forward, head bowed, feet shuffling, stopping when she saw the tips of his boots, slowly looking up to meet the master's angry, dark glare. Her heart was pounding. She had imagined this moment at times, but it was far worse than she had ever imagined. She had always thought that if she was discovered, it would be by Mrs. Walters, and she knew she could get around the kindly woman. But the master would not be so easy to convince.

Grayson could see how frightened the girl was and took a deep breath, calming himself before he spoke. "Sadie, come into the drawing room. I have some questions I would like to ask you." The walk to the room gave them all a minute to prepare themselves. Sadie was still dragging her feet, dreading the upcoming interview.

Grayson seated the women on the settee across from him. "Sadie," he said firmly, waiting until the girl looked at him. "You know that Miss Blake is missing." The girl nodded, trying to look away but his eyes held hers. "And I know that you know something about that." She started to shake her head, but he held up his hand and she stopped short, sitting up straight and stiff, tears spilling over her eyes and down her cheeks.

Grayson couldn't help the stir of pity he felt for the girl but pushed it aside, speaking sternly, "Sadie, you are going to tell us what happened. You gave Mrs. Walters a message from her sister when, in fact, there was no message. Why?"

The maid's mouth opened but no sound came out. She tried again, looking every bit like a fish gasping for air. Grayson forced himself to be patient but was almost ready to snap at her when a tiny sound broke through. "I...I...I had to. My Aunt, at Miss Barker's, told me to." She stopped, looking down at her hands twisting her apron into a knot.

Grayson's eyes widened and he looked at Mrs. Walters who returned his surprised stare. They both turned back to the maid. "Miss Barker? What has Lydia got to do with this?" he asked.

"I...I...," the girl stammered again, then, resigning to her fate, took a deep breath and sat back in the chair. There was no point in trying to lie to the master. "Miss Lydia wanted to speak to Miss Sarah alone. My aunt told me to tell Mrs. Walters that her sister needed her and to have George drive her away. The other servants were busy elsewhere and would not interfere."

"Your Aunt?" Grayson asked.

"Yes, Sir. My Aunt works for Miss Barker, and she told me to pass on anything important that is happening here." Sadie's face flushed and she looked down guiltily.

Grayson could not sit any longer. He stood up and paced across the room several times before stopping in front of the girl again. "And Lydia came over here, to speak to Sarah?"

The girl nodded.

"What did she say?" He demanded.

"Oh, I wasn't in the room, Sir. I did not hear anything." Grayson scowled at her and quickly she added, her voice trembling. "I might have heard a bit, from behind the stairs. Miss Barker said something about returning some cufflinks you had left in her room in London." She clapped her hand over her mouth, flushing bright red, clearly embarrassed at what she had just said.

Grayson's groan could have been anger, or pain. *Oh Sarah, my sweet Sarah*, his mind screamed.

Mrs. Walters put her arm around the shaking maid trying to calm the girl while her own heart was breaking for Sarah. "Anything else, dear?" she asked the sobbing maid whose quiet reply could hardly be heard.

"Miss Barker said something about a will. I heard her say, 'He only cares about money. He doesn't care about you. You have to leave." She paused. "And Miss Sarah said, 'all right'. That's all. I went to the kitchen. I made her a sandwich to take with her."

"WHERE?" Grayson could not stop the angry shout. The woman jumped, staring at him. "A sandwich to take with her – WHERE? Where is she, Sadie?" His voice got calmer as he spoke, although his heart hammered in his chest, fear gripping him. He couldn't lose her now.

The maid shook her head, "I don't know. A carriage was waiting. I don't know where she was going. I don't think she knew. She was crying. Miss Barker gave the driver a piece of paper. Maybe it said where she was going. I don't know." Sadie spoke more and more quickly, desperately. It was clear that she was telling the truth and felt terrible for her part in it all.

Grayson stood up, his fists clenched, face as dark and threatening as any storm at sea. His boots hammered the floor as he strode to the door.

"Grayson," Mrs. Walters called.

He turned quickly and said sharply, "I am going to see Lydia. When I return, I will have Sarah with me."

CHAPTER 47

Grayson stalked to the stable, unmindful of the mud splattering his polished boots. He chose a new horse and saddled it himself, too impatient to wait for the groom. He mounted in one fluid movement, walking the horse to the main road, where he released her into a full gallop. Even the chilly wind blowing against him could not cool the tumultuous emotions raging inside.

Lydia was not completely surprised when she heard the pounding on the door and opened it to catch a glimpse of Grayson before he pushed her aside and charged into the house. She had been expecting to see him sometime after he got back and knew he would not be happy, but the anger she felt resonating from him did take her aback for a moment. She wondered how much he knew, replaying her encounter with Sarah quickly in her mind. No one had been there so he couldn't know the details of their discussion. That maid was the only other one in the house and she had been in the kitchen, or had she? It had been convenient to have the girl there to pass on information, but you can't really trust someone who is so easily convinced to spy on her own household for a few extra shillings. What had the girl heard, and more importantly, what had she told Grayson?

Lydia closed the door calmly before turning to greet the angry man. "Why hello, Grayson. I thought you would come to see me when you got home. I have missed you." She smiled her most beguiling smile, but her heart beat harder at the scowl she got in return.

"What did you say to her?" He growled.

She kept the smile on her face and walked toward him, "Grayson, darling, whatever do you mean? Perhaps we should go into the drawing room if you are going to make a scene."

"Why don't we skip the drawing room, and the scene by you telling me right now where Sarah is!"

Lydia managed a surprised look, "Why Grayson, why ever would I know where Sarah is?"

Grayson leaned over until his face was next to hers, eyes blazing, "It won't work, Lydia. I know you were the last person to see her, and I know you put her in a carriage and gave the driver a piece of paper which was most likely the address of the place she went. TELL ME!"

Lydia glared back at the angry man realizing that there was no point in pretending that she did not know, but that did not mean that she was going to tell. She spoke through gritted teeth, "She wanted to go! And not because of me! Don't get self-righteous on me, Grayson. You are the one who lied to her." She smiled when she heard his intake of breath and saw his face blanch. "You know it is true Grayson. You have no one to blame but yourself.

Grayson spun away, feeling the pain of her accusation like a knife in his heart. "I cannot deny that Lydia, but do not think that my deception completely exonerates you. I can explain to her about the will, but the cufflinks?" He spun back, facing her just in time to

312

see the shock cross her face before her mask of innocence covered it again.

"I was simply returning them to you," she simpered.

"And implying that we were intimate in doing so! I did not leave them in your room as you said. You took them from mine when you came there uninvited. How could you say that to her? Do you not have any feelings for anyone but yourself?"

She walked over to him, putting her hand on his chest, looking up at him with unfeigned tears in her brown eyes. "I do have feelings, Grayson. For you. I love you. We are meant to be together. She is wrong for you. I was only trying to help. She will destroy your chance to be everything you want to be."

He pushed her away. "Perhaps you do not understand what I want as well as you think. Perhaps I am content to be a simple sea captain with a happy family waiting for my return." When he said the words, they suddenly felt right in his heart. "Tell me where she is, Lydia," he pled, his anger dissipating. "You and I have been friends all our lives. Will you destroy even that? I must talk to her, try to explain, and beg her forgiveness. Until then I cannot decide anything about the future. You will have nothing of me, not even our friendship, ever again, if you do not tell me now."

They looked at each other, sadness filling their hearts. Tears rolled down Lydia's face and Grayson felt his own eyes stinging. He could hardly hear her words when she stammered, "I will get the address." She walked quickly to the drawing room and returned a minute later to hand him a piece of paper.

"Thank you," he said dully as he read the information on the paper. When he was sure he had what he needed he tucked the paper in his pocket and turned to leave. He stopped for a second and their eyes met, but there was nothing left to say. Lydia watched as he walked out the door before sinking into a chair, burying her face in her hands. He had said he could not decide until he talked to Sarah. There was still a chance, she thought, but her shoulders shook with silent sobs of defeat.

CHAPTER 48

Grayson rode home, planning his next step. He knew the town where Sarah was. If he rode half of the way tonight, he could get to her in the morning and hire a carriage to bring them home that same day. He went directly to the stable where he left his horse with Jeffrey to be exchanged for a fresh one for the coming ride.

Back at the house Mrs. Walters greeted him with tired eyes. It had been a difficult day for everyone. She looked past him as if expecting to see Sarah behind him.

"I know where she is," he said quietly, walking to the stairs. "I need a few things as I will have to stop along the way, but I will return with her tomorrow." He went to his room and quickly put a clean shirt and breeches in his saddle bags, adding his shaving kit and comb. He would not show up for her looking like a saddle-worn vagabond.

On his way back downstairs, Grayson stopped at his study, thinking to take a minute to calm himself. This room reminded him of his quarters on the ship. It was his solace. He went to the large desk against the wall, also reminiscent of the one onboard. He trailed his hand over the familiar wood as he walked around it. Behind the desk he noticed a large object against the wall, hidden under a cloth. Puzzled, he pulled the cloth off to find a large picture he did not recognize. He lifted it up and laid it on the desk. It was a painting of a ship being tossed by a storm at sea. He looked closer and saw "Sea Wolf" painted on it's side. How could the name of his ship be on the painting? Baffled, he turned the picture over and saw an inscription.

Dear Grayson. As with the storm He brought us through at sea, God brings us through the storms of life. May this verse bring you peace in any storms you face. 'And we know that all things work together for good to them that love God, to them that are called according to His purposes.' Romans 8:28 Happy Christmas, from, Sarah

Grayson leaned against his desk, recalling how he had told Sarah that a storm at sea was a time when any man knew that it was only by the providence of God that he survived. But how could he survive this storm? How could he survive the loss of her, go on without her? How could this work out for good? He wiped at the tears that threatened to fall and did something he hadn't done in a long time: prayed for God's help. Prayed that God would help her to understand and forgive him.

Mrs. Walters waited for him at the bottom of the stairs, her face tired and worried. Grayson knew he probably looked the same. He stopped to talk to her wanting to offer her some consolation. "I will bring her back."

"Oh, I do hope so. I do hope she will come back."

"She has to." He told the older woman quietly, "I love her."

A quivering smile touched Mrs. Walters' lips. "I know you do. I'm so glad you finally realized it. Go find her, Dear."

They walked to the door together. Grayson leaned down to embrace the dear lady, a tear spilling over, running down his cheek. "Sarah and I will return tomorrow afternoon," he said as confidently as he could manage before going out the door.

Grayson rode his horse hard, stopping at an Inn a couple of hours down the road. He could not eat and slept only a little. Finally, morning came and he paid his bill and then strode to the stable to get his horse. He mounted quickly and raced down the road, the knowledge that she was close spurring him on. In two hours, he was entering the outskirts of the town. He stopped at the Mercantile to get directions to the house. He would be there in half an hour. His heart skipped a beat at the thought. Soon he would see her, talk to her, and explain everything. He could only imagine how hurt she was by the things Lydia had told her. He longed to take all the pain he had caused her away, to bring her back where he could take care of her and make her happy again.

Finally, he came to some large gates which were closed. It took him some time to explain to the attendant who he was and why he had come. It wasn't until he mentioned Lydia that he got anywhere. There was instant recognition of the Barker name, and the gate was opened. The house was an imposing structure with many sharp steeples and gabled roofs. After tying his horse to a post nearby he rapped the large doorknocker several times and waited impatiently for it to be opened by a uniformed servant. He explained that he wanted to see Sarah Blake making sure to mention the Barker name

317

quickly this time. The man let him in, asking him to wait in the entry. Grayson sat down on a bench beside the door, his fingers drumming impatiently on the intricately carved arm.

Winston found Matilda in the kitchen and explained the situation. "Tildy, there is a gentleman here who says he wants to talk to Sarah. Could you tell her, please?"

"Who is he then? What does he want?" The protective housekeeper asked.

The butler frowned, "He wants to talk with Sarah." Seeing Matilda's scowl, he went on quickly, "I don't recall his name at the moment. I had other things on my mind. It doesn't matter. He looks right enough, and has an expensive topcoat and hat. Seems like a decent chap." The man was getting impatient and huffed, "Just tell her, Tildy. I'll stay close by."

Matilda found Sarah cleaning upstairs, humming quietly while she scrubbed the floor. "Sarah," she called.

Sarah looked up and smiled, "Tildy, hello."

Matilda smiled back at the pleasant girl. She had become very fond of Sarah, such a hard worker and gentle spirit. "Sarah, dear, Winston asked me to tell you that there is a gentleman here to see you."

Sarah's brows immediately drew together in a puzzled frown. "Me? Who would be coming to see me? Did Winston say who it was?"

"Oh, you know that man, always so distracted. He didn't get a name."

Sarah's frown deepened. She stood up, brushing some stray hairs back from her face, leaving a smudge of dirt on her cheek.

"I can tell him you are not available, Sarah," the housekeeper offered quickly.

Sarah shook her head, "It's alright, Tildy. I'll go see who it is."

"All right then, come on along and talk to the chap then." Matilda held out a hand to help Sarah up.

"Yes, I'll meet him and send him on his way." Sarah smoothed her hair and wiped her hands on the long apron she wore as she started down the stairs, stopping when she heard Matilda's groan as she slowly followed. "Don't come down, Tildy. I know it hurts your knees," she told the woman, assuring her, "I will be fine. Winston is probably waiting there."

The housekeeper stopped, "Yes, he said he would stay close by. You go on ahead then and I will be down as quickly as these knees allow."

Sarah waved a hand at her and hurried down the stairs, through a labyrinth of halls and rooms to emerge into the main lobby. It took a minute to adjust her eyes to the bright light coming in from the many windows surrounding the room. There was no one there, not even Winston. Perhaps she and Tildy had tarried so long that the visitor had left. That would suit her just fine. She let out a sigh of relief and immediately saw movement beside one of the windows. A large form, silhouetted against the sunlight turned towards her. She could not make out who it was and moved closer.

Grayson turned when he heard the soft sigh, barely able to make out a maid across the large room. He watched the girl lift her arm, shielding her eyes as she began to walk slowly toward him. Something about her movements made his heart jump. Sarah? He moved quickly forward needing to know, stopping abruptly when he heard her voice call out, "Winston? Matilda told me that you said there was someone here to see me." She continued walking and called again, "Winston?"

Grayson could see her clearly now and his heart hammered in his chest. "No, Sarah, it is not Winston."

It was her turn to stop short, the familiar voice resounding in her head. It can't be! She was imagining things again. How many times had she thought she heard that voice in these past weeks?

Grayson moved over to stand in front of the frozen girl and couldn't stop his intake of breath when she finally lifted her emerald eyes to him, watching them widen in shock when they met his deep blue gaze. It was as though they had just collided at the bottom of the stairs in the hotel all over again, both stunned, trying to breathe.

Sarah's hand touched her throat as she whispered, "Grayson?"

The sound of her sweet voice saying his name was his undoing. He could not stop himself; he reached out and pulled her into his arms, his heart flooding with

320

relief. He had found her. She was safe. He gathered her closer, resting his head on hers, his throat tightening. He swallowed hard, rasping, "Yes, Sarah, it is me. Thank God I have found you."

Sarah felt the deep voice rumble in her ear that was pressed against his chest. She couldn't breathe and tears sprang instantly to her eyes. She felt so safe with his arms around her, like the time in the storm, but… Her brow puckered, but… She couldn't think, not like this, so close to him. She pushed against his chest, and he immediately dropped his arms.

She stepped back slowly, still dazed, stammering out, "What are you doing here?"

"I have come to find you Sarah, to talk to you and take you home where you belong. I want to explain."

Sarah's mind was clearing, reverberating with the sound of Lydia's voice – *he has aspirations, you will hold him back, he never cared about you, he only wanted the money.* It was so clear again, like living it all over with him standing here. The pain flooded her, and the tears pricked sharply behind her eyes. She blinked, refusing to let them fall, shaking her head, "You do not need to explain anything, Grayson. I understand."

He moved closer, pleading with her, "But you do NOT understand, Sarah. I need you to listen to me, let me explain. Please."

Sarah's heart pounded. She felt herself yielding, wanting to listen, to hear what he said, but it wouldn't do any good. It would only make things harder. He had already made everything harder by coming here. She looked at his face, so strong and beautiful, his long dark hair brushing against his chiseled jaw. So many memories of him looking just like that flashed through her mind. She had missed him so much, his confidence, his strength, his tenderness, even his gruffness. In all this time of trying to forget, the memories had barely dimmed. Now she would have to try to forget all over again.

Grayson took advantage of her silence, stepping closer to her, and taking one small hand in his. "Sarah," his voice cracked, his throat tight and hurting. He swallowed, "Sarah, come with me somewhere where we can talk. Just hear me out. After all we have been through, won't you give me that? Where can we go?"

Sarah stared up at him, her eyes glistening, afraid to blink now in case a tear overflowed. From the corner of her eye, she saw movement at the back of the room. Winston and Matilda! Were they standing there, watching? Whatever else, she did not want an audience, whether she convinced Grayson to leave now or let him stay and have his say. Quietly she capitulated, "We can talk in the garden. Come with me." She turned her hand to take him and lead him out of the house.

CHAPTER 49

Sarah let go of Grayson's hand as soon as they got outside, the heat of his touch sizzling up her arm. He did not reach for it again but walked quietly beside her. Although it was Fall, the sun was shining and neither of them noticed the slight chill in the air.

They followed a cobblestone path, finally stopping in a clearing under a small grove of trees, next to a rose garden where the fragrance of some late-blooming flowers still scented the air faintly. Sarah led him to a white gazebo with lattice walls and a couple of ornately curved wrought iron benches inside. Sarah sat down while Grayson walked briskly around, his boots clicking on the slatboard floor. He finally joined her on the bench leaning back to turn towards her. She did not look up but kept her eyes fixated on the hands that lay folded in her lap.

He took a moment to study her. A white cap covered the large bun of thick blonde hair on top of her head, but a few long curly tendrils had escaped to caress her delicate neck and the sides of her face. She wore a plain gray dress covered by a heavy navy apron, the clothes of a servant. Although they were cleaner and fit well, the image of a waif in a faded brown skirt and yellowed shirt flashed into his mind. Here she was, a servant again. Pain gripped him. He had gone to take her away from that! Or had he? He pushed the question away, not wanting to think about why he had really gone. He continued his perusal. Her eyes were still lowered, long dark lashes fanning out against the soft skin below.

Some of her deep golden tan had faded, leaving her skin like rich cream. Her cheeks were no longer hollow but gently rounded with a touch of pink heightened by the brisk air. She was still slim but no longer gaunt. The hands folded in her lap had not changed much, still slightly rough, nails short and square. They were hands that knew hard work and weren't embarrassed to show it. And yet the same quiet peace and contentment exuded from her.

Grayson gazed at her, breathing in the sight of her. She was more beautiful than ever and yet his same Sarah, as lovely and content in servant garb as she was stunning yet humble in a beautiful gown of sea green. "Sarah," he said softly, "Look at me."

It was a request, not a command, but something of his captain's tone came through and Sarah's heart caught in her throat. She had always loved the strength and confidence in his voice. It was impossible to refuse him. Slowly she turned her head, lifting her eyes to meet his.

The sun touched her eyes turning them golden green, and without thinking, Grayson said softly, "Hello, Cat-eyes."

Her heart fluttered at the nickname but at the same time a spark of anger flared. She stood up walking sharply away from the bench. Grayson was surprised to see the tiny green darts forming in her eyes. He jumped up to follow her, reaching out to touch her shoulder, "Sarah, what…"

Before he could say more, she yanked her shoulder away from his hand and spun around on him, "Grayson, stop." Her voice was strong and firm. She continued quickly when he opened his mouth, "There is no reason for this anymore. You do not need to flatter me. Try to win me over with sweet words. You have what you want. I have a position now. Your responsibility to me is done. Your inheritance is secure."

Grayson groaned, pushing his hands through his long hair. Here it was, the time he had dreaded. "Sarah, it is not what you think. I know what Lydia told you but that is not how it is."

"You lied to me," she stated factually. "You told me you came to free me because we were family. Even that was a lie. We aren't really family. You knew how much I longed to be connected to some family, knowing my parents had both died." Her voice broke and she swallowed before going on. "You said you came because a dying woman asked you to." She took a breath before adding quietly, "Because you cared."

"I DO care, Sarah!"

"About your money! Not about Bethany's dying wish, not about being my family, not about me! I finally thought… after all those years with the Tompkins, knowing I was worthless, nothing to them," she paused for a breath, "I finally thought… that maybe there was something worthwhile in me, maybe something worth rescuing, but it wasn't true."

She turned away from him but not before he heard the catch in her voice and saw the glint of tears in

325

her eyes. He felt her pain like a knife in his heart, her pain at his betrayal. With a deep sigh he turned back to the bench, sitting down heavily, leaning forward resting his head in his hands. What could he say? How could he fix this? He was surprised to find himself saying a quick prayer again.

His voice was very quiet when he spoke, and she had to turn to him to hear what he said. "I cannot deny it Sarah. I came because Bethany forced me to, threatened to deny me my rightful inheritance if I did not." He had to move and got up to go and stand in front of her before he continued, pleading with her to understand. "But it was not just about the money. It was about my father and mother, the property that had been in my family for generations! Bethany was going to divide it up and sell it. I had to stop that!"

He watched her. Her face was white, her eyes huge, but she was listening to him. He could see her thinking, digesting. He went on more calmly now, knowing he could not hold anything back. "I will admit that even so, the money did matter to me. I am not entirely noble. I like my way of life and my status. I did not want it to change. But I did not know you then, Sarah." He moved closer to her, and she did not move away. He looked deeply into her eyes, his own burning from the tears he forced back. He spoke earnestly, "I didn't know you, Sarah. How could I care? I am not like you. I am not naturally caring and kind." He paused, taking a deep breath, struggling with his next words, "But I did care after I met you, more than I could have ever imagined caring about someone else's misfortune. I wanted to get you away from those people, wanted to see you happy and free. I even wanted to tell you the truth." He paused briefly, "But after I met you, I wanted you to think well of me. I wanted you to think I was generous and kind. I liked the feeling that someone thought of me as more than a wealthy, arrogant fop. I was too proud to tell you." He couldn't go on and turned away from her, but not before Sarah saw the glint of tears in his eyes.

Her heart broke for him, and she lay her hand on his bent shoulder. "You could have told me about the will, Grayson. I think I would have understood. An inheritance is an important thing and should stay with you. It is your history, your birthright. You could have told me."

Grayson turned, reaching out to take both her hands in his, "And I should have. I know that! I can't change what I did but I am terribly sorry for deceiving you, terribly sorry for the pain I have caused you. Please forgive me, Sarah."

Sarah held onto his hands, looking at him and loving him more at this moment than she had ever thought possible. "I forgive you Grayson. I understand. I am so grateful for everything you have done for me. Whatever the reasons, it was still a sacrifice to come all that way to rescue someone you did not know and risk bringing them back into your home. Thank you."

Relief flooded Grayson's heart at her words, the heavy burden he had been carrying lifted off his shoulders. He smiled softly, humbled by this woman's ability to forgive all the wrongs that had been done to her, even his. "Thank you, Sarah. I am so glad to have this behind us. Now I can take you home with everything open between us. "Come," he pulled on her hands.

Sarah's smile faded and she pulled her hands back speaking seriously, "I am glad to have this behind us also, Grayson. Now we can part with everything open between us."

A puzzled frown replaced Grayson's joyful smile, his dark brows drawing together in confusion. "Part?" He held his breath waiting for her to answer.

CHAPTER 50

Sarah was quiet, dreading what she had to do next. With a deep breath she said, "I cannot go back with you."

He could tell by her voice that she meant it, but he was baffled by it. He shook his head, denying what she said. "Sarah, you don't mean that." He stated it as a fact, but fear was rising inside him.

Sarah looked down at her hands, fidgeting with her dress. Her voice was quiet but determined as she continued, looking back up at him. "I will always be grateful to you, and I too am glad that we do not have any lies between us, but I still do not belong in your life."

Grayson dragged his hand over his hair, a deep, frustrated groan coming from his throat. He opened his mouth to protest but Sarah spoke quickly, "I am happy here, Grayson. The people are kind. They appreciate my work and I feel worthwhile. It feels good. I am supporting myself. I am independent and I like it. You are free to go on with your life unhindered by me."

When she paused for a breath, Grayson quickly protested, "Sarah, you are not a hindrance to me."

"Not everyone feels that way, Grayson. I know that you are announcing your engagement to Lydia at Christmas. She is right for you. You belong together. She will be an asset to you, help you to fulfill all your aspirations to go into politics, and maybe even be Governor someday. Having a family member like me will only hold you back."

"What are you talking about? Those are Lydia's aspirations! I have never wanted to give up the sea for a desk and I have not proposed to Lydia!" His voice became louder as he spoke, anger breaking through.

Sarah spoke calmly, ignoring his outburst. "She wants the best for you, Grayson. She loves you." Sarah took a deep breath, building courage for what she would say next. Looking down at her hands again she said quietly, "I know that she went to London with you. You should marry her, Grayson."

A growl came from deep in Grayson's throat. "She did NOT come to London WITH me! She found out that I was in London and came there on her own. She came to my room to see me, uninvited. She must have taken the cufflinks off my dresser. No matter what she implied, I have never been intimate with Lydia. I would not do that to her. I have some honor, Sarah. You have to believe that," he implored.

With all her heart Sarah wanted to believe it, and deep down she did. She knew this man. He had his faults, but he was honorable and would not hurt his lifelong friend that way. But it did not matter either way. Lydia was the right woman for him. She had the prestige and sophistication he would need in a wife.

Grayson saw her struggling and went over to her, gently placing a finger under her chin and lifting her face to his. "I do not love Lydia. I have never loved her, or I would have married her long ago. I love YOU, Sarah."

A tiny gasp escaped Sarah's lips. Her eyes were wide as she stared unblinking into his before slowly looking down and turning away from him. When had she last heard those words? When was the last time anyone had really loved her? All these years, she had imagined what it would be like to be loved. Now, to hear those words from his deep, strong voice was overwhelming. How could he love her? She wasn't worthy of him. She couldn't move or speak. She felt the warmth of his body behind her and wanted to lean back into it, feel the warmth wrap around her and reach down to those cold places in her heart that had not been warmed by love for so long.

As though he read her mind, he stepped closer, putting his hands on her shoulders. The contact was enough to snap her out of her daze. As much as she wanted to bask in his words and the warmth of his touch, she had to put aside her feelings and do what was best for him. She shivered as the cool air touched her back when she moved away from him. With a deep breath, she collected her thoughts, stilled her pounding heart, and turned back. The sight of the tall man behind her, watching her, was almost her undoing. The strength and confidence he always exuded were mixed with a new touch of uncertainty, humility, and almost fear. She wanted to go to him, comfort him, assure him, but she drew on all the strength she had and said again, "But I am not right for you, Grayson. You..."

He reached out and gently put a finger over her lips, stopping her. "You are perfect for me, Sarah. You are strong and courageous. You love the sea. Your faith and trust inspire me." His eyes roamed over her sweet face, stopping at the white cap covering the bun on the top of her head. Mesmerized, he reached up, removing the cap and dropping it to the ground. Slowly, he pulled out the few pins that held the thick rope of hair, releasing the tresses to fall around her shoulders. He ran his fingers through the strands, loosening them to fall in curls down her back. He stepped back, taking one long strand with him, smoothing it between his fingers as he gazed at her, "You are so beautiful, but you don't even know it. I want to show you." Her breath was shallow, lips parted. He struggled with himself to resist the urge to touch them with his own. He wanted her to want him to kiss her before he would yield to his own desire. He kissed the hair that was burning his fingers instead. Dropping it quickly, he took her hand.

Sarah was a turmoil of emotion, caught in a whirlpool of feelings she had never felt before. Her heart was hammering in her chest, and the hair he had freed was burning against her back.

Grayson turned away, leading her over to the bench, sitting close beside her, still holding her hand, feeling the stiff fabric of her apron rubbing against his. He felt her heart beating in the tiny hand he held. He turned to her, and she looked up at him, not knowing that love shone from her eyes.

Grayson cleared his throat, "Sweet Sarah. You are perfect for me. I love you. I think I have loved you since that day you ran into me on the stairs. I just didn't know it until I came home from London and you were gone, and I realized how empty my life would be without you in it." He hadn't planned it, but the words came out anyway, "I love you, and I want to marry you."

Sarah's mouth opened as if to speak, but nothing came out, so he said it for her, "I think you love me too, Sarah. Don't be afraid to say it."

Sarah searched the recesses of her mind to find some sanity, to squelch the emotions overtaking her, to find the strength to do what was best for him. She looked down to stop the truth from showing through her eyes. Slowly she eased her hand out of his, took a deep breath, "Grayson, what you feel for me is not love. I am a novelty to you, someone different from your usual set. You have become accustomed to looking after me as I have become accustomed to having you take care of me. That isn't love. We don't know each other well enough to know love."

"How can you say that?!" Grayson's voice was louder than he expected, and he lowered it when he continued. "How can you say that, Sarah? After all these months together, all we have been through. We don't know each other well enough to know love when we feel it?! Sarah, you know me better than anyone. You've seen me at my worst certainly and possibly even at my best."

He paused, but she didn't answer, just stared at her own hands twisting in her lap. He covered them with his, quieting them. "And I know you, Sarah." He spoke tenderly, and her eyes were drawn to his. He gazed deeply into them. "I know all the shades of your remarkable eyes, the golden hypnotic cat-eyes, the majestic emerald jewel eyes, sometimes sparking with fiery darts, sometimes clouded with sadness, shimmering with tears, darkened with fear." He gazed into her eyes, and she could not look away. His voice was deep with a hint of awe when he said, "And now, Sarah, looking into them now, I see what I never have before. I see them glowing with love." She looked away quickly, but his voice drew her back. "Deny it then, Sarah. Tell me you don't love me."

She tried to look away, but he cleared his throat meaningfully, holding her eyes with his. She stammered as she began, then gaining more confidence, said again, as firmly as she could, "I do not.... belong in your life."

Somehow, her insistence that they did not belong together made it completely clear to him that they did. Why couldn't she see it? Enough of pleading and cajoling! It all made sense. He could see the uncharted map of their lives as it lay in front of him. He had sailed the seas without the map, but he could chart it all right now, looking back.

"Sarah, stop saying that," he spoke sternly, determined to make her recognize what was right in front of her.

Sarah sat up straight recognizing his captain's tone. "Saying what?"

"That we do not belong together when it is perfectly clear that we do, and you have been saying so all along, whether you knew it or not." Her brow puckered in puzzlement, and he went on, "How many times have you said that there is a reason for everything? Rose has been saying the same thing for years and my mother before her. Every time you say that Sarah, you are saying that we belong together."

"It is not always that easy to understand the reasons for the things that happen, Grayson," Sarah reasoned. "Sometimes we never know."

"But this time we do know!" Grayson stood up, needing to move, feeling agitated. He paced across the gazebo, finally leaning against the lattice across from her. His long frame stretched almost to the roof, and his dark hair stood out starkly against the white wood.

Sarah caught her breath, picturing him at the helm of the ship, that same confident, determined look on his face as he sailed his ship into the endless sea. She soaked in the sight of him, feeling the same sense of security and safety she had on the ship whenever he was near. Her love for him washed over her leaving her breathless. At that moment, she knew that there was nowhere she would rather be than beside this man sailing through the uncharted seas of life.

Grayson sensed her eyes on him and moved back to her side, taking her hands and saying again. "This time, we do know the reason for the things that have happened, Sarah. The chain of events that has brought us to this point is undeniable, especially by you, who are so confident of God's control in all situations, refusing to be angry at Him regardless of all that has happened to you. I have been angry at Him for so many years because he did not spare my mother, but now I can finally see how the chain of events, starting with her death, has worked together perfectly toward this day. If my mother had not died my father would not have married Bethany. If he had not married Bethany, I would not have heard about you. If she had not made the will, I would not have gone to find you and come to love you as I do today.

And it is the same for you, Sarah. If your parents had not needed to send you away, you would never have needed to be rescued and would never have met me and come home with me." He stopped, watching her take it all in, come to the truth of it. Then he added one more thing. "I found the painting you got me for Christmas, Sarah. It is wonderful. I will cherish it forever. And even there you said we belong together in the verse you wrote, 'All things work together for good'. But how could everything work for good if you are not with me, Sarah, if we are not together?"

He saw the sheen of tears in her eyes and leaned closer to her, "Sarah, you know that we do belong together. Will you marry me? Be my wife?"

A tear splashed on his hand, followed by another. Grayson took her face in his hands, lifting it up to him, his heart ripped apart as he watched the tears running down her cheeks. Gently he rubbed his thumbs under her closed eyes, drying the tears. "What is it, Darling? Why are you crying?" He leaned down and softly kissed each eye, tasting the salt of her tears on his lips.

Finally, with a tiny sob, her voice shaking, she said quietly, "I don't know if I know how to love someone anymore. I have not had anyone to love since I was twelve, but now you have come into my life, rescued me from my bondage, and found something worth loving in me." She took a shuddering breath and looked deep into his eyes, "I love you, Grayson, with all my heart, but I am afraid. What if I fail you?"

She was surprised by Grayson's broad smile, "That is impossible, my darling girl. You have just made me the happiest man alive. I may have come into your life and rescued you from the Tompkins, but you have rescued me also. You have brought love and joy back to my life, helped me let go of the anger I harbored, and brought me back to my faith. We are both a little afraid, facing another uncharted voyage." He took her hands in his, smiling into her eyes, "Step on the boat with me, Sarah. Do not be afraid. Take this journey with me. Marry me."

Sarah stared at their clasped hands. Her eyes were shining emeralds when she lifted them to Grayson. A smile hovered on her lovely lips when she said, "Yes, Grayson, I will marry you. I love you."

Grayson pulled her joyously into his arms, and she wrapped hers tightly around his neck. Finally, their lips met in a deep, sealing kiss.

In a minute, Sarah leaned back but stayed in his arms, looking up at him. "Can Rose come?" she asked.

Grayson looked seriously at her, but there was a smile in his voice when he answered. "Well, I was hoping we could get married tomorrow." At her gasp, he laughed and pulled her close again. "Yes, darling girl, Rose can come, and maybe even Mary. I will send my fastest ship right away. You can have whatever you want for our wedding. I am happy as long as you end up my wife in the end."

He leaned down to find her lips again, and she eagerly met his kiss.

Made in United States
Troutdale, OR
12/01/2023